THE COURT OF THORNS AND WINGS

FATED TO DARKNESS
BOOK 2

JEN L. GREY

NAME GLOSSARY

Lira (LEE-rah)
Tavish (TAH-vish)
Eiric (AY-rik)
Faelan (FAY-lan)
Finnian (FIN-ee-an)
Caelan (KAY-lan)
Eldrin (EL-drin)
Lorne (LORN)
Moria (MOHR-ee-ah)
Torcall (TOR-kahl)
Finola (fi-NO-lah)
Rona (ROH-nah)
Dougal (DOO-gal)
Malikor (MAL-ih-kor)
Moor (MOOR)
Struan (STROO-an)
Pyralis (pie-RAL-is)
Brenin (BREN-in)
Hestia (HES-tee-ah)

Erdan (ER-dan)
Sylphia (SIL-fee-ah)

GENERAL GLOSSARY

Ardanos (ard-AN-ohss) – Realm Name
Aetherglen (AY-thur-glen) – Unseelie and Seelie joined kingdom
Cuil Dorcha (COOL DOR-kha) - Unseelie Kingdom
Dunscaith (DOON-skah) – Unseelie Castle
Gleann Solas (GLYAN SO-las) – Seelie Kingdom
Caisteal Solais (KASH-tul SO-lash) – Seelie Castle
Aelwen – (A-el-wen) - River in Seelie Kingdom
Tìr na Dràgon (CHEER na DRAY-gon) – Dragon Kingdom
Cù-sìth (koo-shee) – Wolf-like Unseelie creature

TAVISH

I n a matter of seconds, my entire world had shattered. My heart had been obliterated with no hope of salvaging it because of one simple fact.

Everything had vanished in the blink of an eye.

Tears streamed down my face, and I hunched over, agony piercing my chest and running throughout my body.

I'd made a horrible mistake. One I couldn't fix or take back, even as the king.

Death... that was permanent, even for me.

The only thing that could perhaps get me through the rest of eternity was having someone force Lira into my dreams.

My chest heaved, and I curled my fingers into my hair and tugged. If living every day without her in this world was going to feel like this, I wanted to die.

"Tavish," Caelan said softly, his voice thick with worry.

He'd used that tone only one other time in my entire life, twelve years ago when Eldrin saved me after the Seelie had killed my parents and imprisoned me. I'd been severely injured during the castle attack and woke up to find both my parents dead at the feet of Seelie warriors. Eldrin had rescued me and saved my life and my father's sword for me.

While healing after my rescue, Caelan had become like a big brother to me, tending to me and caring for me when my people rebelled against my reign.

His tone now made my misery worse, reminding me of that time so long ago.

I lowered my hands and rolled up my sleeves slightly to see that the incomplete, magical fated-mate tattoo of delicate vines and leaves interconnected with thorns had spread across Lira's body and mine when we'd come close to cementing our bond. The tattoo cut off abruptly at my wrists, waiting for the consummation of our bond.

Something I'd stopped because I'd believed Lira had to die for me to save my people. I couldn't risk completing the bond. Now I wanted to go back in time and change that moment.

I'd lost so much time with her, pushed her away too often, and exhausted myself with the constant battle of not intervening whenever she was in danger.

And look where it had gotten me.

Would my tattoo fade over time? Because that was the last thing I wanted. Her soul had branded mine, and though it had been for only a short while, I never wanted to forget.

I shouldn't have declared the gauntlet, and I should've saved her instead of watching as she fought for her life. It had taken her getting stabbed in the final battle of the gauntlet to make my sorry wildling self realize how wrong I'd been.

Can someone die of heartbreak? This was a question I would've laughed at had anyone else asked it a mere month ago, but today, this was the question I posed to myself.

"Sunscorched," Finnian hissed as my mattress dipped in front of my head. "You can't die. You're fearless."

My breath caught, and I stood, prepared to drag him away from Lira's body. He had to be careful. She was injured! He didn't need to hurt her more.

He straddled her half-naked body where they'd ripped off part of her shirt so they could tie the towels around her waist to stop the bleeding.

His navy wings were closed tightly behind him, and his light ice-blue eyes glistened. "Lira, wake up. You can't leave us like this. Not *now*. Not when Tavish needs you more than ever." The ash-blond tips of his hair hit midforehead as he bent over her, begging her to come back to life.

But she didn't.

She couldn't hear his plea.

My stomach churned, and something weird and painful inched up my throat like it was trying to come out.

My eyes stayed locked on her, and I could've sworn the shimmer of her sun-kissed complexion had returned. Illusions that I wanted to see, like she was waking and returning to me.

My tattoo pulsed faintly, but I ignored the sensation. It had to be a figment of my imagination. I should probably make arrangements to take her back to the Seelie territory. Her body needed to be buried there so her magic could return to her lands... the way it should be. She deserved that.

I sniffled. "We need to settle things with our people so I can take Lira home."

"What?" Caelan asked, stepping up beside me. He tilted his head, a piece of his dark-blond hair falling from the bun on top of his head. "You can't be serious. If you take her back dead, they'll believe we're attacking. Remember, that was the plan not too long ago."

His words cut deep, and I clenched my teeth, fighting the urge to punch him. I straightened my shoulders and pulled darkness around me, emphasizing my height and magic to him. I gritted out, "You don't dictate what I do. *I'm* your king, and I'm blasting clear on what my original plan was and will carry that guilt for the rest of my existence. I don't need you reminding me. But Lira will be returned to her homeland and family because that's what she deserves. We won't taint her death worse than we already have, and we'll do the right thing... for her."

He flinched. "I don't understand why things changed so suddenly. You two knew each other before she was hidden on Earth, so why didn't you feel this way from the start?"

"It took finding her again to realize what she is to me." This was something only Finnian, Lira, and I knew. Finnian only because he'd suspected it all along, which had irritated me. Maybe if I'd understood sooner that Lira and I were fated, I could've wrapped my head around it and changed this outcome.

I guessed we'd never know.

I pulled up my sleeve, revealing the tattoos on my arms.

Caelan arched a brow. "When did you get that?"

Then I noticed the light pulsing again... as though Lira's heart had somehow started beating again.

I took a few steps toward the bed and shoved Finnian off her, placing myself between him and Finola. If Lira was coming back to life, he didn't need to be sitting on her.

"What the—" Finnian started as I lowered my ear to her chest, ignoring the way the dried blood from the gauntlet stuck to my ear.

"Hush," I snapped... and then I heard the most beautiful sound in my entire existence.

Her heart was beating. Barely. I jerked upright and moved to her left side, where Bran had impaled her with the sword. I lifted her shirt and saw that the gaping hole had closed a little, though blood still trickled from the wound.

"Get the silk thread. We need to mend her wound!" I didn't care if someone was creating an illusion. I'd take whatever they offered as long as I got to spend time with her again.

"Tav, we can, but I'm not sure that will make a diff..." Finnian trailed off like he was searching for how to finish that thought without upsetting me further.

Finola gasped. "No, look. Her fingers are moving." She spun around, her fine, straight black hair blowing back, and hurried to the wooden table I'd once used to play chess with Eldrin. There lay the kit with the gray silk and curved needle to close her wound.

Laughing, Finnian sat beside Lira and shook his head. "I swear, she defies all odds."

Lira did have a tenacity, the likes of which I'd never seen before, but that didn't mean she couldn't die again. "She's still bleeding. We need to stop it if we want her to keep breathing," I bit out.

After placing the mending kit on the side of the bed, Finola narrowed her deep-set eyes and threaded the needle. Then she placed a hand at the base of Lira's wound, not flinching at the gold blood that continued to trickle from it.

Lira had made an impression on more people than Finnian and me. If she woke, it would be interesting to see how many people thought well of her despite her being our enemy's heir.

Finola's light-tan complexion seemed pale compared to

Lira's, proving this wasn't a figment of our imagination.

As the needle pierced Lira's skin, she groaned faintly. My heartbeat quickened, and the fated-mate markings pulsed harder. I reached out and took her hand in mine.

A jolt crashed between us, one that hadn't been there minutes before.

"Lira, you're in our bedchamber and safe." I wanted her to know she was no longer in the arena. "I need you to keep fighting. I can't lose you just when my foolish eyes have finally opened." My voice cracked, and my vision blurred as I remembered how awful the silence had been when I believed I'd lost her. I couldn't lose her again. I wouldn't survive.

"Put pressure on her other wounds," Finola said and nodded toward Lira's stomach and side. She'd been slashed in the stomach, and though the cut wasn't deep, it still bled. Someone had also taken a chunk of skin from her other side, though that injury wasn't as bad as the one Finola was mending.

I released Lira's hand, though every cell in my body protested, but her blood loss was the priority.

"I'll do it." Finnian set his hands on the towel on Lira's side. "Put pressure on her stomach with your free hand. Keep holding her hand—both of you need it."

He didn't have to tell me twice. My touching her alone had made her face soften. Black blood covered her long, wavy blonde hair, and somehow, seeing her bathed in the blood of her enemies did something to me that wasn't very appropriate, especially with her injured and unconscious.

Caelan paced behind us, not saying a word, and I focused on my beautiful mate. I'd give anything for her to open her cobalt eyes and say something to me... even if it was to tell me to get off her.

Biting her bottom lip, Finola continued to work diligently, and my shoulders slumped.

What if she didn't want to be with me? I'd made multiple unforgivable mistakes. My chest tightened, but not as it had been when her heart stopped. It ached and made my insides feel vacant, but even if she didn't want to be with me, at least she'd be alive.

Her eyelids fluttered, and my lungs seized. *Come on, sprite. Open those huge, beautiful eyes.* I needed proof that she was coming back to me more than anything.

She flinched, and her expression twisted in agony.

"Almost done," Finola whispered. "Hold on."

Lira nodded slightly, and my chest expanded with so much hope.

The jolt between us grew stronger, and I wanted to bundle her into my arms and never let her go. No one would ever harm her again, even if she didn't choose to be with me. I wouldn't force her to remain here any longer.

Sweat beaded on her face, and I leaned over, brushing my hand against her skin.

"This might hurt a little, but I need to tie it off," Finola warned. She leaned down and bit through the silk thread.

After a quick whimper, Lira went still again.

Cold tendrils of fear squeezed my heart. "What's wrong?" I leaned down, her heartbeat the only thing grounding me.

"She passed out." Finola grabbed the kit and headed around the bed to Lira's other side. "I don't know how she came back, but she's in a lot of pain. She needs rest more than anything."

Someone knocked on the door frantically. "Your Majesty," Faelan called. "May I come in?"

I didn't want to handle whatever frivolous crisis was

going on, but Caelan and Finnian were here with me, and Eldrin was in prison where he belonged. I had no choice but to handle this, if only to put it off longer. "Come in."

The door opened, and the dark-blue-haired guard hurried in. His gaze went immediately to my bed, and he wrinkled his nose. He wasn't hiding his disapproval of the Seelie princess getting tended to in my bed.

"Do you have a problem with what's going on here?" I released Lira's hand and turned to face the guard head-on. My blood boiled. Since I couldn't kill Eldrin because of my life debt to him, it would be nice to take out my anger and frustration on someone else. "Is that why you came here, to see if my vow during the gauntlet was true?"

"Of course not." Faelan wisely kept his attention on me. He rubbed a hand over his dark armored guard uniform, and his blue wings fluttered gently behind him.

He was nervous about informing me of something, and I didn't have the patience for it.

"If the people want me to talk to them about my decision, that's fine." I didn't like answering to them, but this would be an exception to the rule... anything for Lira. I didn't want to burden her conscience by killing everyone who spoke out against us. She'd blame herself for that. For her, I'd give my people one chance, but that was it. Anyone who continued to show dissent would meet the sharp tip of my blade.

"That's not it." Faelan huffed and glanced out the door as several guards flew past, hurrying toward the prison. "We have a pressing situation, and we need your assistance."

My stomach hardened. The guards wouldn't be rushing like that unless something had gone horribly wrong... like when Lira had escaped. "What is it?"

"Eldrin." He exhaled. "Eldrin has escaped."

Out of every possibility, I hadn't expected that. "That's impossible. Torcall took him to the holding cell." Torcall was one of the best guards we had.

"Eldrin stabbed Torcall in the throat with a poisoned dagger." Faelan scratched his neck. "It was a paralytic toxin, which is why Torcall couldn't scream. Two of the other prison guards stumbled upon Torcall, but he died. With his last breath, Torcall managed to communicate in slurred whispers that Eldrin had gotten away. We immediately began searching but so far have come up empty-handed. We believe he made it out of the castle since no one but Torcall was aware of his escape."

"Then let's find him," I snapped. My blasted cousin had betrayed me once again and, in doing so, had killed one of my most skilled and favored guards. I couldn't kill him, but that didn't mean I wouldn't hunt him down and punish him. I had to make a point to show my people what happened when someone rose against me... like I had to do when I was fifteen.

I turned around, knowing that Lira was in good hands with the three of them. I trusted them, even Caelen, though he wasn't happy with my latest decisions. "Keep watch over Lira. I'll help find Eldrin and make sure my people see that even my blood gets punished. If anything changes—" My words cut off.

"We'll let you know." Finnian placed a hand over his heart.

"I'll send Nightbane here." That beast loved Lira and would protect her with his life.

I pivoted on my heels to leave, but something stopped me in my tracks.

2

LIRA

I was drifting in peaceful darkness when discomfort tugged at me. I tried to jerk away, to remain in this comforting abyss of nothingness, but the tugging strengthened to a yank, and pain flooded into me.

Desperate to escape the agony, I tried to fight, but nothing worked. My body began to hurt in a way it hadn't when I'd descended into peacefulness, a place I was desperate to return to.

My suffering continued to intensify.

A faint buzzing filtered through my brain, taking the edge off. A comforting sensation settled over me, and I stopped fighting.

The sensation was familiar, reminding me of something.

I racked my brain to remember *what*. It suddenly seemed important, but then the torturous agony strummed through my body, and my head fogged, making it hard to ascertain anything.

"Lira..." A deep, sexy voice resonated from miles away. "Bedchambers... safe... keep... fighting." The words kept going in and out like I was going through an area with bad cell reception. "Can't... lose... you."

Then an image of a man seared my brain.

Hair the color of darkness and eyes a stormy gray that made me feel things I didn't understand. As if those two attributes alone didn't make him the sexiest man I'd ever seen, leathery onyx wings spread out behind him, contrasting with his pale skin.

Then a name clicked into place.

Tavish.

He'd stopped the gauntlet to save me, risking his people turning on him because of what I represented to them.

The *Seelie.*

Despite the agony, I stopped fighting the yank. I would gladly suffer through hell as long as I got to see and talk to him again. He deserved a thank-you for what he'd done for me.

Something stabbed my side, increasing the discomfort on top of the agony. I focused on the buzz, using it as my anchor, but then it vanished.

My breath caught, and I wanted to cry out for him, but I couldn't form words. I whimpered, but then I faded back into the darkness, where pain couldn't reach me.

A worried tone tugged at my consciousness, and agony washed over me again, though it had improved slightly. This time, as I tried opening my eyes, my lids fluttered. I stirred, and the warmth in my chest swirled toward the side of me that radiated pain.

What had happened to me?

Memories of the gauntlet slammed back into me. Bran

had stabbed me in the side—both he and his sister, Rona, had fought with every intent of killing me. Little did either of them know that they'd succeeded, even though I'd taken the blighted wildlings down with me.

My heart ached as I remembered that I had murdered Rona. I wished I could take it back, but I might as well wish that I didn't need oxygen to breathe.

Futile.

I would carry her death with me for the rest of my life, knowing I'd killed someone who'd believed they were doing what they had to do to survive. The same as I'd done, but why should I feel justified in taking her life?

"If anything changes—" Tavish's voice broke.

The heartbreak in his voice shook me. I couldn't keep doing this to him. I needed to open my eyes and thank him. If it weren't for him, I wouldn't be here now.

Focusing on stirring, I couldn't make out what they were saying anymore. I couldn't believe how hard I had to struggle to do something so simple.

My chest *yanked* hard, the way it sometimes did when Tavish left my proximity. Everything inside me screamed, and I rasped, "Tavish."

The entire room became silent, and the mattress dipped on my right side. Someone took my hand. The buzz thrummed back to life. Tavish.

"Sprite?" he whispered, his hand squeezing mine.

I swallowed, but my saliva might as well have been sandpaper. My throat was dry from physical fatigue and the dirt and sand of the arena floor. Yet, with his touch, the warmth spreading from my chest heightened, allowing my eyes to crack open.

Our eyes locked, and his stormy gray ones caused my

heart to gallop. There was something in them I hadn't seen before, though I couldn't clearly label an emotion.

"You gave us a scare." Finnian was perched by my feet, giving me an exhausted smile. "And it's nice to hear your heart beating once again."

Tavish's head jerked in his direction, and he scowled. "She just came to, and that's the first thing you say to her?"

"What?" Finnian's brows furrowed. "She came back from the dead. I'm telling you, that's something. No one else here can say that."

I tried licking my lips, but it didn't accomplish anything since everything inside me was bone dry. Still, I tried to focus on what Finnian had let slip. "I died?" The peaceful darkness now made sense.

"That's what it sounded like, but maybe your heart just became very weak." Finola patted my arm. "But we're mending you."

I turned my head toward her, only to see her holding a hooked needle and thread. Golden blood covered the needle, telling me everything I needed to know. Mending me must mean stitching me together.

I lifted my head a little and stared at my injured side. The skin was closed with gray silk stitches, and the bleeding seemed to have stopped. But that wasn't what worried me. It was the black blood that coated every other inch of my body.

Dammit, I had nightmare snake and Unseelie blood all over me. The ickiness brought up the horror of the final gauntlet.

"What's bothering you?" Tavish leaned forward, scanning the bed.

I flinched, the pain intensifying for a second. "I'm

drenched in blood and in your bed." He should have put me on the floor. It would've been easier to clean.

"Where you're supposed to be." His jaw clenched, and his irises smoldered.

My heart skipped a beat. I didn't know what had changed, but I *really* liked him saying that.

"Your Majesty." The dark-blue-haired guard cleared his throat. "I *hate* to interrupt you, but Eldrin..."

Tavish hung his head, and I could see the weight of the guard's words impacting him. Eldrin had a way of sneaking up and ruining the precious moments we shared.

"I can go in your stead," Caelan offered.

I located him against the wall next to the bathroom door, and my lungs seized. I hadn't noticed him until he'd spoken.

Tavish sighed. "As much as I want to accept that offer, I can't. With Eldrin's new status, I need to be part of the search."

New status? I didn't like the sound of that. I wanted to panic, but before I could ask questions, Tavish bent down and kissed me gently... in front of everyone here.

Butterflies took flight in my stomach, and if I hadn't been covered in blood, I would've deepened our kiss.

"I'll return as soon as possible," he vowed, cupping my face. Then he turned to address Finola, Finnian, and Caelan. "You three, stay here and keep guard, and Faelan will join me. I worry Eldrin will attempt to finish what he started."

A lump formed in my throat, making me more desperate for water. I hadn't ever been this parched before, not even during the second trial when I'd almost been burned to a crisp.

He released his grip, and I wanted to beg him to stay.

But I refused to become the sort of needy woman who couldn't survive on her own. "Just hurry back."

The mattress moved, adjusting to him standing, and he paused. "That will be my motto from here on out, sprite."

He hurried to the door and left with Faelan.

When the door shut, Finola walked around the bed to my other side while Finnian dropped to the spot next to me on my left.

My body jarred, and I hissed as my wound pulsed.

"Easy. She may be mended, but she's still injured." Finola *tsked* and rolled her eyes as she settled by the side of me that wasn't as brutally injured.

He winced. "I wasn't thinking. Is there anything you need?"

Two things that seemed equally important leaped into my mind. One took precedence, and my mouth answered based on survival first. "Water." Some dirt and sand kicked into my airways, causing a coughing fit. Each time I coughed, it felt like my stitches were going to rip, and nausea roiled inside me.

Finnian readied to jump from the bed, but Caelan growled, "Stop moving and stay put so you aren't bothering her injuries more. The last thing we need is Tavish becoming more unreasonable about her."

Unreasonable.

That word hurt coming from him, especially since he had more influence than most with Tavish.

I could hear Caelan filling up a glass as I continued to hack. My eyes burned with unshed tears, and I was beginning to believe I would never stop coughing.

"Here, let's sit you up so you can drink easier, and I can tend to your final injury," Finola said, wrapping an arm around my back and under my armpits. She helped to raise me up. My sides screamed as she slid me back so the bed's pillows could keep me upright.

Once I was settled, Caelan handed me a glass. With each cough, a little water spilled from the side and hit Finnian. Instead of getting flustered, he helped guide the cup to my lips. I took a huge gulp, and the relief was immediate. The warm spot in my chest sparked, almost in sync with the sip that eased my chest as it slid down.

I couldn't get over how miraculous the water was here.

Each gulp made my chest feel lighter, and even though the pain remained, I could handle the agony better. Once I'd drained the glass, Finnian took it from me and held it out to Caelan.

Caelan gritted his teeth then asked, "Do you need more?"

Even if I did, I was certain I didn't want to ask him for *anything* else. "No, I'm good."

"This is going to pinch," Finola said and jabbed the needle into my side.

I whimpered, caught off guard as the needle broke through my skin. At least on Earth, they numbed people before stitching them up, but I knew better than to say anything. I refused to be seen as weaker than they already considered me.

I leaned my head back, feeling the sticky blood that coated me. I needed a distraction. "What's going on with Eldrin?" Out of everyone here, he was the one who truly got under my skin, and I hated it. Every time I saw his face, the horrible way he'd hidden in the shadows and attacked me in the tub surfaced in my mind.

Finnian beamed and raised a hand. "Something that I never thought would happen, and I'm so blasting glad it did."

"Easy." Finola paused. "Don't jerk the mattress, or I could hurt her."

I snorted but covered it with a cough. My muscles screamed in discomfort as if Finola wasn't putting me through enough torture on her own. A tear trickled down my cheek, and I brushed it away, hoping no one had noticed.

Caelan did, and he wrinkled his nose. He hated me more now than when I'd arrived.

"Okay, I'll stay still." Finnian lowered his arm slowly to his side. "Eldrin wanted to kill you, and Tavish stabbed him and declared that he was officially a prisoner. After all these years, I'm thrilled that Tavish finally tired of his antics and did something about it."

"Don't celebrate too early." Caelan rubbed his temples.

Hmm, did fae get headaches like humans? That was my mom's tell before a migraine came on.

Finola stabbed a little harder with the needle, and I tensed. I bit the inside of my cheek, trying to relocate the pain so it wouldn't overwhelm me. I took in a shaky breath, wondering if she'd be sewing me up for the rest of my life. At this point, it sure felt like it—though I wasn't trying to be dramatic. "What do you mean?"

"Whether we like it or not, a lot of people here respect Eldrin, and Tavish turned on his own blood, the man who saved him." Caelan paced in front of the bed. "Between that and interfering with the gauntlet and informing everyone that you're under his protection, Tavish will have to be careful with his next moves, especially since Eldrin might have escaped."

My world tilted. "Tavish did all that?" I didn't remember much after he'd stepped in and protected me. I'd been disoriented. Hearing how much he'd risked for me turned my insides gooey.

"It's not a good thing for him, though it puts you in a remarkably good position." Caelan smacked his lips like he tasted something bad. "You get protection while he has to prove to his people all over again that he's worthy to lead them."

"Caelan, leave her alone." Finnian slowly swung his legs over the mattress and stood. His face tensed, and he crossed his arms. "She almost died, and you're being a wildling. She didn't force Tavish to do anything, so the issues you have are with *him*. Not her."

My heart expanded, and when Finola placed the silk in her mouth and bit off the end, I wanted to cry with relief. I wasn't sure how much longer I could've taken her poking and prodding, and I wanted Tavish to return so Caelan could take his sulky ass out of here. Though I did appreciate his concern for Tavish. That alone made me like him better.

Caelan huffed. "That doesn't change that Eldrin will use the situation to his advantage like he tried to do twelve years ago, but this time, Tavish is aiding the Seelie princess. Eldrin's claims could carry more weight."

"When he stabbed Eldrin?" I asked. Tavish had mentioned a disagreement between them, and he'd had to put Eldrin in his place. "What happened?"

Finnian frowned. "Eldrin claims he's the rightful heir, even though he didn't receive the royal magic. Eldrin's father was the eldest brother, but he passed away before the magic was inherited. When Tavish's grandfather perished, the magic transferred to the first direct blood descendent— Tavish's father."

I scoffed, causing my body to ache a little more. "Eldrin wasn't passed over. That's how the royal blood works." And a part of me believed Fate had intervened. I couldn't fathom Eldrin as king. It would be disastrous for everyone.

Either way, it was irrelevant and not worth focusing on. There was no question Tavish held the royal magic and was the rightful king.

Someone knocked on the bedroom door, and I froze.

Could it be Eldrin?

"Finola, I've brought Nightbane as requested," an unfamiliar female called from the other side of the door. "Do I let him in?"

A threatening growl had me wanting to rush to the door, but as soon as I tried to move, my sides stung, reminding me that I had a lot of healing to do.

"Yes," Finola answered, standing and grabbing the hilt of her sword. She lifted it like she suspected an intruder was on the other side of the door.

When the door opened, the cù-sìth came barreling into the bedroom. His glowing green eyes focused on me, and his dark fur with green-tinged ends flattened from where it had risen on his neck. He stalked toward me, taking a moment to look at every person. A deep growl rattled through him as if he were trying to figure out who'd injured me.

The door slammed shut without the woman even saying goodbye, but I didn't blame her. Nightbane was a huge animal that instilled fear in others.

Now that he was here, there was only one thing I wanted to do. "I'm going to take a bath." Though it might not be smart with my injuries, I needed to get the blood off me. "Nightbane can come in the bathroom with me to keep an eye out."

Finola nodded. "Good idea. Finnian or Caelan can grab you a gown and tell a castle maid to come in here and change the sheets."

"I'll handle that." Caelan rolled his shoulders like he couldn't wait to get out of here. "I'll be right back."

I slowly moved to the edge of the bed. My tunic had been ripped into a crop top, and my leather pants were molded to my skin. By the time Caelan exited the room, I was on my feet.

When I glanced back at the gray sheets, I saw the blood smears I'd left all over them. I doubted there was a way to clean them.

"Don't worry, Lira." Finnian winked. "We'll take care of it, and if you need us, just yell."

Nightbane came to my side, and I tangled my fingers in his fur, breathing in his pine and wet-soil smell. He whimpered, rubbing against my hip as we made our way into the bathroom.

My eyes adjusted to the soft candlelight, and I strolled to the tub with its frosted bottom and stepped onto the elevated platform it was centered on.

I turned the faucet lever, and aqua-blue water poured from the spout. From the closet to the right of the tub, I took out a fluffy gray towel and placed it on the side. Then I slowly removed my clothes, my muscles feeling like they were pulling apart at my sides.

Once undressed, I stepped into the tub, trying to ignore the shadow-hazed wall on my left, which looked like a dark forest loomed behind it. A chill ran down my spine as I searched the shadows for Eldrin. The one comfort I had was that Nightbane lay at my side, unconcerned.

I'd hang on to that.

I sat in the tub, enjoying the way the water made my skin tingle, and leaned my head back, waiting for the tub to fill. A huge dark lantern lit by a candle hung above me, reminding me of a starry night.

As I submerged myself in the water, the blood disappeared like magic, and my skin felt clean and refreshed while the pain disappeared. The warm spark inside me thrummed again.

Once the water had risen past my breasts, I turned off the faucet and got clean. I wasn't sure how long I remained in the tub, but when I finally got out, I didn't hurt anywhere near as much as I had before. I dried off then realized I didn't have the gown. I needed Finola to meet me at the door and hand it to me.

Nightbane suddenly stood and growled, and I jerked to a halt, my muscles moving painfully. I yelped and gripped my injured side, causing the towel to fall from half my body, leaving me naked and exposed.

Terror tried to choke me, but I screamed, "Help!"

3

LIRA

I looked around the dark room for something to use as a weapon. There was nothing in sight, and I wished I hadn't removed the daggers I'd hidden in the toilet tank the night I'd tried to escape.

Nightbane snarled and moved toward the door as it opened.

My breath caught as Tavish rushed into the bathroom with his sword drawn. His eyes widened, and he took in my state of undress before looking around for my tormentor. He shut the door and raised his sword, ready to strike.

The beast wasn't concerned with the bathroom but rather with whoever was in the bedroom.

"Is everything—" Finnian started to say from outside the door, and the knob turned.

I snatched up the side of the towel, ignoring my aching muscles as I covered my entire chest. My face heated from Tavish seeing me like this. I didn't want to add anyone else to the equation.

Tavish froze. "Do *not* come in here. Lira is in merely a towel."

"Which is why I'm trying to hand her this gown," Finnian responded without worry, opening the door enough to slide his arm through and hold out the dress.

I snagged the gown from his hand, and Nightbane ran into the bedchamber. The beast snarled, and I heard another man yell. He didn't sound like Caelan or, unfortunately, Eldrin.

Not wanting anyone else to enter, I moved to shut the door even before Finnian had removed his arm.

"What the blast?" he groaned.

I grimaced and opened the door slightly. "Just remove your arm so I can get dressed."

"Aw, why should Tavish get—"

"Finnian, be quiet," Caelan called from the bedroom. "Or do you want to die?"

Tavish moved beside me with his teeth clenched and his sword sheathed. He was upset, and I couldn't blame him.

Deep, menacing growls sounded from Nightbane, but I didn't hear an attack. More like he was warning the others to stay away.

I'd freaked out over nothing. Figured.

"When Nightbane became anxious, I thought..." I bit my bottom lip. I hated the shiver that shot down my spine. I wanted to vanish.

Tavish's expression smoothed, and he cupped my face in his hands, forcing me to look him in the eye.

"Hey, I'm not upset with you. If you were alarmed, you did the right thing." His nostrils flared. "My issue is with Finnian and all the things he says."

He was comforting me, and I wanted to return the favor. "He only says half the stuff he does to get under your skin. Maybe if you ignored him, he'd stop pulling your leg."

Forehead wrinkling, Tavish stared at me as if I had two

heads. "Sometimes, I have no idea what you're trying to say to me. Earth is such a strange place."

I laughed, the sound light and reminding me of my old self... and then the ache of missing my sister and parents squeezed my heart. I tried to push away the sadness and focus on the present. "What I mean is that Finnian likes to annoy you."

"Yes, and if he's not careful, I'll wind up losing my temper and killing him for it." His eyes narrowed and flashed with darkness before his face softened. "Is he the reason for your sudden sadness?"

I shook my head, not wanting to get into it. I tightened my grasp on the gown, my face warming as I remembered I was standing here in just a wet towel. I lifted the light-blue gown and smiled. "But if we don't get out there, he'll continue to make comments, and I'd rather he not die on my watch."

Tavish's Adam's apple bobbed as his gaze darted downward. A warm knot formed in my stomach—a knot I'd experienced only around him, which had gotten me into this whole mess to begin with. My attraction to him had been instantaneous, and my goal had been simple—a New Year's Eve kiss—the very thing that landed me here.

As if Finnian wanted to tempt Fate and his death, he knocked on the door and cooed, "What are you two doing in there? Several of us are still out in the chambers, waiting for you. If—"

"Step away from the door, Finnian, or I swear, I will end you without a morsel of remorse," Tavish snarled.

Nightbane continued to snarl, and Caelan sighed and said, "No wonder the Seelie managed to banish us."

My chest constricted. How could my biological parents have done that to these people? What had the Unseelie done that had doomed them to this future? As if living on the ruined dragon lands weren't enough, my people had to eliminate Tavish's parents and put me on Earth, where I'd forgotten about my life here. A whole slew of questions attacked my brain.

Yanking the door open, Tavish stalked out, and then I heard a *smack*.

"Blighted abyss!" Finnian exclaimed. "What was that for?"

I chuckled and tensed, waiting for the agony, but it never came. Then a chill in the bathroom caused me to shiver, and goose bumps sprouted all over my skin. I hated being in here alone.

Breath quickening, I slipped the gown on and scanned the room every few seconds, imagining Eldrin's creepy-ass eyes staring at me from the corners.

I enjoyed the fact that the gown was looser than the other ones I'd worn, which had belonged to Tavish's mother. I suspected they'd raided someone else's clothes that fit me better.

Running my fingers through my hair, I entered the bedchamber, happy to be with Tavish and Finnian and not alone in *there*—until my gaze landed on Struan.

The memory of his smirk and chuckles as my wings had been bound flashed in my head. Even though he hadn't harmed me, he'd stared at me with complete hatred... more so than most of the other Unseelie who lived here, which spoke volumes.

Refusing to show my hesitation, I straightened my shoulders and lifted my chin. I wouldn't cower to him. That was what the guard wanted.

Also, it helped that Struan was backed against the wall near the door to the hallway. Nightbane was hunkered down, his fur high on the nape of his neck. I hoped Struan desperately needed a change of underwear.

"She's *alive*?" He frowned and blinked like he couldn't believe his eyes. "But she was severely injured! This is impossible."

"Why is *he* here? Is he a snack for Nightbane, who's such a good boy?" Now Nightbane's reaction made sense. The beast had seen what Struan had done to me before throwing me into the arena. He must have sensed my fear and associated it with the guard.

I wasn't complaining.

"He's the last guard who saw Eldrin while he was in the castle." Tavish rolled up the sleeves of his black tunic.

My attention went straight to the vines and thorns that had magically appeared on him at the same time they had on me.

Tavish lowered his hands, resting his right one on the dark, smooth hilt of his white-tipped sword. "And I wanted to make sure he heard the same message everyone in the arena did so there's no chance of a misunderstanding." He smiled without warmth, and his irises turned almost the same color as his wings—onyx.

Struan wrinkled his nose. "About the Seelie wildling?"

"The Seelie *what*?" Tavish gritted out, and he drew his sword, preparing to swing.

Caelan huffed from beside Tavish. "Is this necessary? People aren't happy about what happened. You can't expect them to celebrate that the gauntlet is over, especially when they discover that Lira is alive."

A warm hand landed on my shoulder, and I looked at Finnian, who winked. He mouthed, *Don't fret.*

"Yes, it's more than necessary—it's a blasting require-ment." Darkness swirled around Tavish, and the temperature dropped several degrees. "Lira is no longer a prisoner. She is free to go where she wishes without being harmed. If anyone disobeys that, I'll kill them. No questions asked. Do you understand?"

I should have been angry with Tavish, but instead, my shoulders lightened. He was protecting me the only way he knew how, even if he was misguided. Fear had been his tactic for so long, and it was the one thing his people associated with him.

"Yes, Your Majesty," Struan murmured, though his body was rigid.

Nightbane bared his teeth and pawed at the smooth floor, his lime eyes glowing brighter.

Glancing at the beast, Tavish nodded and focused back on the guard. "I hope you do. And if any of the other guards do anything to harm her, you'll be held responsible as well."

His mouth dropped. "What? That isn't fair!"

"Fair isn't my concern. Lira's safety is." Tavish arched a brow and tilted his head.

Chest heaving, Struan made his displeasure obvious, but he didn't say anything more.

"See?" Finnian whispered in my ear before bumping me in the shoulder.

My body jerked, and I winced. Luckily, I swallowed my moan.

"Now that we've settled that topic, tell me what happened with Eldrin." Tavish leaned back on his heels, his left arm crossing his body and cradling his right elbow. "I want to hear every detail."

A muscle twitched in Struan's neck. "Eldrin walked past me toward a window, informing me that he was in a hurry. Then he flew out."

"Interesting." Tavish tapped his lips. "You and Eldrin are close. He didn't tell you any more than that?"

"Oh. Um..." Struan's forehead wrinkled, and he wrung his hands. "He told me he had to go to the village and that he hoped to be back."

Yeah, I suspected the nightfiend had said more than that, given Struan's prickly behavior.

"The village. Good." Tavish placed the sword back in its sheath. "That helps a lot. You're dismissed."

I opened my mouth to object, but Finnian stepped in front of me, blocking my view of Struan. He mouthed, *Quiet.*

Anger heated my blood. Yeah, I'd teach the prick exactly how quiet I could be after Struan left the room. I didn't want to cause more friction for Tavish by throwing a tantrum.

The door to the hallway opened, and Nightbane snarled. Teeth clacked as he snapped, and Struan yelped, slamming the door behind him.

"What the hell was that?" I snapped, shoving Finnian in the chest. My sides still ached, but not to the point where I wanted to cry and vomit, which was progress.

"Sprite, be careful." Tavish flew and landed at my side within a second. "Your injuries. We don't need you bleeding anymore. I worry you won't survive it."

My pulse fluttered. "I'm feeling better."

"We still can't risk you reopening the injury." Tavish pivoted to Finnian and growled, "And what did you do to her?"

He lifted both hands. "Nothing. She wanted to confront Struan, and I told her to be quiet."

My blood cooled to a normal temperature. "What? You knew he was evading the truth?"

"We knew before he came in here." Tavish cupped my cheek and smiled tenderly. "But we needed to listen to him for show and to make my stance about you clear so the guards can't claim there was a misunderstanding."

"Now we put Finola on him to watch his every move." Caelan placed his hands behind his back. "Which we hope will lead us to where Eldrin is hiding. I suspect we'll have him back in the cell within three days, if not less."

Okay. That sounded like good news. Then a thought slammed into me. "But my parents and sister. He threatened them. What if he's heading to Earth to kill them for revenge?" Panic clawed at my chest, and I felt as if I couldn't breathe. Had I put everyone I loved in danger by living?

"Blighted abyss!" Tavish kicked at the floor. "With you nearly dying, I'd forgotten his threat."

"I can go check on them." Finnian's wings fluttered. "I went to Earth with you once before, so as long as you tell me how to get there, I should be fine."

I hated that I was a burden, but I wouldn't reject his help. I needed to make sure Eiric and my parents were safe. "Or I can go."

"You can't go anywhere." Tavish shook his head and stepped closer to me so that our arms touched. "Just like I can't—I need to deal with the turmoil in the kingdom. Finnian, when you get there, you can't stay long, or you'll risk losing your memories. You need to bring them here so we can protect them from Eldrin until the threat is over."

"I'll be fine." Finnian rubbed his hands together. "Besides, Earth is interesting. It's been years since I visited."

Caelan crossed his arms. "This isn't for pleasure. It's a mission."

"Noted." Finnian beamed.

Tavish went over the instructions on getting to Earth while I turned toward the bed, wanting to sink into the mattress. Navy sheets had replaced the bloodstained bedding, and it looked so inviting. But with the way Caelan kept darting glares at me as he listened to Tavish and Finnian's conversation, I didn't want to lie down and make myself a target.

Instead, I stared out the large windows the men stood in front of. The sky was clearer than it'd been since I'd arrived, the stars twinkling and the full moon shining down on the dark village.

After a few minutes, the men dispersed.

Finnian came over and hugged me. "Don't worry, Lira." He held my gaze. "I won't be gone long, and I know what I'm doing. Trust me."

The realization that I did trust him crashed over me. "Be safe."

He released me and squeezed my arm. "I will." He headed out with Caelan on his tail.

"I'll tell Finola to select someone she trusts to stand guard tonight over your room," Caelan said as he exited into the hallway. "We don't need Eldrin sneaking in and undermining your word."

"Sounds good." Tavish ran his hands through his hair and sighed. "We both know I can't kill him, so it's best to have people guarding me who can."

As soon as we were alone, Tavish excused himself to take his own bath.

Alone in the room, I couldn't resist the bed with its fresh sheets. Fatigue hit me, weighing me down. I crawled onto the mattress on the side closest to the windows.

Nightbane jumped onto the bed and lay down at my feet, and I listened to his breathing and fell fast asleep.

I woke, and something immediately felt off. I took in the room and found Tavish standing by the windows, staring out toward the village and the ocean. He had his hands on the back of a wooden chair, and his shoulders were hunched.

He resembled a defeated man.

"Did you want me to sleep on the floor?" My throat thickened. I hadn't considered it, but now that the trials were over and after risking so much, maybe he didn't want me lying next to him. I uncovered myself and threw my legs over the side.

"Of course not!" He turned to me. Something fell from his cheek onto the chair.

Was it a tear?

I'd come between him and his cousin, and I hadn't considered how that might make him feel. "I'm not sure how to make this better. I never meant to cause a disagreement between you and your only family."

He straightened, and his eyebrows lifted. "Is that what you think has me upset?"

I nodded. "Don't get me wrong. I appreciate you stepping in and protecting me, but I understand—"

"*Protecting* you?" He laughed bitterly. "I wish I could claim that was what I did?"

The sound reminded me of the man he'd been when I arrived here. I'd missed something, and it must be important, judging by this change in him.

I swallowed, realizing the truth. "You still plan to kill me." That had been his plan from the very beginning—to kill me in front of the Seelie. My mouth dried.

He moved toward me with a scowl on his face. "Is that a statement or a question?"

A whimper lodged in my throat, and my lungs refused to fill with air.

He repeated his question and added, "Because if it's a question, you'd better be prepared for the answer. I'm done hiding things from you."

For some reason, I needed to hear him say it. "It's a question." I needed to find a way to construct a barricade around my heart once again.

Before I realized what was happening, he'd closed the distance between us and lowered his mouth to my ear. Then he whispered.

LIRA

"Y ou're safe with me forevermore, sprite."
His lips brushed my earlobe, and I shuddered. I
breathed in his amber and musk scent and grew dizzy.

"If you let me, I'll spend the rest of eternity making up
for what I put you through, but even then, it won't be
enough." His voice broke at the end.

This had to be a dream because Tavish would never
speak like this to me. It was impossible. I shook my head,
realizing that someone had to be using illusion magic on me.
I leaned back, trying to come to my senses before I wound
up with a broken heart.

Straightening, he let out a shaky breath and grimaced.
"I don't blame you for not wanting anything to do with me. I
kidnapped you to kill you, and I've put you at risk too many
times to keep count. It took losing you for me to finally come
to my senses."

I lifted a hand, and my heart squeezed. "Stop, *please*.
Don't make this harder than it needs to be."

"I understand I may be too late, but I blasting need to
say it anyway." He clutched his chest. "I know how risky

this is for me, of all people, to say, but Lira, I'm so sorry for everything that happened to you. I don't care if my apology causes me to owe you something substantial because I already plan to make things right between us for the rest of my existence."

A lump formed in my throat. I'd never dreamed he'd say *anything* like that. My heart fluttered with the hope that this was real.

I needed to wake up, so I pinched the inside of my wrist. A sharp pain stabbed me, but nothing changed.

"If waking each day to grovel at your feet will help you forgive me one day, I'll gladly do it." Tavish's hand tugged at his thin gray tunic. "If pulling back all the darkness so the sun can rise and melt the snow from the only sanctuary my people and I know, I'll make it happen. Just tell me what I have to do to keep you in my life. If it's within my power, I'll do it without question, and if it isn't, I'll find a blasting way to make it happen. At the end of the night, I'll give up whatever it takes as long as you stay with me."

The world tilted underneath me, and I wrapped my arms around my waist to anchor myself to this strange, new reality. "Tavish, I—"

"Don't say anything. Not yet." Tavish bit his bottom lip and took a hesitant step closer. "This might change how you feel, but I need to be honest."

The hair on the nape of my neck rose in warning, so I nodded, afraid to speak.

His eyes lightened to silver. "I wish I could say I regret kidnapping you, but I can't."

I started, not expecting that.

"If I hadn't, I wouldn't be here with you now, and that's unfathomable. I'm a selfish, entitled moron who regrets everything that happened to you, but I can't find the remorse you deserve for bringing you here and setting off this entire chain of events." He hung his head like the guilt weighed on him. "Which gives you every right to hate me and every reason to get far, far away from me." His eyes glistened as he stared into my eyes, warning me away. "If you want to leave, you're free to go. I won't make you stay. I just hope you don't for my own selfish sake."

The little bit of a wall I'd constructed around my heart shattered. His giving me the freedom to decide whether to stay or leave made things desperately clear, even though my head screamed *no*. "I want to stay, but I fear what might happen to us." The simple truth couldn't be ignored. Even if I wanted to leave, I couldn't. Not now... not with him saying these things.

He winced. "You should want to get far away from me. In fact, I should make you." A tear trailed down his cheek as his irises turned stormy. "For your own safety, you should leave now before I change my mind and refuse to let you go. I'm struggling—and knowing it's best for you to leave is the only thing forcing me to say the words. If you don't leave and change your mind later, I won't be strong enough not to hunt you down. Do you understand?"

Why did the sound of him hunting me down thrill me? I was tempted to try it just for the thrill of seeing his desperation to retrieve me, but even considering doing that made me feel guilty.

At the end of the day, I wanted him to know I felt the same way. "I understand, and I'm not going anywhere." I wiped the stray tear from his face. "You're right, though. You're the reason for everything I've gone through since you brought me here, so why the sudden change?"

"I struggled with your situation the entire time, but you were Seelie, and it was easier to hang on to that hatred. I felt a pull toward you, but I thought that maybe if you went away, I wouldn't struggle anymore." He flinched. "But the more time we spent together, the stronger the tug became—until I had to open my eyes."

He huffed but didn't pull away. "You met every challenge that came your way head-on, even when the odds weren't in your favor. You showed empathy, strength, and a resilience I never knew existed, and the way it pained you so much to kill one of us despite how we treated you forced me to open my eyes and actually see *you*. I hate that it took me so damn long." His jaw clenched.

And that was what I needed to know. "This moment right here, with you opening up to me and baring your soul, made it all worth it. If you feel for me half of what I do for you, there's no question where I need to be."

He caught my hand, and the buzz from his touch warmed my body even more. He whispered, "Some of my people will still want to kill you. You'll still be at risk here, and your parents will eventually come for you. My guards may not be able to fight them off, so you'll have to make a stand. That's too much to ask."

"It's not." I stepped into him, our chests touching. "I don't even remember them, Tavish. My parents are the ones on Earth, the ones Finnian is fetching. They raised me when my biological ones passed me off without a second thought. Standing up to them won't be hard because they're strangers."

"They won't be for much longer." His free hand touched the top of my sparkly sea-green wing. "Your magic is returning, which means your memories will be restored at any moment."

The way he touched my wings almost had a groan slipping out. I'd never felt anything so intimate before, but I'd had wings for only a few days. That had to be why. Still, need burrowed deep in my stomach.

"I've given you no reason to want to stay here. It's merely the fated-mate bond forcing you to speak this way." He scanned my face, taking in every crevice.

"Fated mate?" Finnian had alluded to some sort of connection, but he hadn't named it. Is that what he'd meant?

He sighed. "Right. You don't remember. It's when a soul is halved and placed in two separate people. They're only whole when together, and it's Fate's way of marking the perfect person for you. It's rare and precious, and the magical markings indicate what we are to each other and also make it clear to everyone around us. It causes the buzzing between us and the urge to be next to one another. The connection makes us want to be together, even when it's bad for us."

The explanation made so much sense, and somehow, it made me even more certain. "I could say the same for you, but I know that's not true." I cupped his face, lifting his head so he stared into my eyes. "You took care of me in your own way, even when you didn't want to. You saved me from a guard who wanted to disfigure me when you didn't have to. You had me stay in your bedroom instead of a horrid prison cell that smelled of bodily fluids while giving me a comfortable place to sleep, clean clothes, and a bathtub."

"I made you sleep on the floor, and you were attacked in the tub." Tavish's jaw clenched. "If only I could kill my cousin—"

"You did what you could with the debt you owe him." I placed a finger over his lips, wanting him to allow me to finish. He had to stop beating himself up so much. "You clothed me, fed me, and allowed Nightbane to stay with me to protect me. You kept me safe, even from your own people."

He winced. "I should've done it sooner. You never should have suffered through the gauntlet."

"I believe the gauntlet is the reason my power has started coming back." Until I'd been forced to protect myself and get through perilous situations, I hadn't shown any changes. "And if you hadn't kidnapped me, we wouldn't be having this moment. It sucks that it took all that for us to get here, but if we can move forward stronger together, then everything will have been worth it."

"Don't say that. What you went through was unbear—"

I was tired of him talking, so I kissed him.

He froze but didn't pull away, so I brushed my tongue over his lips, needing to taste him.

"Blast," he groaned, opening his mouth to allow me entrance.

I slid my arms around his neck, my sides aching a tad, but not enough to make me stop. The taste of what I could only describe as velvet night and frosty air made me want more. My fingers twined into his hair as I pressed my body to his.

We'd kissed like this only once before, and it'd been cut short when he noticed the magical tattoo on my chest. This time, nothing would stop us, even if I had to take the lead.

He wrapped his arms around my body, pulling me flush against him. Then he dropped his hands and tried to step back quickly.

I let him go as a sharp ache shot through my heart. "Did I do something wrong?"

"No." He adjusted the large bulge in his pants. "That's the problem."

"How is that a problem?" Suddenly, I felt like I was

back in English class where all these strict rules existed, but there was a list of crazy exceptions you had to memorize.

He lifted both hands and ran them through his hair. "Because you're injured, and kissing me like that will ruin my self-control. I can't risk hurting you again."

"You won't hurt me." I fisted his tunic and pulled him toward me. My body was uncomfortably warm, and there was one thing that would fix that issue.

As soon as he was back within reach, I kissed him. He groaned, pressing his hardness into my stomach. I gasped as need soared through me.

He stopped moving. "Did I hurt you?"

"No, but if you keep stopping, I'm going to hurt *you*." I pivoted on my heels, dragging him with me, and shoved him onto the bed.

Nightbane's lime eyes glowed, and he snarled at Tavish.

"Come on, boy." I released Tavish's shirt and clicked my tongue, wanting the beast to obey me.

Thankfully, he did, and I led him into the bathroom. If he was going to threaten Tavish when he already had reservations about him touching me, Nightbane needed to stay in a separate room until it was safe for him to be with us.

When I opened the door and told him to go in, the beast tilted his head like he didn't understand. Somehow, he realized I had no intention of going in there with him. "It's okay. It won't be for long."

He scoffed but went into the bathroom, allowing me to shut the door behind him.

When I turned back to the bed, I found Tavish where I'd pushed him, but his face was lined with worry.

Walking back to him, I lifted both hands. "If you don't want to kiss or..." I trailed off, feeling my face flame. I wasn't even sure what to say because I didn't want to sound like I expected more than he was willing to do. I didn't want to pressure him.

"Sprite, there is *nothing* more I want than to be buried inside you. But you're hurt, and I lost you once already. I can't risk it."

His words lit a fire inside me, and it had nothing to do with embarrassment. He wanted me, though I doubted it compared to how much I needed him. "The pain is barely a discomfort now."

He sat up and motioned for me to come to him.

My legs moved of their own accord. When I reached him, I waited for him to give in, but instead, he lifted the left side of my shirt and inspected my injury.

His jaw dropped. "That isn't possible."

I glanced down to find that the gaping wound from earlier was now a mere scab. "I... I don't know how that healed so fast. But I told you I'm not hurting like before." I had my own questions about that, but there was something way more pressing on my mind.

Emboldened by his words and his shock, I wrapped my arms around his neck and straddled him.

"You're going to be the death of me," he murmured. "And I'll cherish each moment of dying." Then he kissed me, and this time, it was different.

No restraint.

Instead of moving his hand from my side, he reached up and cupped my breast as he devoured my mouth. Each stroke of his tongue had me needing more, and I rolled my hips against him.

His fingers gently rolled over my nipple, causing me to arch. I'd never been this turned on before, and I felt like I might implode if we didn't get there faster. I reached down and yanked the hem of my gown over my head, baring my body to him. He was worried that I didn't want this—that I didn't want him—and I wanted to make it very clear that I did.

Now both his hands cupped my breasts as he leaned forward and kissed my neck and then moved downward. He wrapped one arm around my body and paused, whispering, "I'm going to lower you onto your back."

I nodded and folded my wings in, and he moved me slowly and gently, making sure not to grasp my side. My blonde hair spilled over the pillow as he kneeled between my legs, lazily scanning me. "You're the most beautiful woman I've ever seen, Lira."

His inability to lie and the adoration on his face had my chest expanding uncomfortably. There were so many things I wanted to say, but I settled on something I could actually get out. "Show me."

He smirked, looking more handsome than ever before. "Gladly."

Sliding his body onto mine, he lowered his head and took my nipple into his mouth. One hand slid between my legs, spreading my lips apart. His tongue flicked my nipple as a finger slid inside me, and his thumb hit the most sensitive spot I'd ever experienced.

I moaned, wrapping an arm around his shoulder, needing his body closer. I slid my other hand into his pants and held his dick. I wasn't sure what to do, but Eiric had talked to me about some of the things her lovers liked, so I began to stroke him.

"Blast," he groaned, and I froze.

"Am I doing it wrong?" I hated to ask. He'd probably been with many women, and I didn't know what I was doing. "I'm sorry. I've never—" I tried to take my hand away, but he caught it with the hand that had been supporting his weight.

"You're doing it perfectly." He lifted his head, staring into my eyes. "Have you never done this with anyone before?"

I shook my head. "So if I'm not—"

"Thank gods." He let out a shaky breath. "I haven't either, and I'm only doing what I think you might enjoy."

The pressure that had been almost suffocating me vanished. "You're doing great. So you're a virgin too?"

His face turned a faint purple. "That was why Finnian teased me about finishing fast. I've never felt any sort of attraction to anyone... until you."

"I was the same way." My cheeks hurt from my huge smile.

"Then we can share this with each other." His smile was genuine and free, like our burdens had left temporarily, and the air between us sizzled.

His mouth crashed over mine as he continued to finger me and rub my clit while I stroked him to the point of becoming dizzy. Suddenly, the friction intensified, and pleasure exploded inside me. My breathing turned ragged as his fingers quickened, driving my body further over the edge.

When I came down, somehow, I wasn't satiated. I wanted *more*. He had control, and now it was my turn.

I pushed him down, grabbed the waist of his pants, then removed them. The need started pulsing between my legs again as I ogled him. He sat up and scooted to lean against the wooden headboard of the bed, removing his shirt and tossing it aside as I crawled over him.

My head spun with *need*, and I positioned myself over him. Before I could lower myself, he cupped my face.

"If we do this, you're *mine* forever. No Seelie or dragon can come between us. I won't allow it." His gaze leveled with mine. "Any man who touches you dies. Do you understand?"

Instead of answering him with words, I kissed him and bore down on him. His tip slipped inside me, and he hissed against my lips. The reaction made me feel sexy and in control, so I slid down farther and whispered, "Kill them all." If that was what it took for me to be his, I'd gladly accept the risk.

His lips turned up, and he gripped my waist below my injury. After he slid in another inch, we paused, allowing my body to adjust to his.

Our mouths collided as his hand caressed my breast.

Inch by inch, we connected slowly. When I thought I couldn't fit any more, my body somehow proved me wrong. Then he filled me, making me feel more complete than I knew I could feel.

I rocked my hips gently, and he leaned back and groaned. His eyes fluttered, and I wanted to make him feel like that even more.

Each time I moved, it hurt less, and it wasn't long before only pleasure coursed through my body.

He lowered his head to my breast, his tongue working my body the same way I worked his, and we began moving in sync. Each movement became faster, and sweat slicked our bodies. I sank my nails into his back near the base of his wings, causing his body to shudder.

"Lira, I can't wait much longer," he rasped.

The need in his voice had the pressure intensifying in me once more.

I moaned as ecstasy flooded me, and Tavish leaned back and shook with his own release. Something in my chest snapped open, and emotions that weren't only mine filled me whole.

Gods, I love this woman, Tavish said, but it was inside my head, and his orgasm melded with mine.

My head spun as we continued to chase our release, and I replied, *I love you, Tavish.*

His eyes opened, locking with mine, as the pleasure somehow intensified even more. Something settled inside my chest, warming a place I'd never noticed before. His love mixed with mine, and I realized we both felt the same.

There wasn't a question anymore.

We stilled, but I didn't move, wanting him to still fill my body. The thought of us not being connected bothered me. I felt closer to him than I'd ever felt with anyone else.

"You're stuck with me forever, sprite." He grinned, raising his left hand to show me the tattoo had continued down his hand and around his ring finger.

I raised mine, finding the same marks, though I hadn't felt the burn like before. "I could say the same for you, *nightmare.*" Without the nightmare, the two of us wouldn't be here.

He smirked and pulled me into his arms, anchoring me to his chest, but my head turned fuzzy, like something was off.

Tavish's voice popped into my head. *Lira, what's wrong?*

Before I could answer him, something *yanked* me from the present and tossed me into oblivion.

Darkness surrounded me, similar to when I'd been injured, but it wasn't the same. My stomach churned with unease. I gathered my bearings, knowing that physically, I was next to Tavish. The faint buzz of our bond pumped through my blood, constricting my throat.

There was no telling how Tavish was reacting.

I needed to talk with him, but there was only silence around me.

Then the darkness around me changed into a vision.

I stood in the center of a forest with green, leafy trees all around and a sun twice the size of Earth's beaming on me.

I lifted my head, enjoying the heat on my skin, when I heard a familiar voice call out, "Lira, you know that's not fair! You're using your magic to hide your scent."

My heart thumped as I spun around and flew deeper into the thick treetops.

I looked forward to my semiannual visits with Tavish. Even at nine, I'd felt a kindred spirit in him, and ever since I'd been able to fly, we'd played chase. It had started by accident when I was young and shy around him and tried to get away. Now, I enjoyed the thrill of him chasing me.

I'd cut a sharp left when arms wrapped around my waist. Tavish's boyish face beamed, the sharp edges that were so clear on the man I'd gotten to know since my capture not yet present. His silver eyes sparkled like the weight of the world and future hadn't crashed onto his shoulders, and my younger heart squeezed with an echo of the magnitude I felt today.

"That's not fair!" I squealed, trying to scowl but not succeeding. "You used the darkness to cloak you."

"And you used your water to hide your scent." One hand released me, and he booped me on the nose. "All's fair in a chase, sprite. You should know that by now."

I rolled my eyes, pretending I was annoyed, but I didn't pull it off. The best I could muster was mashing my lips to hide my smile. "And that's why your name should've been Thorn and not Tavish." I wrinkled my nose at him to look more menacing. "Because you're prickly and cause pain."

"Ah... but that's more fitting for a Seelie than me," he teased.

An unfamiliar voice called his name.

His smile dropped, and he released me, fluttering his wings. "I must leave. It's time for us to head home, but one day, we won't have only hours but forever to chase one another."

My little heart skipped a beat, though I didn't comprehend why. Instead, I straightened my shoulders to appear composed. "We'd better go."

The two of us flew back toward the voice that had called him, and we reached eight people standing together, four on each side, facing each other.

My breath caught as understanding of who they were washed over me.

My biological parents stood in the middle on one side, and the two people flanking them had my mind tensing. Even though they didn't look quite the same, there was no doubt they were my adoptive parents on Earth.

Dad's and Mom's skin was the same shade as on Earth but with a faint golden glow that made them look other-worldly, especially with their pointy ears.

Across from my two sets of parents stood Tavish's parents, flanked by Torcall and Finola. Two of the eight I had known in my human life, but the Unseelie and Seelie royals were just returning to my memory.

"It was an honor visiting with you again." Tavish's mother bowed her head, her long white hair slipping over her slender shoulders and almost blending in with her skin, which resembled the color of the snow that covered their kingdom.

The Seelie queen returned the bow, her hair the same shade as mine—medium blonde. It waved down her golden dress, emphasizing the golden freckles on her cheeks and her emerald-green eyes.

My favorite color.

"I'm excited about the potential of our kingdoms finally joining and becoming one." The Seelie king puffed out his chest and turned his cobalt eyes on me. "Lira is strong and smart, so she will be able to rule over the two kingdoms as one."

All my life... at least on Earth... people had known I was adopted. I'd become used to standing out with Eiric and my parents. Seeing my biological parents caused my chest to squeeze. I was a blend of them both, having my mother's hair and the same shade of eyes as the king, as well as his sun-kissed complexion.

"As is my son." The Unseelie king's jaw clenched. His gray eyes hardened, the edge in them matching the look I'd often seen in Tavish's today.

"That's fantastic, seeing as we'll be ruling together." Tavish cleared his throat and winked at me. He leaned toward me and whispered, "Don't worry. I'll never be that grumpy."

Before I could see what happened next, the image around me changed.

I lay in a massive bed with ten pillows underneath me. My biological parents sat on the edge of my bed, telling me good night. The moon hung high in the cloudless night outside the window to my left, where the view was partially obstructed by a sizable pink tree that reminded me of the cherry blossom trees Japan was renowned for. The most unsettling sensation was the contentment and love my younger self felt for them.

The memories sped up as I relived each one.

The next ones seemed more familiar as faces, feelings, and places started to feel like home.

Then they stopped, like a dark cloud hovering over me, yanking me back into the present.

"Lira." Tavish's voice shook in tune with my body. *I need you to wake up.*

My body thrummed as my consciousness settled back over me, and I choked as pain and terror settled into my heart and limbs.

Agony, that didn't belong to me... but Tavish.

I cracked my eyes open enough to see Tavish leaning over me, and the chill of the room confirmed I was still naked.

Of course, my magic would choose *the first time I had sex* to bring my memories back.

"Sprite." His head lifted, his stormy eyes lightening with hope. "Thank gods. I knew we shouldn't have completed our bond until you were fully healed. I'm so sorry yet *again*." His love, remorse, and concern replaced most of the fear.

My heartbeat quickened, and my cheeks stretched into a smile. "With all your apologies, you'll never get out of the debts you owe me, thorn."

His head jerked back, and the twinkle in his silver eyes returned like some of the memories I had experienced moments ago.

"What did you just call me?" he whispered.

"Thorn?" I lifted a brow. "Is that not okay?"

"You remember?" The corner of his lips lifted.

"I remember you chasing me." I wondered if that was why I had wanted to run earlier and liked the idea of him finding me. "And you were cheating with your magic."

He laughed warmly, his expression smoothing more into one of boyish charm. "Only because you used your water to wash away your scent. It's only fair when both of us can use our magic and not just the one." His face turned solemn. "But love, are you okay?"

I thought about that. The warm and refreshing spots in my chest were stronger than I had ever experienced... except for when I was younger. I had never noticed the warm spot when I was younger. Maybe because it had always been a part of me that I'd never accessed. But coming back and having my magic reactivated, I could feel that I had two different types of magic within me. I'd never done that before, and I wasn't sure how or why I was now.

Knowing Tavish needed comfort, I lifted my head and

kissed him. *I'm more than good and would actually be perfect if your arms were around me.*

I suppose I could oblige you with that. He nipped at my lips and settled beside me, pulling my back against his chest. Neither of us attempted to get dressed, and his body curled around me. Now that we'd completed the bond, the buzzing had grown into a jolt, and it felt natural to be nestled into him like this.

He peppered my neck with kisses, and I exhaled, completely content. And this time, I fell into a comforting sleep surrounded by the touch, scent, and taste of Tavish.

A whimper and scratching sound stirred my consciousness. My body thrummed with warmth, peace, and comfort, so the last thing I wanted was to open my eyes and move from this spot, but the whimper grew louder.

Awareness washed over me, and my mouth dried.

Nightbane.

I'd put him in the bathroom and forgot to let him out after we had sex.

Even though Tavish's body was cooler than mine, the jolt between us warmed me so much that I didn't need covers. I inched slowly from Tavish's arms and tiptoed to the bathroom.

At the door, I turned the handle slowly so as not to make a noise. When it was about two inches wide, Night-bane shoved his nose through the crack, forcing the door the rest of the way open.

I stumbled back a few steps as Nightbane trotted out, glaring at me. His eyes weren't lime-colored—like when he wanted to attack but worse. They were a dark green, like I'd hurt him.

It was official.

I was a wildling.

"I'm sorry." I hung my head, feeling like I was getting chastised by a parent. "I..." I stopped short, unsure what to say.

"Listen, beast," Tavish rasped sexily. "Don't make my mate feel bad about needing to connect with me. You've cuddled with her many nights while I've lain awake, jealous. It was your turn."

My head jerked in his direction, and I took in his disheveled appearance. Warmth spread through me. Clearly, he was having similar thoughts because his eyes were locked on my naked body, and he was already hard.

Go ahead and put him back in the bathroom, sprite. He licked his lips. *I'm thinking we need more time alone without an audience. Waking up to you naked and covered in fated-mate markings is the sexiest thing I have ever experienced in any realm.*

As my cheeks warmed, my legs took on a life of their own, forcing me to head toward him.

Nightbane huffed, reminding me that Tavish and I weren't alone. Then someone knocked on the door.

My lungs seized, and I searched frantically for my gown. I didn't want someone walking in on us naked.

"Your Majesty, do you want to join us this morning to search for Eldrin?" Finola called. "We're getting ready to leave, and you haven't been down for breakfast."

Tavish scowled, and heaviness like disappointment filled our bond. "Yes, I do," he called back. "Please get someone to bring breakfast to the room immediately and inform them I'll be eating off both plates, so neither better be poisoned."

I spotted the gown crumpled on the floor where I'd pretty much attacked him. I snagged it and slipped it over my body as Tavish searched around the bed for his own clothes.

If it weren't for Eldrin, there's no way I'd leave this bedroom. Tavish stepped into his pants, a frown on his face. *But you won't be safe until he's behind bars, so I'm sorry.*

Enjoying the view, I strolled around the bed, damn near pouting as he slipped on his tunic. He closed the distance between us and placed his hands on my ass cheeks to pull me against him.

I yelped before his lips captured mine, and his tongue slid into my mouth.

I responded eagerly, but another round of knocks on the door had me wanting to snarl.

"I'm coming in," Caelan informed us, and the door opened.

When I attempted to take a step back, Tavish held me in place, moving his mouth so he nibbled on my jaw. My breath caught, and I enjoyed the unexpected sensation.

Caelan's disapproving headshake had me closing my lips altogether. He held black armor in his hands.

Tavish groaned and glared at his friend. "What's so urgent?"

"I thought you might be grateful for me locating armor for Lira." He tossed the top and bottom onto the bed. "I'm assuming she'll be joining us while we search for Eldrin."

My heart rate picked up. I'd been outside the castle only twice. Once when I'd arrived and the other when I'd attempted to escape. The thought of actually learning about the kingdom had my blood pulsing with excitement.

"It's too risky for her to be out there." Tavish frowned. "She should stay here where she's safest."

That joy quickly changed to frustration, and I took a step back, needing distance. "You've got to be joking."

"Why in the blighted abyss would I joke about something like *this*?" Tavish lifted his chin and crossed his arms. "Your safety is the only thing that matters to me."

"And that of your people." Caelan rolled his eyes.

"My people come after Lira." Tavish turned his gaze on his friend. "I need to make that perfectly clear."

Caelan sneered. "Don't worry. You have."

Wow. This was tense, and I needed to refocus on the moment. "He brought me armor so I'll be protected. And I bet most of the guards will be out there searching with you. It'd be good for your people to see us together. Reinforce what you said yesterday and all that." I smiled and batted my eyes, hoping my words would sway him.

"She's right, and if you hide her, you'll make them resent her more." Caelan pointed at the armor. "With her by your side the entire time and with Finola and Moor protecting you, she'll be safer out there than in here."

Moor.

That was the guard who'd taken Torcall's place. My chest constricted.

"I don't—" Tavish started.

"Remember when you said I wasn't a prisoner anymore?" I lifted a brow and rocked back on my heels. "Did you mean it?"

He huffed, and his shoulders sagged. "Of course I did, which is now working against me."

I laughed and kissed his cheek. "Good, then we're settled."

You'd better love me, sprite. His eyes lightened as warmth spread between us.

Oh, I do, thorn. I winked at him and dashed over to the bed, ready to put my armor on.

My heart felt like the moment was perfect. Tavish had listened to what I wanted, to my needs, and we were going to find his cousin together. The way we'd be doing everything else from here on out.

Within an hour, Tavish and I had eaten and put on our armor.

We flew out of the castle's massive front doors, which were rarely used except in situations where the illusion of the castle taking action needed to be had. Then we soared over ground covered in snow so thick it hid the stone path below.

The sky showed a hint of light as snowflakes hit my face, the coldness refreshing and the air crisp with a hint of salt from the breeze that blew in from the sea where the village ended.

Everyone stood outside their homes, which reminded me more of townhomes or apartments than actual cottages. A dusting of snow covered the dark slabs that the houses were made of, making the entire place look pure white except for the surrounding dirt and rocks.

The fifty guards with us separated into teams and began searching each house while Tavish and I hovered in the sky side by side, waiting for Eldrin to be found. Another fifty guards left to search the ruined lands, to be thorough, but Tavish and Caelan believed Eldrin had to be somewhere inside. He wouldn't survive out in the lands for long. The mushrooms were nearby, in a cave with four guards keeping watch since last night in case he showed up. He would eventually need to come for the food. Unseelie weren't made to survive on meat alone.

The longer we stayed in place and the guards continued the search, the more disgruntled the Unseelie became.

A few women glared at me with all the hatred they could muster, and I forced myself to smile back at them, wanting them to see I didn't feel threatened. Still, my heart ached. Would these people ever see me as more than Seelie?

Who's upsetting you? Tavish linked, taking my hand and scanning the almost three thousand people the guards had forced from their homes so we could do this sweep.

The yellow-eyed man from the night I'd escaped spat on the ground, causing some of the snow to melt. He wasn't even trying to hide how he felt about me.

Tavish followed my gaze and snarled, but before he could say anything, something exploded at the far end of the houses.

"What the blast—" a man screamed, but his words cut off as smoke rose from the windows.

Someone down on the other end yelled, "Fire!"

The guards had made it almost to the halfway point, and they all came flying out of the houses with tense frowns on their faces.

Finola pointed at Tavish and me and said, "I need two guards to take them back to the castle until we find out what happened. This could be a threat from Eldrin."

"We'll take them," a woman guard with frosty-blue-tipped hair answered and pointed to the male guard beside her. "Everyone else, go."

Finola nodded, and she and the others flew toward the threat.

My heart raced. *I can use my water—*

That's probably why Eldrin made a fire, Tavish answered, tugging on my hand to take me back to the castle. *To lure you away, knowing how you like to help.*

I tensed, hating how well Eldrin knew me... almost better than I knew myself.

"Go ahead. I'll be right behind you," Tavish said and released me as he drew his sword.

The woman flew next to me while the man remained behind with Tavish, watching our backs.

With a few flaps of her wings, she came super close to me... so much that our arms brushed. She lifted her right arm up like she was readying her sword. Then the weapon vanished and morphed into a needle, which she stabbed into the back of my neck.

Tavish, I connected as fear squeezed my heart. I tried to turn and only managed a half spin. Just enough that I noticed Tavish's eyes widen as I lost the ability to move my wings.

The man flying beside him struck with his right arm. The sword he held shortened into a dagger and lodged into Tavish's neck.

Arms caught me as I began to drop, but that didn't matter.

All I could focus on was the pain that spiked from Tavish as the edges of my vision darkened.

T he heat of the flames burned through the frost magic I blanketed our kingdom with. After the Seelie had killed my parents and taken our lands, we hadn't had the strength to create a veil, so I'd done the only thing I could to make them and the dragons never want to visit—I'd made the land dark and cold, the two things they hated most.

My gaze remained on Lira. Her safety meant the most to me. I wanted to ensure she never experienced another ounce of torment or agony. I feared what the future held when her parents and the dragons learned of her return, but I purposely pushed that from my mind. I wanted to focus on the present and remediating the situation here before we had to address anything else.

Lira's sea-green wings were bright and warm, marking her as different from us, but through the thick snowfall I'd created to control the fire, she looked like the sun, calling me home.

When Ailsa's head snapped toward Lira, cold terror choked me. I followed the guard's gaze, searching for the threat. Fear that wasn't my own slammed into my chest, turning the warm spot of my and Lira's bond almost the same temperature as my frozen magic.

My attention landed back on Lira to see that the sword Ailsa had been holding had vanished. She dropped something sharp that dripped with golden blood.

No.

Had Eldrin turned one of my father's most loyal guards against me?

Lira turned her head toward me, but not all the way. However, I noted the panic in her eyes.

I reached for my sword at the same time that Keir's hand rose with his own, both of us ready to attack and save Lira.

As I began to move forward, Keir's sword jabbed at me. The end of the sword would hit my armor, and I turned to slice at him instead. Then the sword changed like Ailsa's had, and a dagger stabbed me deep in the throat.

Lira's wings slowed as pain took over my body, and I watched helplessly as Ailsa wrapped her arms around my mate.

There was no doubt, given the angle of the dagger, that I'd be dead in seconds.

I tried to force my wings to move, but I was already dizzy. My body dropped toward the snow-covered ground at the base of the castle.

As I landed on my back, staring up to watch Lira being carried off toward the sea, Keir grinned and spat. His spittle landed on my chest, adding more insult to injury, but they'd already done everything they could to break me.

My people's shrieks filled the air, and wings flapped toward me.

"You're no king." Keir wrinkled his nose before flying away.

I'd believed the day I lost my parents was the bleakest of my entire existence. Not anymore. It was today.

Eldrin had convinced two of my most trusted guards to turn on me and take Lira. Worse, I couldn't save her. She'd trusted me to protect her, and here I was... dying.

I'd failed her once again.

"My king," a woman murmured as she kneeled beside me.

All I could do was watch the three of them get farther away and focus on my fated-mate connection with Lira. The spot became hot, but not like the normal warmth of our connection. Was this what it felt like when someone with a fated mate died? The separation was like searing apart our two souls that had been connected.

"Lira—" I rasped, but I wasn't sure if it was audible. Even though the bond burned, I held on to it because it was the only thing I had now that she'd been taken from me.

More people surrounded me, all sorts of hands touching me, but I didn't hear what they were saying, nor did I care what they were doing to me. There would be no saving me.

Finola appeared above me. She scanned the area for threats before focusing on me.

"They took Lira," I strangled out, using most of the energy I had left. Finola was now the only one I trusted to ensure Lira remained unharmed.

Her face strained with indecision.

"Go save her," I growled, the vibration causing the dagger to tear more of the muscles and likely an artery in my neck, but that didn't matter. I would be dead in seconds anyway. In fact, I was surprised I hadn't died yet.

Huffing, Finola nodded. "Moor, guard Tavish and take him somewhere comfortable. I'll gather a group to chase after Lira."

Moor pressed his lips together like he might object until Finola nodded at me.

"Be careful." Moor hung his shoulders. "I fear there might be more to this attack."

I wanted to yell at them to stop talking and obey their king, but when I tried to open my mouth, I couldn't.

"Tavish!" Caelan cried. Two of the women gathered on my left side vanished as he pushed through and took their spot at my side.

When his gaze landed on my wound, his face blanched. "I'm taking him to his room!" he shouted over his shoulder, and he slid his hands underneath my head and knees and lifted me like a princess.

The way I should have been carrying Lira to save her from danger. Instead, Caelan was saving me.

Air ruffled my hair as the sky lightened to dusk, the sun peeking through some of the dark clouds. Further proof that my magic was weakening.

"What the blast happened?" Caelan snarled, but his eyes remained forward, aimed toward the window in the hallway next to my bedchamber.

"Lira..." I took in a ragged breath, the world spinning around me. The spot in my chest warmed even more. "Kidnapped."

"I'm not worried about her right now." Caelan's jaw clenched as we breezed through a window frame. "I'm upset about my best friend and king getting stabbed in the neck and lying in front of the doors of his kingdom, bleeding out in front of everyone. If the goal was for you to look as weak as possible, Eldrin succeeded masterfully."

Even though his words were true, I couldn't find the energy to care. Not when Lira's life was at risk. She was more important than my ego. At least, the latter could be fixed.

He turned from the hall, throwing open my bedchamber door, and settled me in bed. Lira's wild roses, mist, and vanilla scent filled my nose, and my chest ached deeply once again.

More people ran into the room, but my vision hazed. I had lost too much blood.

"That blade is at an awful angle." Moor stalked around the bed, taking in the left side of my neck. "If we want a chance for him to live, we need to get it out, or it'll keep tearing muscle, and the bleeding won't stop."

"I don't know if that's wise." Caelan winced. "At least not now."

In other words, he wanted to wait until I died but didn't want to say it in front of me. Caelan had always worried too much about me and tended to choose the wrong things to focus on... like me being with Lira when I'd already made up my mind. I'd already accepted that I'd be dead soon. I just needed to know that they'd protect Lira.

"Remove it," I gritted out. I didn't want Lira to wake up and feel me suffering. She'd already be going through so much; she didn't need to worry about me.

Caelan's eyes widened. "Tavish, no. If we—"

With the little strength I had, I gripped Caelan's hand. "I am your king. Don't question me—but I need you to promise something. Something I would ask only of you and Finnian." I had the most trust in the two of them. We'd been friends since childhood, and they'd remained by my side even when my people had risen against me, which had made their own lives hell.

He sighed as he placed his other hand on top of our joined ones and vowed, "You don't have to ask. I already know what you're going to say. Since I will never call Eldrin king, I will do everything possible to find Lira and keep her safe. You have my word." His voice quivered ever so slightly but enough that I heard it.

I nodded. If no one else had been around, I would've thanked him. Instead, I squeezed his hand as hard as I could, hoping he understood.

"Now." I faced the ceiling, staring at the sun that had almost broken through the clouds over the kingdom. All my magic had weakened, and I had no doubt that even the snow was melting. But I couldn't do anything about it.

My bond with Lira seemed to be raging with fire.

"Someone fetch towels," Caelan snapped, not sounding like himself.

"This is going to hurt, Your Majesty." Moor gripped the edge of the dagger.

That alone intensified the agony. My eyes watered, and a gush of something warm ran down and under my neck. This was it. The moment I died. The one benefit was that Caelan and Moor could soon leave my side and hunt for Lira with Finola. Eldrin had to be taking her somewhere to kill her and wait until I had passed.

Taking a ragged breath, I closed my eyes and pulled up an image of Lira. Her warm smile, sparkling cobalt eyes, the warmth of her long blonde wavy hair. The sun-kissed glow of her skin gave her eyes an ethereal glow, and her full, rosy lips screamed to be kissed. Something I hadn't done often enough.

Moor jerked the blade from my neck, and pain obliterated me as it rocketed through my body. Everything hurt, but my neck felt as if it had been ripped open. In fairness, it had.

My vision darkened at the edges, but I stayed focused on the hope and light in Lira's eyes.

Something that resembled sand pressed against my neck, and I opened my eyes to find one of the servants—a new one whose name I couldn't remember—handing Moor towels.

The extreme heat that burned my chest flowed throughout my body, pulsing like some sort of magic from my bond with Lira.

I waited for death to take me as Caelan's eyes glistened and Moor and the woman tried to slow down my bleeding. They worked hard and fast.

My darkened vision didn't get worse, but I closed my eyes, wanting Lira's face to be the last image I saw before I slipped into unconsciousness. I embraced the sensation of our bond and the magic coming through it.

"What's wrong?" Caelan whispered as his hand tensed in mine.

"Uh... nothing." Moor paused. "But his bleeding is slowing. It shouldn't be possible. He's still alive."

At his words, I noticed that the flames that licked within my body had focused all their efforts on my neck and chest. The fire was hot, but it didn't hurt. Now that it had been working for a few minutes, I realized it was uncomfortable... but also familiar.

"We should mend his neck," the woman replied.

"There's a mending kit on the table by the window." Caelan released my hand and disappeared.

I opened my eyes and noticed that the black edges of my vision hadn't retreated.

Caelan and the woman grabbed the kit we'd used on Lira not even two days ago. Taking the curved needle and light-gray silk, she hurried to my side. Her dark-green eyes narrowed as she threaded the needle, and she waved Moor to move to the side. She positioned herself and pushed her long black hair behind her shoulders. Then she pierced my neck with the needle.

Her fingers brushed me, and my skin crawled. I didn't want another woman touching me. It didn't feel right... only Lira.

Caelan took in my reaction, hung his head, and sighed. "Let me do it, Flora."

Hands stilling, Flora wrinkled her brow, but she moved so Caelan could take her spot at my side. Then my friend continued the work, though his fingers weren't as soft nor as kind.

Still, I much preferred this to another woman touching me.

Each jab felt worse than the last. Heat pulsed in the spot, and after a few minutes, Caelan finished. "I'm not sure how you're still breathing, but I'm not upset about it."

"That's reassuring," I deadpanned, but I was as perplexed as he was.

I lifted my head. The world slanted, and a dark puddle of blood stained the sheets. The irony that these sheets had been changed due to Lira's wounds wasn't lost on me. I'd make Eldrin pay for this by taking his wings and eyes.

"Why would Eldrin want you dead?" Caelan's forehead wrinkled. "Your death will weaken all Unseelie magic, especially since you don't have a direct royal descendent."

Eldrin had been pushing me to choose a queen. The thought had repulsed me until Lira came here. He must have been planning for this moment all along.

"I don't think Eldrin wanted you dead," Moor said, turning the dagger over in his hand.

"Why do you say that?" I tried to sit up, but my body

fell backward. Even though I hadn't died, I was still weak, and I despised it.

"This dagger has the Seelie seal." Moor lifted the weapon, revealing a golden hilt with a rose surrounded by delicate vines. Vines like the ones in our fated-mate tattoo with thorns interspersed throughout. Thorns that had been part of the Unseelie seal we'd lost twelve years ago, along with everything else.

Two male guards ran through the open door to my chambers. They both paused when they saw I lay in the bed with my eyes open.

"Your Majesty." The dark-green-haired one sighed with relief. "You're alive."

I didn't like seeing their surprise. If they'd feared I was dead, so did everyone else. I needed my people to know their king was alive. "I am. Is that why you came in here?" Had riots already begun?

"We found Ailsa and Kier." His shoulders straightened. "They were unconscious in the last house that was checked."

"So it wasn't just the weapons that were glamoured. It was the people themselves." Adrenaline pumped through me, and I sat upright. "Are they all right?"

The Seelie had captured Lira, which meant the dragon prince might know she'd returned. Add that on top of Eldrin still not being found, and my entire world was imploding.

"Yes, sire," the tanned man answered. "They've got some injuries, but nothing like... *yours*. What if the Seelie attack?"

"They did. They believe our king is dead." Caelan frowned. "We should be safe now that they have Lira back."

My heart clenched. I threw my legs over the side of the

bed. I didn't care if getting up killed me—I had to get to my mate... before *he* did.

When I stood, I wobbled, and Caelan flew over the bed, helping me stay upright. "What are you doing?" he hissed. "You lost a ton of blood and should be dead."

I glared at him, wanting him to see how close to snapping I was, and growled, "Everyone but Caelan, out."

The others glanced at each other and nodded, then rushed to the door. When the two of us were alone, I did snap.

"But I'm not, and I need to get Lira back." I didn't want the guards to know my plan or what Lira was to me... yet. "I can't stay rational with my mate taken from me."

Caelan tilted his head and huffed. "But she's safe."

Not for long. Not when the *dragon prince* learned she'd returned home. "You know why I need to get her." I stared him in the eyes. If I could reach her before her people learned of her return, we might be able to handle the threat here before taking on the dragons.

He sighed. "But what good will you be if you pass out before you reach the Seelie? And you can't get through the veil. What's your solution for that?"

Eldrin had stolen some of Lira's blood. There should be enough for me to get through and save her. "We need to find the vial." Caelen knew what I was referring to. I'd told him what Eldrin had done to her. Eldrin wouldn't risk carrying that around, and I'd taken him to prison. He'd have it hidden somewhere in his bedchamber or his study.

"You get some rest, and I'll search for it." Caelan pinched the bridge of his nose. "Otherwise, you'll pass out trying to get there and get yourself killed."

"You'll wake me when you find it?" Though the last

thing I wanted was to rest, he was right. To save Lira, I had to heal more. "I need to hurry to her."

"I know."

I stared into his eyes, but as usual, I sensed only truth. "Okay. I'll rest for a bit, but then I must go. Vial or not." If they saw me near the veil, the Seelie would take me prisoner, and then Lira could find a way to get me out. I had no doubt she would.

My legs gave out, and I lay down on the bed again, hating how feeble I was. Unfortunately, Caelan was right.

"I'll go look. Rest," he said, and the door closed a moment later.

And then sleep took hold of me fast.

My body shook, stirring me from a deep rest. I moaned, trying to fall back asleep, needing more rest.

"Tavish, wake up," someone said urgently.

Finnian. He was back from Earth.

My eyes popped open to see his solemn face.

He bit his bottom lip. "There's something I need to tell you."

7

TAVISH

My heart leaped into my throat. Finnian was many things, but when he wasn't smiling or teasing, that meant something was wrong, and I already suspected what this was about. "Out with it," I snapped, grimacing as I prepared to sit upright.

He blew out a breath, and his wings tightened behind him. "I went to the location on Earth you told me to go." He placed a hand on his chest like he was bracing himself for the news he had to deliver.

I sat upright, waiting for agony to strike, but felt only a slight ache. Still, the news made my stomach churn. "Are they dead?"

"I... I don't know."

"How do you not know?" My body tensed, and my wings spread out.

Finnian scowled and inhaled. "Because they weren't there."

Either I'd injured my head, or he wasn't being clear. I needed answers now. "Then why are you here?"

"Where's Lira?" he asked, scanning the room.

My chest ached painfully. "You don't know?"

His brows furrowed. "Know what? I came straight here. I knew you and Lira would want an update immediately."

My head hung, the weight of the loss of my fated mate crushing me. "The Seelie..." I'd never struggled for words before, but this void I felt without her beside me made even breathing hard. "... took her."

Finnian stumbled back and blinked. "How?"

"They set the end of the village on fire, diverting the guards away from us, and they glamoured themselves as two of our guards and offered to protect us." I clenched my hands into fists. I couldn't believe I'd been so careless and foolish. Of *course* they'd figured out that Lira was here. Her magic had returned, but I'd thought we'd have more time.

The door to my bedchamber opened, and Caelan and Nightbane hurried into my room. Caelan froze by the door as Nightbane rushed into the room, sniffing... no doubt searching for Lira.

"You woke him?" Caelan shook his head and entered. "I had hoped you'd come looking for me first. Where are the humans that Lira's so fond of?"

"Wait." Finnian rubbed his temples. "Lira's gone? The Seelie have her? And you're just *sleeping*?" His face blanched.

If I didn't trust him with my life, I'd want to kill him for caring about Lira so much. However, I needed everyone to care enough to bring her back home. "Not anymore, I'm not. I need you to get back to Earth and find them. The last thing she needs is to learn that you didn't bring them here and protect them. Why didn't you wait for them to return?"

"Their dwelling was wrecked from some sort of fight. Chairs were overturned, and a rectangle-like apparatus was shattered on the floor." He lifted both hands. "They had already been taken."

Blighted abyss. Everywhere I turned, our situation became more dire. If I'd left Lira alone on Earth, this could have all been prevented, but that wouldn't have kept her from coming back to Ardanos. Her parents would've eventually handed her to the dragon prince. We might never have met again, and if we had, she would've already been wed.

My usually frozen blood blazed with heat at the thought of her married to anyone but me. If I didn't get her back, I had no doubt that the dragon prince would demand her hand despite her being fated to me. I feared it would make him covet her more and use her as a tool to weaken me and bend me to his will.

I couldn't stay here any longer. I needed to get to her before the Seelie forced her to complete an oath they'd had no right to make on her behalf.

"Are you going to get out of bed anytime soon to find your *fated mate*?" Finnian's nose wrinkled. "Or are you leaving that matter to me as well?"

I wanted to punch him, but he was right. I couldn't lay here and waste more time.

"Have you lost a wing?" Caelan's face turned a new hue of gray.

I stood, and the world swayed ever so slightly but nowhere near as badly as before.

"Tavish, what are you doing?" Caelan asked just as Nightbane tilted his head back and howled.

The desperate howl resembled a sob, and for the first time in my existence, I actually understood what the beast was going through. He loved Lira, and he wanted her here with us.

With numb legs, I headed to the creature and copied what I'd seen Lira do to him, a motion that always left me puzzled. I patted his head. The beast's cry cut off, and its glowing lime-green eyes narrowed as it stared at me. The encounter was awkward and off-putting, so I dropped my arm to my side.

Clearing my throat, I straightened. "Don't worry, Nightbane. I'll bring her back."

"You've been stabbed in the neck, so forgive me if I have a hard time believing that," Caelan growled, marching toward me. "You're going to pass out before you even reach the village."

"You were *stabbed*?" Finnian's voice rose ten octaves higher. "Why didn't you inform me of that? I'd—"

Caelan moved the neckline of my tunic to the side, and he gasped, "How is that possible?"

"What?" I reached up and touched the stitches. My fingertips ran across the lumpy scabs that had formed there. Thankfully, the pain had disappeared, and my life was out of danger.

"You're almost healed." Caelan blinked repeatedly. "You should be dead, not standing here with scabs. I don't understand."

Finnian stomped his foot. "Why didn't anyone tell me you were injured?"

"Because you came straight to him without checking in with anyone else." Caelan dropped his hands and glared. "A guard informed me that they saw you flying by like a dragon fleeing from water. We'd just found Ailsa and Kier unconscious in one of the homes that had been cleared."

He flinched. "I never considered that the Seelie would be here." He ran a hand through his hair. "No wonder you were sleeping. I shouldn't have—"

I didn't have time for theatrics. "I appreciate your concern, but I am more than well enough to retrieve my mate." My attention landed on Caelan, and I asked, "Did you find the vial?"

Caelan hung his head. "I didn't. I searched his room and study with Nightbane and didn't find anything. He must have it on him."

My heart sank. I'd hoped he would be too wary to keep it on him, but clearly, that wasn't the case. However, that made me more determined to find a way to retrieve Lira. He could pass through the veil into Seelie, and I doubted he'd leave her alive if he caught up with her. He'd kill her to get to me and weaken the Seelie royals.

My connection to her was still warmer than normal, but not hot like when they'd been stitching me up or as I'd fallen asleep. It wasn't the usual warmth of our bond, indicating she was still unconscious. There was no way I could alert her to the problem, and I had no comfort that she was all right.

I spread out my wings and hurried to the door. "There's no time to waste. I need you two to find Eldrin and do as you see fit. And make sure our people stay calm in my absence. When that is resolved, we need to find Lira's Earth family." I knew they were a priority for her, so we needed to focus our attention on them as well.

"You're going *alone*?" Finnian's mouth dropped. "Tavish, you've always been confident, but that's rather foolish. What are you expecting to accomplish?"

I had to hope that the Seelie listened to Lira. That was all I had. I trusted that Lira would help me, and even if she couldn't, I'd find a way for both of us to escape. I could use illusions and nightmares to get my way—something I couldn't do as a young boy when the power of the royal line had yet to be transferred to me, leaving me weak. "The guards are needed here to chase down the threat, and everyone saw me get injured. No one will notice that I'm gone, so it's best if I go alone."

"You may be better, but you lost a lot of blood." Caelan gestured to the bed.

There was a significant amount of blood on the mattress, but not nearly as much as Lira had left after she'd been stabbed in the side. "I'll grab something to eat on the way." I lifted my chin, staring down my two most trusted friends. I understood that they were worried, but I had a say over what happened here.

"I'm going with you." Finnian spread out his wings. "At least to make sure you get there safely. How will it benefit Lira if you get dizzy and weak from blood loss and die on the way there? Then how are we expected to save her?"

I hated that he had a point. I'd improved, but my strength hadn't completely returned. Yet, the longer I remained here, the more the risk of losing Lira forever increased. "Fine. But once I get there, you leave."

Caelan rubbed a hand down his face and moaned. "If his strength weakens, make sure you take him somewhere safe."

"I will." Finnian placed a hand over his chest and nodded.

I gritted my teeth, not liking being coddled. However, none of that mattered as long as I reached Gleann Solas.

"Change into some clean clothes while I get you both something to eat." Caelan huffed, making his disapproval clear. "I suggest something more peasantlike so the Seelie might not recognize you at first."

He was right. If they caught me, I might not be beaten immediately if they didn't realize who I was. I'd be more likely to die, but they'd take me to the holding cells first for the royals to attempt to question me.

I marched into the bathroom and headed to the closet. I had an outfit stashed in here in case I ever needed to escape and didn't want anyone to notice me. I grabbed the frosty-blue casual tunic and plain leather pants, along with a towel.

Heading to the sink, I wetted the towel and removed the black blood caked on my neck. As I wiped away each spot, I noted there wasn't even a scab. My skin had completely healed, and my magic had already strengthened once again. I could easily cover the land in darkness and frost, but I didn't want to do too much too quickly.

I'd only napped for an hour and a half, so Lira and her captors should be arriving in the Seelie lands in the next hour or so. They'd be moving slower due to carrying Lira's weight.

After quickly changing into the new clothes and placing my sheath around my waist to carry my sword, I headed back into my room and went to the table where the mending kit sat. I took the small blade and went back into the bathroom, where I removed the stitches. By the time I finished, Caelan had returned with the food and a jug of water.

I went to the windows and opened the one on the left, closest to the edge of the spiked mountain. Thankfully, my people weren't used to sunlight, so their eyes should be more sensitive, and Finnian and I could fly to the west without being seen.

"Be careful, you two, and I'll tell the guards not to bother you." Caelan sighed. "Just return as fast as you can."

"Don't worry. I don't want to be around the Seelie lands any longer than I have to," Finnian reassured him.

I didn't bother to respond and instead flew out the window.

Finnian was right behind me, the two of us flying close to the castle underneath the section of windows. Each flap of my wings became easier as adrenaline pumped through me, masking some of the fatigue.

Within a few minutes, we were over the hill and flying low, just above the ruined lands, to prevent anyone from spotting us.

I scanned the area for signs of Eldrin. However, all I saw were rocks, dirt, and volcanoes. Nothing that signified any sort of life.

"Do you really believe he's out here somewhere?" Finnian asked as we approached the edge of the island where we'd soon fly over water.

That question had been plaguing me. I didn't understand how he could live out here, especially since I'd pulled back my magic from the entire blasted desolate island to force him back here because of his affinity for cold and darkness, the same as me. "I'm not certain, but they're checking the village in case someone is hiding him." I hated that some of my citizens were still loyal to Eldrin, but most of his followers had died in the last gauntlet because they'd been traitors who had risen against me.

"Once we get Lira back, we'll return and make Eldrin pay for his betrayal." Finnian wrinkled his nose as he caught up to me. "I told you I didn't trust the blasting wildling."

He had. Many times. But I'd needed to believe that Eldrin had changed and learned his lesson after the one time he'd moved against me. "I won't make that mistake again. He just—"

"Saved you." Finnian rolled his eyes. "Something he likes to remind you of regularly."

We flew past the last bit of land and over the beautiful sea-green water. My heart squeezed. The color matched Lira's wings... further proof of her connection to water. "None of it matters. Once I save Lira from her kidnappers and bring her back home with me, I'll allow her to handle Eldrin's punishment. After all, he handled the gauntlet—it seems only fitting that she get some justice."

"You do realize you kidnapped Lira, right?" Finnian smirked and raised both brows. "In the Seelies' minds, they saved Lira from *you*."

I clenched my hands, ready to punch him. "They saw that she was with me willingly, and they still took her."

"Because she's their princess and future queen." He tilted his head like I'd lost my mind.

"I thought you were coming to ensure I made it safely so I could bring her home?" I gritted my teeth, my muscles working. "Instead, it sounds like you're on their side."

He lifted his hands, the wind ruffling his blond hair. "I'm on *your* side. I care for Lira too."

I snarled and fisted my hands.

"Obviously, not like you do." Finnian shrugged. "She's like a sister... the sister I always sort of imagined." His voice cracked on the last word.

My anger vanished as quickly as it'd come. Finnian had a baby sister who had never been born. Slaine. His mother hadn't been strong enough to birth her, and both of them had perished. His father, overcome with grief, died a couple of years after our arrival in these ruined lands that we'd been forced to call home.

Caelan's parents had been killed during the Seelie attack, and while the three of us had already been friends, our losses had strengthened our connection. Something most fae didn't understand because we tended to live forever.

We flew on in silence. I wasn't sure what to say. Finnian seemed lost in his thoughts, and my mind circled around Lira.

The spot in my chest that connected me to her flared as if she were waking. I was both relieved and upset that she was coming to because I wasn't sure what would happen when she woke. I pushed myself harder to get to her.

Lira, I connected. I'd give anything to hear her voice, but instead of a response, a sensation like the one we'd experienced when she'd regained her memories soared between us. Her emotions mingled, confirming what I'd suspected.

The rest of her memories and magic were returning now that she'd entered Seelie land.

"They just arrived," I rasped, flying faster than ever before.

"Tavish, wait up!" Finnian cried, but the fact she was there and might need me pushed me harder. "Nothing bad will happen to her there."

He was right. Her parents wouldn't harm her... not at first. They'd want to understand what had happened and learn what we'd done to her here.

I slowed enough for Finnian to catch back up to me.

After a few more minutes, our bond leveled back out as she went back to sleep.

I needed to touch and see her... needed to make sure she was okay.

After what felt like hours, the Seelie territory appeared.

The moon shone down on the bountiful land now that night was upon us. I could see green trees and a village nearby. A huge mountain hovered in the distance, with a massive field to the east, where some of the best fruits in the kingdom grew.

Down below, the ocean rolled up to the shore, crashing in miraculous waves. I'd bet Lira had enjoyed playing in them as a child.

"Guards!" someone shouted from the edge of the village. "Unseelie are here!"

My head snapped toward the tree line, where a man soared into sight. He yelled again just as something buzzed across my skin, startling me. I searched for the guards the fae was alerting. I needed to cloak myself and Finnian in darkness.

"Tavish!" Finnian exclaimed. "I need help."

I spun around to find Finnian pounding on something invisible between us. Cool flickers of my darkness wrapped around me but didn't extend to him as if there was a barrier between us. I tried pushing my shadows toward him to cover us both.

"The Unseelie are here!" someone shouted behind me. "Attack!"

Then something hit me.

8

LIRA

My eyes fluttered open, and instead of finding myself in Tavish's dark and frosty room with windows overhead that overlooked the sky, I found myself staring at a white ceiling.

My mind fuzzed as panic clenched my throat. I turned my head to the left and found a large open window the size of the wall. A tall tree grew through it right inside the room, full of flowers with pink petals that reminded me of cherry blossoms from back home but were called silathair here in Ardanos.

This was my childhood bedroom. But even though it held good memories, I needed to get back to Tavish. It felt strange and wrong being here without him.

"Lira," a familiar feminine voice gasped. "You finally awoke. We were worried."

Mother?

I blinked, my attention drawn to the other side of the room to find Mother, Mom, and Eiric sitting on pink-rose-petal cushions made from the gigantic flowers that had been grown in my room for seating.

Some of the tension released from my chest as I sat up, the room spinning slightly. "You're safe! Thank goodness. Did Finnian find you? And where's Dad?"

Something tingled in the back of my mind, like I was missing something important, but I couldn't yet grasp it.

"Finnian?" Mom's brows furrowed. "Who's that?"

"The person Tavish sent..." I trailed off, my mind still misfiring.

"The Unseelie king sent someone for you." Mother turned to Mom and Eiric, lips pursed. "We need to alert Erdan and Brenin that Lira has awoken."

"I'll locate someone to inform the king. I'll be back momentarily," Mom replied, heading toward the door.

"Thank you, Hestia." Mother ran her hands over her long sky-blue dress.

Eiric glided over to me, her forest-green wings spread out behind her. Even though she still looked like my sister, the wings, pointed ears, and glistening skin threw me off.

Was this a dream or reality? And if it was reality, how had I gotten here? I scanned the room again for Tavish.

Eiric sat on the edge of my bed, like she'd done back on Earth, and took my hand while saying, "Olvin, Alor, and Talise retrieved us. Granted, we didn't remember them, and we assumed the people who kidnapped you had come back for the rest of us, but once we made it back to Gleann Solas, our memories returned. We've been so worried about you, and it took us a bit to track you down via your magic."

Mom returned just in time for my head to clear and the room to come into precise focus. I'd been knocked out, and Tavish had been stabbed. He was injured badly, and I needed to be there with him. "Tavish." His name flowed off my tongue, and a sob built in my chest.

"Oh, love." Mother's sparkly blue wings fluttered as she

flew to the other side of my bed. "Don't worry. He can't come here. The veil will protect us—not that the Unseelie can rival our magic." She leaned over and squeezed my hand.

I shook my head as the room closed in around me. "That's the problem. I need to go to him." The image of the way the guard had stabbed him in the neck flashed into my mind, and my breathing became erratic. "He's hurt. I need to be with him!"

"Hopefully, the nightfiend is dead." Mom's nose wrinkled as she marched to the end of the bed and stood in front of a large opening to the bathroom. "If he's not, it'll be my pleasure to end him myself. But don't fret, Lira. We can't watch him die, but we won't allow him or anyone else to harm you again."

"*Harm* me? That's not what I'm worried about." I searched our bond and found it muted, and I raised my left hand and saw that our fated-mate tattoo was still in place. *Tavish?* I connected, needing to hear his voice even if only in my mind. I had to know he was safe, but all I got was silence. I threw the emerald-green covers from my body, preparing to leave and go find him. If he couldn't answer, I had to make sure I was by his side, especially if he was injured.

"What are you doing?" Eiric's eyebrows rose.

"Going to check on him. He was hurt." My chest ached uncomfortably from my worry over what Eldrin could be doing to him if Tavish was on his deathbed. "I need to be beside him."

Mom pushed me back onto the bed. "Lira, you need rest. You were given a sedative, and it knocked you out longer than it should have. We aren't sure what the Unseelie nightfiends did to you, but—"

I didn't have time for this. "Stop talking about them like that. Tavish means everything to me." I raised my hand, pointing at the magical tattoos. "He's my fated mate."

"Blighted abyss." Mother shook her head as a breeze blew into the room and floated around her. "I had hoped that getting you away from him would undo the illusion, but he has stronger magic than we suspected. He located you on Earth and messed with your mind, and he has managed to keep an illusion of a fated-mate tattoo on your body."

"What are you talking about?" My back straightened, and I tried to calm my breathing. Overreacting would make getting out of here take even longer. I needed to bide my time until I could search for him.

Mother's wings fluttered as she perched on the bed next to me. "Fated mates are rare. So rare there are only ten known in all of fae existence. Do you really believe that the man who kidnapped you would wind up being your fated mate?"

"He didn't want us to be fated mates." My pulse quickened. I didn't enjoy the way she'd downplayed my emotions. "Me being his mate has made things far more challenging for him."

"Lira, illusions are the Unseelies' strongest form of magic, and Tavish is the expert on creating them." She shuddered. "More so than we expected, especially without ties to their native lands. Had we known that, we never would have hidden you on Earth. A decision that proved futile, seeing as you still wound up in his possession."

I wanted to kick and shout, but I gritted my teeth. With my royal parents, any sign of irrationality would turn them deaf to anything I had to say. I knew what I felt for Tavish. Those emotions couldn't be manipulated. "Mother—" I started, but the double doors to my room burst open, and Father and Dad hurried in.

At the sight of the two very striking men standing next to each other, a flashback of Tavish and me as kids surged into my brain. "Thank Fates," Father sighed as he hurried to me.

Eiric moved from beside me, allowing Father to take her spot. He threw his large arms around me, and his earthy scent filled my nose, grounding me. My vision blurred with happy tears. I couldn't believe I'd forgotten about him.

He held me close to his chest, where I could hear his steady heartbeat.

Then his hands froze. "What did the Unseelie wildling do to you?"

"We were just discussing that." Mother *tsk*ed. "She's under the illusion that the blazing Unseelie king is her fated mate."

I stiffened and pulled away so that Father's warm brown eyes could see the truth in mine.

"He *is* my fated mate," I said slowly and confidently so there was no question that I spoke the truth. After all, a fae couldn't lie.

Father dropped his arms and furrowed his brows, then burst out laughing. "You've always been one to make the perfect joke. How I've missed that."

My stomach clenched, and I looked at Dad. He knew me better than either of them now.

His amber eyes darkened in disappointment. "She's not jesting, My King."

Laughter cut short, Father frowned. "Either way, it doesn't matter. The illusion will wear off, and you've been promised to the dragon prince. So, fated mate or not, you can't be with him."

Skin crawling, I inched away from him, putting me closer to Mother. Once upon a time, the three of us had been close, but that wasn't the case anymore. "Tavish is the only man I want to be with. I won't marry the dragon prince. Besides, I didn't make any vow to the flamers." I had the right to choose who I wanted to marry and be with.

Father took a few steps back from me. He glanced at Dad then Mom. "Did the Unseelie fiend bring the right person back because that can't be my Lira? She'd know better than to make an asinine statement like that."

"That's Lira, Your Majesty." Dad bowed his head. "She's lived on Earth longer than Ardanos at this point and may need time to reacclimate to this realm."

"And you know how good the Unseelie are with their illusions," Mother added, patting my arm. "I'm sure it'll wear off the longer she's away from him."

I hated how they were all speaking as if I wasn't present. I'd opened my mouth to tell them they were all wrong when Eiric caught my eye and shook her head faintly. She mouthed, *Not now*.

A part of me didn't want to listen to her, but she was good at reading the room and knowing when to push and when to back off. For Tavish, I needed to handle this situation right for *us*.

Tavish.

Our bond was lukewarm, the way it felt when he was asleep. I wished I could talk to him, Finnian, or Caelan—someone who could update me on everything.

"The guards informed me that there was no way Tavish could survive, so none of this matters." Father beamed. "The Unseelie will weaken more and never cast our lands into darkness ever again."

Darkness.

That was what had caused the attack. The former Unseelie king—Tavish's father—had cloaked the dragons' land and ours in darkness, like Tavish had his kingdom. But the Seelie and the dragons weren't meant to live in complete darkness. We required light.

"You do realize that the king and queen who cast the darkness over our lands have died?" As soon as the words were out, I knew Eiric would be scowling at me, but I didn't regret saying this. "None of the living Unseelie actually harmed us."

Eiric hung her head, confirming my suspicions. I had a way of running my mouth, but I couldn't remain silent while he spoke so harshly of my mate's people. They'd become what they were because of their circumstances.

"The wrongs and rights of the royals pass on to their people." Father's forehead was lined with confusion. "Every person in this realm understands this, and you're the Seelie *princess*. You shouldn't be speaking such nonsense."

"It's Earth, my king." Mom pressed her lips together. "They believe in those foolish ideologies she speaks of, and we lost our memories, so we couldn't make sure she was raised in the proper way of the Seelie."

Mother sighed and pressed her shaky fingers to her lips. "Maybe the dragons were right to be angry with us. She would've been better off staying here."

A memory flashed through my mind of me as a little girl, begging my parents to allow me to stay. Even though a portion of me had wanted to experience the human world, I hadn't wanted to forget them or my place in Gleann Solas. They'd been fearful for me ever since Eldrin had injured me while I'd been healing Tavish.

My blood froze.

I'd saved Tavish, not Eldrin. Eldrin had merely taken Tavish from the holding cell, cloaking him in shadows.

The life debt Tavish believed he owed his cousin wasn't legitimate. Eldrin had used the situation to his own benefit. No wonder he wanted me dead before I regained my memories.

A guard rushed into the room, and his face blanched. I didn't recognize this guard, but there was something oddly familiar about him... like he might be someone I knew.

"King Erdan and Queen Sylphia, guards near the eastern veil have arrived with two Unseelie fae in their midst. They're taking them to the prison cells." The male guard's rich blue eyes sparkled. "One of them came through the veil on his own, though we aren't certain how or why."

My stomach dropped. "It must be Eldrin."

Dad's head snapped toward me. "Why do you say that?"

I swallowed, trying not to relive Eldrin's attack on me in the tub. "He cut me and took some of my blood in a vial."

"And *Tavish* allowed that to happen?" Mom asked, lifting her chin. Her dark-brown eyes turned almost onyx, and her fingertips turned red, evidence of her fire magic.

That question was a punch to the gut, though he deserved the censure. "He didn't know it was happening." Even as I provided the answer, I knew they wouldn't believe me.

"Another illusion spell." Mother shook her head. "It was probably Tavish himself who did it."

I clenched my hands, wanting to punch something. Everything I said, they refused to believe, making me feel like I was still ten, though I'd been gone for over twelve years.

"It's time we get some answers." Father expanded his

huge chestnut-brown wings that matched the color of his hair and darted out.

Mother, Mom, and Dad followed, leaving me alone with Eiric.

Eiric flew to the door and shut it then returned to my side. She took my hand, linking her fingers with mine.

That was all it took for the sob that had been caught in my chest to release and the tears to stream down my face. Fae weren't supposed to show emotions—the belief was that it made us look weak—but I didn't agree. Emotions also made us strong, and right now, I needed to let my feelings out before I did something more rash and exploded.

"L, what happened with him?" she asked, clearly wanting to hear what I had to say.

I sniffled as I looked her in the eye and whispered, "He kidnapped me, and things were rough for both of us for a while, but then he saved my life while risking his people turning against him. It's not an illusion. He's my fated mate."

"Okay." Eiric nodded, squeezing my hand tighter.

My breath caught. "You believe me?"

"You may be impulsive, but your intuition is like no one else's I've ever known." She leaned her head against my shoulder. "If you say he's your mate, I believe you. That doesn't make anything easier—in fact, it's going to make all of this harder—but we'll figure it out together."

I smiled, though my chest ached with agony and longing. "Because that's what sisters do." I couldn't fathom Eiric not being here beside me. I loved her so much.

"You might be a princess, and I might be the daughter of the two highest royal guards, but you aren't getting rid of me." She lifted her head, narrowing her eyes at me. "You still feel like as much of a sister here in Gleann Solas as you did on Earth, and I know my parents still think of you as their daughter."

"I'd never want to get rid of you three. You're my family too."

I hugged her tightly, thankful she was safe and sound. I'd been so fearful that Eldrin had taken her and I'd never see her again.

Eldrin.

The bastard was here.

Hot rage spread throughout my body, causing my limbs to stiffen. I needed to see the pompous prick now that he was captive here. I didn't want anyone else to have the privilege of killing him.

Determination flooded me, and I dropped my hands.

"What's wrong?" Eiric tilted her head.

"If Eldrin is in the holding cell, I need to see him and confirm it with my own eyes." I flapped my wings, heading toward the wooden double doors.

"As long as we don't get in the way," she replied, following me.

Opening the doors, I glanced back at my room. It hadn't changed at all since I'd left. It looked like a shrine to the child they had given up. The walls were painted pink, and the lanterns danced with blue flames.

It represented a version of myself I barely remembered anymore.

Pushing the nostalgia from my mind, I found my door unguarded. I wasn't a prisoner here... yet.

We flew down white hallways with flowers of every color growing along the walls. The floral scents soothed some of the anxiety inside me as we took the long hallways to the prison area. Unlike the layout of Tavish's castle,

Seelie prisoners were held at the opposite end of the castle, nowhere near my parents' room or mine.

When the white walls morphed into the gray stone used for the prison cells, I heard the murmur of voices ahead.

"You're sure the veil went back up after you brought them in?" Father asked. "We need to ensure they can't enter and surprise us."

"We're sure, Your Majesty," a male guard responded. "We used some of the reserved dead Unseelie royal blood to recover the break."

"Then it's time to wake the nightfiends up," Father commanded.

The answering chuckles reminded me of the way the Unseelie had sounded when they were preparing to torture me. My skin crawled, but I tried to push past that trauma.

"Let me have the first kick," a guard said.

My fated-mate connection with Tavish warmed.

Kicking noises began, and the fated-mate bond came to life. Pain flowed from Tavish into me, and a lump formed in my throat.

Tavish? I mind-melded, desperate to know what was happening. *You're alive?*

Lira? Tavish replied, the warmth of his hope surging inside me. *Stay in your room. I'll find a way to reach you. Trust me.*

"That's not just an Unseelie." Mother gasped. "I can feel his power. That has to be the Unseelie king."

A guard inhaled sharply. "That's impossible. Brielle said she killed him."

"Yet here I stand," Tavish growled. "Here to take back what you stole from me."

My mouth dried, and my wings moved faster than ever before as I soared down the hallway to reach him.

"Though I'm relieved you're breathing for the fate of magic, our guard didn't intend to stab you the way he had. He'd only meant to incapacitate you, but still, *you* stole *my* daughter. There is *nothing* here for you," Father growled. "Move, everyone. This is personal, and I will handle it on my own."

"Aw, Tavish. The Seelie king is going to get his hands dirty." Finnian chuckled, but his voice seemed stilted, betraying his nerves.

Of course they were both here. Now I had to determine a way to get both of them out.

The sound of a sword being unsheathed had my blood boiling. I reached the door and took a sharp right just as Father raised his sword.

Tavish stood with his chin high and back straight until his stormy eyes focused on me.

Father's gaze was locked on Tavish with hatred glistening in his eyes.

Mom, Dad, Mother, and the guards turned their heads my way. I reached Tavish just as my father jabbed the sword forward, aiming for Tavish's arm.

No. I refused to let him injure my mate.

9

LIRA

"Lira, no!" Tavish exclaimed as I soared into Father. Even if I'd wanted to listen to him—which I didn't—his warning would've been too late. My chest and arms slammed into Father's a few inches before the blade would have made impact, and Father fell to the side. With my right hand, I shoved the sword upward so that it missed Tavish's leg as Father crashed to the stone floor, with me landing on top of him.

Though he'd been my cushion, the impact hurt. My knees hit the stone, causing a throbbing that I would feel later when the adrenaline wore off. But that was the least of my worries.

Finnian laughed. "I love how she makes an entrance wherever she goes."

Chains clanged together as Tavish tried to get to me, and my heart leaped as my wings lifted me from my father and toward him.

I buried myself in his chest. His arms wrapped around me, but his head remained lifted. The jolt of our connection sprang to life, and tears that I didn't want to release burned my eyes.

Silence descended, and a large hand grabbed my arm, yanking me from Tavish.

"You *foolish* girl!" Father shouted, digging his fingers into my arm. "Get away from the wildling right this second."

Tavish dropped his arms and hurt panged in my chest.

He connected, *I don't want you to get hurt, and he doesn't see things rationally. Believe me, the last blasted thing I want to do is release you. Being apart from you has been pure agony.*

Father spun me around, his face flushed with the gold of our blood.

Tavish's rage flowed into me, mixing with mine, but our connection also clenched with his concern for my well-being.

"Have you forgotten everything you've ever known?" Father spat and dropped his hand like he couldn't handle touching me any longer. "He's *Unseelie,* and you're betrothed. Do you know what the dragons would say if they learned of your blasphemous intentions?"

I straightened my back, standing between the two of them. Mother stepped behind Father, shaking her head at me, telling me to stop and stand down. Both of them conveniently acted like they were my parents again.

But that was the thing.

They didn't get to give me up for twelve years and expect me to come back and fall into the same dynamics. I wasn't ten anymore, and frankly, they'd lost that privilege when they forced me to live on Earth even though I'd begged them not to make me.

"There is nothing blasphemous going on here. He's my

fated mate, and I will protect him with my life if that's what it takes."

The four guards who remained in the room gasped as the warmth of Tavish's love and the cold tendrils of his fear clashed inside our connection.

"Don't listen to her ramblings." Father glared over his shoulder at them. "She was taken, and there's no telling what the Unseelie did to her. She's not of sound mind and needs time to reacclimate."

I hated that my attention darted over his shoulder to the guards. Unlike the Unseelie, who wore dark armor, the Seelie soldiers wore golden armor with intricate designs. Three of the guards were men, and one was a woman who was lithe and as tall as the other three.

"She doesn't know what she speaks of, and her manners and loyalties to our people were forgotten during her time on *Earth*." He spoke the last word as if it were a curse. "She will remember her place. She just needs time." He took two steps toward me, using his half-foot height advantage to bring home the lingering threat in his voice as he wrinkled his nose at me.

"If you harm her, I will ensure that you experience the same pain you bestow upon her," Tavish vowed in a low growl. "Father or not, you don't get to touch my mate with reckless intentions or insult her. The wrongs you've committed against the ones I love continue to add up."

Father placed a hand on my shoulder and shoved me out of the way. His strength caught me off guard, and I flew into the stone wall, injuring my shoulder.

Eiric rushed into the room and helped me to my feet as Father placed the tip of his sword to Tavish's neck.

A scream lodged in my throat as cool, refreshing magic swirled inside me. I'd begun to push it toward Father to force him back when Dad stepped up beside him and said, "Your Majesty, think about the consequences of killing him. The unbalance will be catastrophic."

Arm shaking, Father exhaled and lowered his sword.

I yanked back the magic, not wanting him to know that I'd planned to use it against him. I'd do whatever it took to save Tavish because I refused to live without him.

Dark skin glistening under the lantern lights, Dad turned his gaze on Tavish. "Release Lira from the illusions you placed on her. If you care for her at all, give her that."

"Believe me, when this all began, Tavish wished the bond was an illusion he'd cast on her." Finnian nodded his head in Tavish's direction and then mine. "But what they have is real. I know it's hard to fathom, but they *are* fated mates."

Mom shook her head, causing her curls to hit her shoulder. "The same illusion could be placed on you. Your statement holds no merit."

"Then listen to my words." Tavish's stormy irises darkened as he held my father's gaze. "Lira is my fated mate. I would die for her the same way she proclaimed she would die for me. Our souls merged into one. I love her and will have her as my wife *forever*."

My heart raced at his proclamation. We'd never discussed marriage, but his words made perfect sense. It wasn't even a question.

"It isn't an illusion. Do what you must to prove that, but let me be clear." I clenched my hands at my sides. "If Tavish or Finnian is harmed, I won't forgive you." That decision would have me allying with the Unseelie in every way because Father would have declared war on me.

"As if I care about that." Father's nostrils flared, and his head snapped toward me. "Your forgiveness isn't something

I need or desire. I am your *king*, and you will abide by what I say since it is *law*. Now go to your room and don't come out until you remember your duties and who you are."

My blood boiled, and I wanted to lash out. Ignoring the way my chest heaved, I refused to budge from my spot. "I'm not a child."

"Then stop resembling one," he snapped.

"She fears you'll hurt them." Mother spoke slowly and placed a hand on his shoulder. "If you give her the reassurance she needs, I'm certain she will happily oblige."

"We are the rulers, not her. She doesn't get to dictate the terms." Father lifted a hand. "Take Lira to her room and ensure she remains there."

As all four guards headed toward me, I shook my head and widened my stance, preparing to fight if needed. "This is wrong. Tavish hasn't done anything to you or the Seelie. Just like your decision right now goes against what I believe in, and that shouldn't be a reflection of me and what I stand for."

Go with them, Tavish connected. *Don't put up a fight.*

What? No! I tore my gaze from them to him. *I can't leave you like this.*

Father's wings spread out, and he glared at me in a way he'd never done before, not even when I was an insolent child. "It's in your best interests to remain silent from this point forward."

Listen, Lira. I don't want you to leave either, but we don't need them watching you. Tavish's eyes lightened to the light-silver shade he showed when we were alone. *Because we* are *getting out of here, and I need you to pretend to be the good, obliging daughter until then. Do you understand?* His face blanched, and he shared the strength of his determination through our bond. *I came for you, and we'll leave here together. Trust me on this. We need to work together to get out.*

When the guards reached me, I exhaled.

Eiric stood as tense as a statue at my side.

I shook out my hands, ignoring the way my shoulder panged with discomfort from the wall's greeting. Then I took a step back and lifted my hands as they reached to grab me.

"I'll go back to my room of my own accord." I shuffled a few steps back, though the yanking in my chest tugged me toward Tavish.

Sprite, I swear to you that he won't kill me. If he was going to, he would've done it moments ago. He needs me alive so that our magic remains in balance. Seelie can't continue without Unseelie, and vice versa. It's the way of our realm.

He was right. That had been their intention in bringing the injured Tavish here as a boy. Though, when I'd found him all those years ago, they hadn't mended him yet. They'd planned on someone tending to his wounds. They'd merely wanted him to remain as weak as possible so he couldn't use his newfound power from his parents against them. And with the injuries he'd sustained, they hadn't been able to place him in chains to lock his magic. I'd learned all that after Eldrin had rescued Tavish from the holding cell.

I turned to head out the doorway as Eiric's brows rose. Instead of speaking, she followed my lead and soon we were flying down the hallway back toward my room.

The guards stayed on our wings, and the hair on the nape of my neck stood on end from their attention.

Every flap I took away from Tavish made my heart clench more, and my entire being wanted to turn around and race back to him. My mate was captured and in danger, and leaving him behind was the last thing I should be doing.

The Seelie king is just threatening me, Tavish connected. *I feel your struggle, and I swear to you, I'll be fine.*

But this isn't right— My words cut off as the connection between us cooled, and my chest almost went back to the normal temperature it'd been before we completed our fated-mate connection. I froze midflap. *Tavish?*

Eiric stopped a little in front of me, realizing I wasn't beside her.

I'm here, love, he replied, but the connection still felt strange.

"Why are you stopping?" the tallest guard rasped. "That isn't what King Erdan ordered."

I bit the inside of my cheek, needing a distraction from the terror knotted in my stomach. My desperation to be with Tavish was damn near overwhelming, yet I couldn't do a damn thing because of my biological parents.

I wished they hadn't discovered that I'd returned so that Tavish and I could be together, hunting down the real threat—Eldrin.

I thought you were dead. Our connection cooled. I needed to hear his voice again so I could make sure that those last words hadn't been a figment of my imagination.

A moment passed, and just as I was about to turn around and rush back to him, he answered, *They put chains on our wings, and now my magic is restrained. I feared we wouldn't be able to speak like this anymore, but I'm blasting glad we can.*

The memory of those chains and their effects popped into my head. Having my wings restrained had felt claustrophobic. I could only imagine how he and Finnian were struggling.

I hadn't noticed that we were already back at my bedroom door. I pushed the double doors open, wanting the guards to leave me alone. Hot rage burned inside me, and I wouldn't be able to hide it much longer.

The four guards stood at my door, glancing at each other.

"I came back to my room like a good little girl." I crossed my arms, letting sarcasm drip from each word. "Is that all?"

The woman guard smirked. "You three, head back. I'll keep watch on Lira a little while longer." Her auburn hair reminded me of embers sparking, contrasting with the pink walls. As she stepped into my room and stood closer to me, I noticed that her eyes resembled flames in the dark of night.

"Should one of us remain with you, Sorcha?" the shorter man with cobalt hair asked.

"We'll be fine." She nodded at the door. "I'll alert someone if anything goes awry. Go back to the king and queen to ensure nothing happens with the Unseelie. Their presence here will affect the veil eventually."

The three of them nodded and left, and I made my way to my bed and sat, folding my wings and crossing my legs like I had all the time in the world. In fairness, as an immortal, I kind of did.

Eiric cleared her throat. "She returned here as requested."

"Which alarms me." Sorcha tilted her head, examining me. "How could you protect an Unseelie? Especially the king? If I were you, I'd want to kill him myself rather than remain fated to him."

My last bit of restraint was damn close to snapping. I wanted to grab the bitch's hair and yank.

Lira, what's wrong? Tavish connected.

A guard is telling me that if you were her fated, she'd kill you. My breathing quickened as the anger took over.

It's a test, he replied. *She wants you to react. Stay strong and don't fall for it.*

Shit. He was right. Even though I didn't feel completely fae, I had to remember how things were here. Fae played with words and tested each other's intent. "Well, I'm not you. However, I understand that Father needs to be in control, so I will behave." Until we had an escape plan.

She lifted a brow. "That's good to hear, but I find it hard to believe after what we saw in the holding cell."

"I don't remember asking for your opinion, nor am I obligated to explain myself to you." Even though this was going against what Tavish had asked of me, I would never gain respect if I didn't stand my ground. "Even though I've been on Earth for the past twelve years, I'm still a princess and will not tolerate your disrespect."

Her shoulders relaxed as if I had passed the first set of tests. "Very well. Please alert me if you need anything."

"We will." Eiric leaned against the wall in the corner of the room.

Sorcha bowed her head slightly to me before stepping into the hall and shutting the doors behind her.

As soon as the door clicked, Eiric fluttered over to the spot next to me. She leaned back and asked, "What was the sudden change of mood back there? You were all gung ho about not leaving him, and now we're just going to chill in your room while they do whatever they want?"

I had to choose my words carefully. The last thing I wanted was to get Eiric involved in my escape plan. However, I couldn't stay here, Seelie or not, with Father and Mother more than willing to hand me over to the dragon prince. "Insisting on staying would have made things worse for Tavish and Finnian. I didn't realize it at first." My voice had thickened, and I paused, trying to hold myself together. "So I walked away to make the king feel as if I was obliging his command, hoping to eliminate some of his wrath."

Pain shot through the connection, stealing my breath. It wasn't the worst pain I'd ever felt, but they were hurting Tavish.

A lump lodged in my throat. *What's going on?*

Nothing I can't handle, he replied. *Stay in your room, please. Don't come here, or neither of us will get free.*

Tears rolled down my cheeks, and I took a shaky breath.

"What's wrong?" Eiric asked, taking my hand in hers. "You're suddenly crying."

Another jolt of pain had a sob breaking from my chest. "They're hurting him."

"What?" She glanced around the room. "How could you know that?"

I gripped my chest. "I feel his pain. It's coming through our fated-mate bond."

"That's both fucking cool and terrifying." Eiric wrapped her arms around me. "But I'm sorry. You heard Dad—they won't kill him."

As if that made it better. I didn't want him to feel any sort of pain. *I'm sorry.* I didn't care if I shouldn't say those words to Tavish. He was hurting because of my father, even though the king knew what Tavish was to me. What sort of parent could hurt their child in such a way?

You tried to protect me, sprite, he replied as another jabbing pain shot between us. *That means more to me than you'll ever know. I love you. Nothing will ever change that.*

I buried my face in Eiric's shoulder, holding on to the

one person from this kingdom who seemed to be on my side. *I love you too, thorn.*

Our bond warmed from the love he felt despite the agony still coursing through me.

I wasn't sure how long it lasted, but eventually, fresh pain stopped flashing through our bond. *Tavish?*

I'm okay. I just need sleep, he replied, and the bond cooled further, but the part in my chest that had the warm magic flared to life.

It had to be due to the lack of warmth from Tavish.

I lifted my head and Eiric frowned. She wiped a tear from my face and asked, "What can I do? I don't know how to fix this."

"You did the only thing you could, and I love you for it." I squeezed her hand, unsure what I would've done if she hadn't been here. She'd been my protector all my life, and now it made sense since she was the child of the Seelies' two strongest guards.

She pressed her lips together. "You know I'll always be here for you and on your side."

"And the same goes for me too." I bumped her shoulder to lighten the moment. I didn't want to worry her, or she'd watch me more closely. I needed to play a part with her from this moment forward and not involve her in our plan. In order for my plan to work, I had to ensure that she remained unaware and innocent so she didn't get accused of anything.

Someone banged on the door, and my stomach dropped. I reached up, wiping the tears from my face, needing a moment before letting them in.

The doors opened, revealing Father's towering frame.

His gaze landed on my face. The warmth in his eyes was still gone as he stalked into my room.

"I need to speak to my daughter alone," he commanded, not bothering to acknowledge Eiric's presence beyond that comment.

She hesitated, unsure whether she should go, and Father's calm demeanor snapped.

"Leave now, or you will be punished," Father bit out, turning his steely gaze on Eiric.

She lifted her chin to say something that would seal her fate. She was a glutton for protecting me, but even if she took his wrath, it wouldn't help.

So, instead, I beat her at her own game and wielded my finger like a weapon. "Don't take your frustration with me out on her. She's merely concerned about leaving me alone with you."

He refocused on me and said, "It's not her place to be concerned with your well-being around me and your mother."

I nodded toward the door, telling her it was okay to leave. The warm spot in my chest next to my bond with Tavish seemed to intensify, but it was probably my imagination, especially with Father being here.

Eiric hesitated, but when I leveled a stern look at her, she obliged, but I knew she wouldn't move from the spot right outside my door.

Father watched our interaction, his face flushing

golden, clearly not liking that Eiric was accepting my permission and not his orders.

When the door shut, announcing he and I were alone, silence hung heavy between us.

He arched a brow and ran a hand through his chestnut beard as if waiting for me to begin the conversation.

The two of us were in a standoff, but I wasn't the one who'd barge into his room, so I sat on the bed and crossed my legs as I waited for him to begin the conversation. He might be centuries older than me and more experienced with this sort of situation, but I had one clear advantage: I truly didn't want to say a damn word.

I was rather positive I could spend the rest of my days happily never speaking to him again. I had fond memories of the times we had together when I was a child, but as I looked back, it was me being bossed around by him and not in the way Dad had done on Earth, where it had been for my safety. My father had been determined to mold me into the woman he wanted me to become, and any time I'd stepped out of line, he'd found an effective way to punish me, either by isolating me from others or keeping me from the water I cherished.

Time ticked by, so I spread out my wings and lay back on my bed with a yawn. It was late, and with the cool night air blowing into my room, the thought of drifting off to sleep was welcoming... or would have been if Father hadn't been hovering over me.

"Is this a game to you?" he spat like something tasted bad.

"Game? No." I sat back up, refusing to chance him seeing me as a coward. "You're the one who came here and demanded that Eiric leave. I assume you have a reason other than to scowl at me." I crossed my arms, meeting his gaze head-on.

"You humiliated me in front of the Unseelie nightfiends and the queen and guards." His neck corded. "I was hoping you would admit that your actions were wrong."

"If you're asking whether I regret preventing you from stabbing my *fated mate* in the arm, the answer is no." I couldn't lie, and I didn't want to mince words with him. He needed to know that my loyalty was with Tavish and for the good of both the Unseelie and Seelie people. I didn't believe it had to be one or the other but that we should find a way to live in harmony. "Do I hate that running into you was the only option? That answer is yes, but I doubt you would've listened if I'd asked you not to stab him."

His breathing quickened, and he closed his eyes as if to choose his next words. He exhaled and gritted out, "Princess or not, you don't have the authority to challenge your king and father. Your mother and I make the decisions for all the Seelie people, and you're no different from the rest."

In other words, this was a dictatorship. Even though I understood that, the human Lira couldn't stand the idea of not having a voice in the actions that related to me. The two worlds I'd lived in were grossly different and conflicted in a way that made me want to scream and shout.

The only thing keeping me from telling Father where to go—not that he'd know the reference to hell anyway—was Tavish's request. I clearly didn't belong here, and more importantly, I couldn't remain in a family or society that would keep my fated mate captive. I needed to be with him. The tug in my chest was hard to ignore; the only thing I wanted to do was run to him and hold him in my arms.

The pain he'd experienced at my father's hands made talking to Father with any sort of respect harder.

I swallowed the scream in my throat and tried to remain somewhat calm. "Even though he's my fated?"

"*I* am your *king*. And *you* are to *wed* the dragon prince." He spread his wings out as if to look imposing. "The Unseelie king is none of your concern. Do you understand? Or do I need to make you?"

"I understand." I lifted my chin, meaning those two words, but that didn't mean I agreed or gave a damn. So I gave in to the game that most fae enjoyed, and in this moment, I did too, because I wanted Father to feel the same sense of betrayal as I did. "You've made everything perfectly clear." I forced a smile to hide some of the venom I couldn't completely eliminate from my voice.

"Thank the Fates." His wings lowered, and his shoulders relaxed. "I feared you would continue to be irrational, but this proves your fae heritage is part of you and merely needs time to resurface. I'm so relieved because if you have an outburst like that again or go against me or your mother, you will be punished in the best way I know."

Understanding his threat clearly, I couldn't swallow past the lump in my throat. I'd revealed my hand to him, and the best way to punish me was through Tavish. We'd both made our fated-mate connection clear.

A slight smirk crossed his face as he suspected I understood the hidden message. It was the same expression he wore when he made the opposition crumble.

I struggled to reconcile the man who stood before me with the one who had taken Mother and me to the waterfalls where the three of us had spent the day laughing and using our magic together... or the man who'd taught me to dance for the solstice parties once I was expected to take part in the balls. Even though we'd had tense moments, he'd never talked to *me* like this... only the people who challenged him.

There were so many things I wanted to say to him, and none of them were nice or good, so I forced my lips to stay shut. Instead, I yawned, hoping he'd get the hint and leave me alone.

His face softened, and some warmth returned to his eyes. "You've had a long couple of weeks, and I never intended for you to reacclimate to Ardanos quite like this. It might do you well to take a bath, change, and get some rest. We can meet for breakfast and hopefully spend better time together."

That was the last thing I wanted, but maybe if he focused on me, he would spare Finnian and Tavish some of his spite.

Despite knowing I wouldn't be able to sleep, I desperately needed time alone to clear my head. Since I'd woken up here, I hadn't had time to process everything that had occurred. "That sounds good to me."

He smiled. "Now there's my little girl." He gestured to the closet next to the bathroom door. "And it'll be nice to see you back in Seelie garments."

I nodded, though I didn't want to remove these clothes. They were the closest thing I had to Tavish.

When he bent over, I tensed, ready to defend myself. But he kissed my cheek, his beard tickling me the same way it had the last time he'd kissed me, right before I left for Earth.

Tears burned my eyes, and I wasn't sure if it was from fond memories or the irony of the situation. The last time he kissed me, I hadn't wanted to leave him, but now I wanted to be as far away from him as possible. Still, my heart ached for the relationship we'd lost and may never have again.

"Good night, darling." He leaned back and touched my arm. His eyes glistened in a vulnerable moment.

In less than a minute, he'd gone from happy to think he'd broken me to tearing up at having his little girl back. The two emotions felt like whiplash, but I had to remember the way of the fae. They loved with all their heart but being feared meant more to them than anything. In that way, he was no different from Tavish, and maybe I would've been the same way too, if I'd remained here, but Earth had allowed me to see a different path... one with mercy and compassion.

With as steady of a voice as possible, I replied, "Night, Father."

He backed away, and I hoped, for her sake, that Eiric had overheard the end of the conversation and wouldn't be camped outside the door.

I headed to the closet to the right of the bathroom just as Father opened the door to leave. Eiric was missing, and I exhaled in relief.

Thankfully, the wardrobe had been updated with outfits to fit my adult body. My hands ran over the gowns, and I noted the golds, blues, and greens that were predominately my future wardrobe. Then I came to the section with my nightclothes, which were all nightgowns. I shouldn't have been surprised, seeing as they were similar to the ones I'd worn with Tavish.

I removed a white silk sweetheart-cut gown with a matching thin jacket, then locked the bedroom door and headed into the bathroom, eager to cleanse myself of the day.

The moon shone through the window over the white

tub and lit up the entire bathroom. My feet hit the cool, sparkly sea-green tiles, and I noticed a white, fluffy towel hanging on the rack beside the tub. I turned on the water and stripped off my clothes. I needed to take off the Unseelie outfit and wash off the Unseelie smells if I wanted them to believe I was conforming so that Tavish, Finnian, and I could escape as soon as we had the chance.

Not waiting until the tub filled, I stepped in and settled down in the corner, looking out the window. Lights glowed from the windows of the cottages at the bottom of the hill, and another mountain range towered behind them, giving a majestic view. The high fae who worked in the palace lived in this village. Only the high fae could hold jobs as advisors, guards, or any other important station within Caisteal Solais or protecting Gleann Solas.

The water tingled, providing relief for my tense muscles, and my eyelids grew heavy. But the more refreshed I felt, the more the lack of warmth from my connection with Tavish came to a head, and the strength of the strange, warm magic in my chest took on a whole new life. I shouldn't get to feel this sort of comfort when he was chained against his will.

This had to be similar to what he'd experienced when he was forced to play his role while I took part in the gauntlet. The knowledge that a guard could enter his cell at any time and kill him while I sat here safe in a tub had my skin crawling.

I held my breath and dunked my head under the water to get clean. Even though Tavish had told me to listen and behave, I couldn't sit here and not check on him.

My water magic pulsed in my chest, wanting to be let out, but I didn't have time for that. I stepped from the tub and let the water drain as I toweled off. I quickly slipped on the nightgown and grabbed a wooden-handled brush with thorns as the bristles. I ran it through my hair, despite there not being any tangles, and set it back on the countertop made of vines that resembled the ones in my fated-mate tattoo. The ache of his absence stole my breath once more.

Determination and adrenaline pumped through my body. I stepped back into the bedroom and tiptoed to the door, then placed my ear against the wood. I held my breath, listening for sounds of anyone walking by or guarding me. After a few minutes of not hearing any sounds that concerned me, I determined the time to move was now.

Taking the lantern that sat on the thorned nightstand, I walked into my bathroom, shut the door again, and locked it. If anyone came inside while I was gone, I hoped they believed that I'd fallen asleep in the tub.

I moved to the wall between the countertop and the tub, squatted, and pressed the latch underneath the vined bottom drawer. A thorn poked my finger, and the wall in front of me separated into a door and opened. I stepped inside the dark secret passage and forced the door closed.

I lifted the lantern as I stepped into a cobweb. A chill ran down my spine, but I remembered that no spiders actually lived in Gleann Solas. It had to be dust.

Taking deep breaths, I began the journey toward Tavish.

With each step, the warm magic inside me continued to pulse steadily. I wasn't sure what was going on. I'd felt a pulse like that only a few times, and usually when I was injured.

I was fine.

My bare feet brushed the cold stone floor, and I regretted not putting on any shoes.

I was moving at a slow, steady pace when a voice startled me.

"Did you hear about how she injured the king to save the Unseelie thornling?" a deep voice spat.

I spun around and lifted the lantern, expecting to find someone behind me.

I was all alone.

A raspy male voice replied, "Yes, and I can't believe she didn't get punished."

"The king always had a soft spot for her," the other person replied.

I wanted to laugh. If that was the king being soft, I felt sorry for the Seelie people.

"I heard the Unseelie king took a beating for it."

The humor died, choking me.

Tavish had said it wasn't bad.

The urgency to reach my mate had my feet moving faster than was safe. Still, I didn't slow down. I *needed* to reach him.

Panting, I ran down the passage, keeping my footsteps light. I didn't want to chance anyone on the other side of the wall hearing me. If they informed my parents, they'd know what I was up to. Right now, I hoped they wouldn't consider that I'd use the secret passage to see him. After all, it was forbidden for me to be in it alone. The last time I used it, they'd assumed Eldrin had kidnapped me from my room when he saved Tavish.

Even though I sprinted, it felt like hours had passed before I reached the hidden door that led to him. As long as they'd kept him in the holding cell...

Shit. I hadn't even thought that far ahead, but I was here. There was no turning back now.

Even though I wanted to burst in, I forced myself to

take a deep breath and control my breathing. Then I placed my ear to the wall.

It was late, past midnight at this point, so there shouldn't be anyone with Tavish. But who knew what they'd do with me here and two Unseelie in their prison?

I forced myself to wait longer. I needed to be more certain than ever that no one would catch me in there, or I would most definitely be watched for the foreseeable future.

When I couldn't take it any longer, I squatted like I had when I was a little girl and pricked my finger to open the door.

When it opened, my breath caught.

A vise tightened around my heart. I'd hoped that Father wouldn't have done *this* to my fated mate, but that had been my foolish human side taking control.

Tavish's eyes were swollen and black, and he lay in a thick black puddle of blood.

Unable to stop myself, I hurried over to him. With shaky hands, I touched the injury on his side and saw that it was still oozing blood. He'd been hurt hours ago, and he was still bleeding.

The warm spot in my chest flared, and my body took control. I placed a hand against his wound, and the warm spot in my chest pulsed, the warmth moving from my center down toward my hand as the buzz of our connection sprang to life.

Memories of a similar thing happening the last time we were in this situation almost twelve years ago took root in my mind as the magic reached my palm and warmed where I pressed it against his injury. The yank of the fated-mate connection flared.

Tavish groaned and muttered, "I need Lira."

I'm right here, I connected, fearful of saying anything out loud since a guard could pass by at any time.

His eyes fluttered open, and when they focused on my face, they widened in surprise. *What are you doing here?* He scanned the room. *How did you get in here without alerting anyone?*

With my free hand, I placed a finger in front of my lips.

His brows furrowed, and he touched his own lips. *Do I have something on my face?*

My chest loosened a little, but luckily, I was too upset to actually laugh. *No. On Earth, it means to be quiet, and you were talking in your sleep. There's a secret passage in here that only the royal family is aware of, and I doubt they considered I'd use it.* I nodded toward the door I'd forgotten to close after seeing him like this. Then I realized that something else was wrong—no one was snoring or making witty quips at us. *Where's Finnian?*

They took him to another cell. Tavish's breath caught as his attention went to the secret passage then back to my face.

The buzz between us intensified to a jolt as the warm magic swirled from my hand into his side. His irises lightened to silver, and need built within me. His injury was the only thing keeping me sane and holding me back from being all over him.

Is he as poorly off as you? I tried to focus on the threat at hand, which included Finnian. Getting lost in a world where only Tavish and I existed had become second nature to me.

No, but they did hurt him, Tavish answered while placing a hand over his wounds. *You shouldn't be here. I'm fine.*

Like hell I shouldn't. I gritted my teeth and smacked his

hand away. *You're injured, and I can't stay in my room while you suffer, especially when our link wasn't warm anymore and you weren't responding. I thought something awful had happened to you, and clearly, I wasn't wrong.*

They weakened me, but I'm not at risk of dying. This isn't like you being in the gauntlet—the very game I created and had to watch you actually die from. His face twisted in agony.

So this is you punishing yourself by suffering through these beatings? No wonder he only allowed a few people to be close to him. For someone who had everyone believing he was heartless and to be feared, he wanted to beat himself up for everything. *If that's why you want to lie here and suffer, then you're foolish.*

He lifted a brow and winked. *With the way you're making me feel, I sure am suffering. I never dreamed that someone touching my wounds could feel so exquisite.*

That brought me back to the present, and I moved my hand to see if what I suspected had occurred. Smooth, pale skin had replaced the wound.

Tavish tilted his head to look, and his face turned a shade paler. *You healed me. How is that possible?*

This confirmed what I suspected had happened twelve years ago. Eldrin had helped Tavish escape, but I'd actually healed him. *I... I don't know, but Tavish, this isn't the first time I did this to you. The night you were here twelve years ago, I snuck into this same cell and found you with horrible injuries. I didn't realize what I was doing, but like now, something inside me took over, and I was healing you when Eldrin came barging in.* Now probably wasn't the time to tell him, but he needed to know in case something happened to me. He needed to know he didn't owe Eldrin nearly as much as he thought he did.

Tension lay thick between us, and fear choked me. I didn't understand the emotions that wafted through him, and I hated that I'd thrown out the information without realizing it could change our relationship.

What if he didn't believe me, or he thought I was trying to pit him against his cousin? Even though I spoke the truth, I'd seen what denial could do to people.

I tried to control my ragged breathing as I removed my thin, lacy jacket and yanked at the cool, refreshing water magic inside me, hoping I could control it as well as I had when I was a little girl. It'd been so long since I'd attempted to use it. A faint mist came out of my fingertips, and I cleaned the blood from him, wanting him to look untarnished when my father saw him in the morning.

After I'd cleaned him off, Tavish caught my wrist, stopping me as he sat upright. His chains clanked faintly as he adjusted himself, and he pulled me to his chest. With his free hand, he cupped my face, and his expression softened into pure adoration.

I don't blasting deserve you, sprite. You snuck in here and healed me as a child, even then, going against your father by aiding the enemy. All I've done is accuse you of betraying me—even as a child—and stalk your dreams to find you in the hopes of killing you. Maybe you'd be better off without me. Every person I've trusted has betrayed me, and every decision I've made has been wrong. You deserve someone worthy, though I'll kill any man who tries to take my place or dares to touch you.

The thought of him even thinking of letting me go had me sliding over his body and straddling him while my mind blurred. He didn't get to think about leaving me. I gripped his chin between my thumb and pointer finger, forcing him to look into my eyes. I connected, *You aren't allowed to let me go. You are the person I want. You've been placed in a horrible situation, and you did the best you could with the information at hand.* The yanking in my chest came to an all-time high, and the need to connect with him overwhelmed me. *If you ever think about letting me go again, I will punish you. Remember, you're going to kill anyone who touches me, and if you don't, I'll do it for you.*

He smirked and placed a hand on the back of my neck, bringing me down for a kiss. His lips brushed mine, and I sucked in a breath at the jolt between us. I licked his lips, begging for entrance, and he opened to me. Our tongues collided, and his velvet feel and frosty night taste filled my senses.

Between seeing him like this and the words he'd said, I needed to connect with him. The desire was so strong that I rocked my hips against his crotch. His hardened dick hit perfectly, causing my back to arch.

You should go, he connected as his hand slid under my thin gown, caressing my nipple.

He was suffering the same conflict as me, knowing we shouldn't do this, but something overrode our common sense. With all the trauma, we *needed* to connect. Even if I truly wanted to leave, I couldn't walk away from him... and I didn't want to.

My fingers tangled in his hair. *If you don't want—*

I'm not sure I can let you go, he replied, kissing down my face and my neck until he hoisted me up so my nipple slipped into his mouth, and his chains didn't make a sound. His tongue glided over my breast, and he slipped a hand between my legs.

When his fingers slid against me, he moaned faintly. *Fates, you're already ready for me.*

That I was, and the thrill of doing this where we

shouldn't added to the excitement. I nodded, moving slightly back to tug his pants down. He lifted his hips enough to lower them so his dick sprang out, revealing how huge and ready he was.

I shifted my weight and slid onto him. As he filled me, it didn't hurt like before, though I felt like I couldn't hold anymore.

He leaned his head back and bit his lips to hold in his groan.

He was blasting sexy and *mine*.

I rocked my hips, and the fated-mate connection between us opened wide, our pleasure mixing together. I panted, and he captured my lips with his. We kissed each other to hide our noises.

Each time I moved against him, he somehow hit deeper and deeper. He gripped my thighs, spreading them farther apart so I could take more of him. Our teeth hit each other as my pace increased since he couldn't move without risking making louder noises with his chains.

One hand slipped back into my top to caress my breasts again as he placed the fingers of the other hand against my clit. I rolled my hips against him, that touch sparking a fire inside me.

I love you, Lira, he connected, his hands and mouth working my body. *Always and forever.*

You're my everything now, I replied. The pleasure heightened between us, and our emotions mingled. I continued, *We're each other's. No matter what it takes. Promise me.*

The corners of his lips turned upward as he kissed me harder. *I promise. You're never getting rid of me, sprite.*

Our orgasms slammed through us, and I clung to him as our bodies rode out the pleasure and our souls connected. A sense of peace filled us as we felt complete once more.

Maybe this time hadn't been slow and romantic, but it'd been raw and exactly what we needed after our cruel separation and the challenge to our relationship. After a few minutes, our bodies calmed down, but I refused to move, needing one more moment.

He kissed me tenderly, pressing our sweaty foreheads together.

I never realized I wouldn't hate being a prisoner the entire time, he teased.

I rolled my eyes, but the corners of my mouth tipped upward. *I'd still prefer to be in your bedroom so we could do this more than once and stay in each other's arms the entire night.* The thought of leaving him to return to my room made my heart bitter. No one should keep us apart.

It's our bedroom. Not mine. Not anymore. Everything that belongs to me is yours, including the crown. Warmth exploded through our bond from the magnitude of his love for me. *And we're getting out of here soon, which is why you need to return to your room even though it's the last thing in Ardanos I want. But getting out of here and determining a way that you'll never be taken from me again is more of a priority.*

Right. If I got caught tonight, it would make our escape harder, which would prolong this problem, and Father would take out his frustration on Tavish. *Fine, but I need to know if they hurt you like that again. I need to be able to trust you, or I'll lose my mind.*

He sighed and nodded. *I'll tell you. I wasn't trying to trick you. I didn't want to risk you doing something foolish, though...* He kissed my lips. *I really enjoyed your visit, and it was something we both clearly needed.*

My heart shattered at the thought of walking back to my room. But I'd already risked staying here too long.

I'll be fine, and we can talk throughout the day tomorrow. He brushed a finger along my cheek. *And I get to smell you as I sleep.*

Footsteps sounded outside the room a little ways away, and I stood quickly. Tavish lifted his bottom, pulling up his pants, and I snagged my thin jacket with his bloodstains from the ground.

Go. Hurry, he replied, his eyes darkening with concern.

Hurrying on my tiptoes, I was thankful I'd forgotten to close the door. It would have taken a moment to open it. I darted into the passage. Tavish and I locked gazes right before the door shut completely, and then another one opened.

Sweat beaded on my brow, but it wasn't from sex this time. I'd almost gotten caught, and somehow, I'd escaped in the nick of time.

I grabbed the lantern I'd left behind when I'd opened the door and hurried back to my room. Still, I worried what the late-night visit meant for him.

Is everything okay? I connected, trying to prevent my legs from spinning around and racing back to him.

Finnian. They brought him back. Tavish didn't sound happy. *He's hurt, but don't come back. He'll be fine. No one but the two of us should know about your healing magic. Not even my trusted friend. I suspect the guards will be watching us more closely now that we're together.*

Mouth drying, I wanted to march to my parents' bedroom and tell them everything they were doing wrong. I despised the way they were treating Tavish and Finnian, but that was the crux of the problem. They didn't want me to care about those things, so it'd only make them unhappy with me.

I made it back to my bedroom and was relieved that it appeared like no one had tried to check on me. I washed my jacket, not wanting evidence of Tavish's black blood on my clothes. The water here washed it out, proving it had to be magic.

After that, I crawled into my bed. The place that had once comforted me made me feel like a prisoner in my own world. I lay on several fluffy pillows and closed my eyes, picturing Tavish. He was the one thing that made sense in this completely foreign world.

A knock on my door had my eyes popping open. I expected to find Tavish next to me in the bed with Nightbane at my feet, but reality swooped in.

I was in Seelie lands, and my beastly friend wasn't here.

God, how I missed my animal companion.

"Princess Lira, the queen and king are requesting your presence for breakfast. They've asked me to help you get ready, as there is a special visitor. May I enter?"

I glanced at the open window, considering the consequences if I flew away and didn't show up. They hadn't informed me about a special visitor last night, and my pulse quickened at the fact that they'd sprung it on me at the last second. Leaving wasn't an option. Not with Tavish and Finnian trapped here.

I threw off the covers and strolled to the door. When I opened it, I found a gorgeous woman who seemed somewhat familiar. Her straight, dark-blonde hair contrasted with her sky-blue dress, and she glided into the room like she knew it well.

Of course she did. She worked here.

"Lira, it's so good to see you again." She smiled, but no warmth entered her aquamarine eyes.

I tilted my head, trying to figure out who she was.

"I'm Gaelle." She tossed her hair over her shoulder. "I'm sure you don't recognize me. You've been gone for so long and formed an interesting connection with the nightfiend king."

Out of everyone, it would be Gaelle. I remembered her now. The one high fae who was close to my age and had tried to seduce my father numerous times, wanting to bear his child and help her own social standing. She was the type of fae who would do anything to get what she wanted, just like Eldrin.

"Ah, that's right." I forced a smile, though my blood ran cold. She was always nice to me, but she enjoyed collecting information as leverage against other people and to elevate her position in society. The less I talked, the better.

"So, Earth—" she started, but I cut her off by going into my closet.

"Did he specify a certain dress, or may I wear anything of my choosing?" I asked, pretending I hadn't heard her.

She followed me into the closet and ran a hand along the intricate dresses. "No, and I think this would look amazing on you." She removed a white gown with gold woven into the lace, emphasizing the breasts and waist.

I didn't care what I wore as long as it kept my father from focusing on me, and I knew Gaelle wouldn't risk the wrath of her king by allowing me to present myself in an inappropriate way.

She removed the dress and held it open for me to step

into, and I froze. I wasn't used to people helping me dress anymore, and now that I thought about it, Tavish didn't have that either. I wondered why.

Forcing myself to not act awkward, I dropped the nightgown from my body and tried to ignore the way goose bumps spread across my arms as I stepped into the dress. It fit me perfectly, brushing the floor and emphasizing my cleavage.

"Perfect." She removed some shoes made of vines and set them down for me to slip into.

When my outfit was settled, she waved her hands over my face, and the tingle of glamour slid across my skin. Then she grabbed a brush and braided my hair before pulling it into a twist.

I stepped into the bathroom to glance in the mirror; I didn't recognize the woman staring at me. Yes, the eyes were mine, as well as the features, but with jewelry emphasizing my pointed ears, it was as if she'd used magic.

In fairness, she had.

I noted one major issue: She'd hidden my fated-mate markings.

I moved my hand to unglamour the very thing that proved Tavish and I belonged together, but Gaelle caught my wrist.

"Trust me. It's for the best that your marks remain hidden." Gaelle lifted a brow, and her forehead creased with concern. "Your parents' guest will cause all sorts of abyss if he sees them."

The truth ringing in her words gave me pause.

"You should hurry. We don't want to upset the guest or the royals." Gaelle gestured.

I gritted my teeth, wanting to correct her that I did not, in fact, care if they got upset, especially since my fated-mate mark was hidden, but her worry seemed genuine, and I swallowed my words. I marched out the door and turned toward the dining hall.

More fae buzzed around, working and stealing glances at me as I passed, and I forced my back to stay straight as I flew past them like I didn't notice.

After making the turns, I found the opening to the dining room. I slowed, preparing myself for whatever stood on the opposite side of the wall.

As I breezed over the threshold, I noticed two people at the table. Father sat on one end, seeming too big for the chair made of roots and the leaf he was perched on. Mother looked more natural and dainty sitting on his left, her legs crossed.

When my attention landed on the third man, the world stopped, and so did my heart.

Each time I blinked, the prince of the dragons reappeared, standing by the middle of the table, his amber eyes locked on me and a scowl on his face.

What the fuck was he doing here?

The dragon prince kept his intense gaze locked on me. My breathing caught as I tried to keep my emotions in check, not wanting to alarm Tavish. Though I had no intention of keeping anything from him, I didn't want him to panic when there wasn't a blazing thing he could do while locked in the holding cell.

The other sensation that had my lungs moving freely again was my relief that I hadn't fought Gaelle's suggestion to glamour the fated-mate marks. They would have enraged the man I was supposed to marry, and though I was proud of them, it wouldn't bode well if Prince Pyralis learned about the bond while Tavish was imprisoned.

The timing of Prince Pyralis's visit seemed odd. My parents had vowed to retrieve me from Earth a few weeks prior to when I'd be wedded to the dragon prince. Tavish had brought me back three years earlier than planned. The agreement was that Pyralis and I would wed when I was twenty-five to ensure I could come back at full strength to protect myself if needed. We had time to determine a way to free me from that vow.

Pyralis's chiseled features tensed as he rubbed a hand through his short, caramel-brown beard. "This is unacceptable."

My back straightened. I understood that not every man would find me attractive, but he didn't have to be so damn rude about it. "Well, you aren't the most attractive man I've ever seen either."

"Lira!" Mother exclaimed as her head jerked in my direction. Her jaw dropped, and Father glared at me.

"I'll take that as a compliment, seeing as I'm not truly a *man*." Prince Pyralis smirked. "I'm a beast, which you'll learn all about shortly."

The idea of learning anything about him had bile churning in my stomach. I refused to think of any man but Tavish in that way, and the dragon prince's suggestion made me feel dirty.

Sprite, are you being harmed? Tavish asked, the bond tightening with his concern.

So much for trying to contain my emotions. My blood ran cold. *Prince Pyralis is here.*

Silence hung in the bond before frigid fear blasted through our connection. *If he touches you, I'll make sure his death is slow and painful.*

I relished his threat, my heart skipping a beat. A month ago, it would have sent me running, but now I wanted to run to Tavish and bury my tongue in his mouth. I was changing, and I wasn't sure who I was anymore. *Don't fret. He won't touch me. I won't allow it.*

Refocusing on the threat in front of me, I straightened my shoulders. "Three years isn't long for an immortal, but I wouldn't consider it short." I tried to relax my shoulders, not wanting Prince Pyralis to realize he was getting under my skin.

Wanting to seem confident despite my shaking knees, I entered the dining room and took the spot next to Mother, turning my back to the doors leading to a massive balcony with an absolutely gorgeous view of the village below.

The prince's face turned red, hinting at the crimson scales he bore in dragon form. "After receiving insult after insult of no communication, despite the vows our families exchanged, I came here to learn for myself if you had returned to Ardanos after all."

Father's jaw clenched. He had to be wondering who'd informed the dragon royals of my return. I had no doubt that the traitor would be punished once Father ascertained their identity.

"We were going to inform you soon." Mother laid a hand on my arm and smiled at me warmly. "We've just gotten our daughter back after twelve long years, and we wanted a moment to celebrate with her before announcing her return to the masses." Her fingers dug into my skin when I didn't respond immediately.

Good. Let them fret for a moment, wondering if I would play along with their ruse. They wouldn't want the prince to learn that Tavish had kidnapped me while I was in hiding. The fact would reflect poorly on their strength and intelligence.

The silence hung thick, and Mother took in a choppy breath.

This time, my smile wasn't forced because I enjoyed gaining a little control over my parents. If I wanted to, I could out them for everything they'd done, but that would only put a larger target on Tavish. "Yes, I've needed time to acclimate to my magic and wings again. The last thing I'd ever want is for you to see me as weak, Prince Pyralis." My voice lowered into a deep threat, so I batted my eyelashes in tune with the flutter of my wings, trying to come off as sweet as possible.

But there was no lie there. The dragon prince needed to see me as a force. One that would make him think twice about coercing me into a contract I'd never agreed to personally. Free will wasn't relished here in Ardanos, but I'd grown up on Earth long enough that I refused to give up certain freedoms and have someone else decide my life *for* me.

"You're fae. Not dragon." Prince Pyralis scoffed. "You'll never match me in terms of strength and size, so don't flatter yourself."

I bit the inside of my cheek and ignored the way I wanted to ball my hands into fists and lunge at him. What was it with all these men thinking I was inferior to them? They'd all have another think coming... thing coming... whatever version of the saying fit since both were technically correct in this day and age.

What is the blasted ashbreath doing to you? Tavish linked.

Being condescending, nothing more. I refocused on the dragon prince. "Ah... yet I'm smaller, lither, and possess an affinity for water." I placed my hands on the table and wiggled my fingers, emphasizing my point.

Father's neck corded.

Prince Pyralis pursed his lips. "If I didn't know any better, I wouldn't believe you were the same girl I met all those years ago. That girl acted more like a lady than the woman sitting across from me today. However, I suspected Earth would have that impact on you." His steely gaze cut to my parents.

My departure from this realm must have been a point of

contention between the two royal families. I'd always assumed that the dragons had been informed, but based on these interactions, I'd assumed wrong. "There is a big difference between ten and twenty-two. A child is easily manipulated whereas a woman has the ability to think on her own."

Head jerking back, Prince Pyralis wrinkled his nose with disdain.

"That's *enough*, Lira," Father said sternly. "Prince Pyralis, if you're certain you don't want any breakfast, then I'd love to show you this year's harvest. It has been very bountiful, and I'd be honored if you took some items back so that you and your parents can enjoy our delicacies."

"I'm certain my parents would appreciate the gesture." Prince Pyralis brushed the front of his golden-threaded shirt, which he wore with crimson slacks designed as if they were scales.

My heart dropped into my stomach as I realized why Gaelle had chosen this dress. The gold in my dress matched the color of his tunic.

Discomfort wafted through my bond with Tavish.

I hated that there wasn't a way for me to reassure him. I could only imagine how he felt, knowing my betrothed stood before me. If I were in his shoes, I'd be going out of my mind. *He's leaving with Father. They're going on a tour around the kingdom.*

Father stood, his wings expanding to his sides. "Excellent."

Prince Pyralis bowed his head ever so slightly at me and said, "It was interesting seeing you again, Lira. I hope when I see you next, we'll have a more pleasant conversation." His pupils elongated, emphasizing the dragon locked inside him.

A chill ran down my spine, and I tensed to hide my discomfort. There wasn't a way to respond to that comment without upsetting him or my parents, so instead, I bowed my head back at him. I didn't care if that gave him a sign of respect as long as it got him far away from me.

Seeming appeased by my gesture, he strolled to the end of the table, and when he stood next to my father, I realized how gigantic the dragon prince truly was.

He was at least eight feet tall.

When he exited through the doorway into the hallway with Father, he had to duck his head. Even though I didn't find him attractive, I couldn't look away. I'd never seen anyone that tall before.

As soon as they disappeared from sight, Mother turned her entire body toward me. "Are you trying to cause the dragons to go to war with us?"

I rolled my eyes. Mother did have a flair for the dramatics when we were alone with no onlookers. "We're allies. They wouldn't do that."

"You haven't been here for the past twelve years. Nor do you understand what happened before you left." Mother huffed. "Our relationship with them is strained."

"How would I know when you and Father never inform me of anything?" I refused to be the villain in her story.

"A woman should know better than to insult family and defy her future husband." Mother's face took on that golden hue that signified her flush. "That's common knowledge, and we weren't informed of his arrival until the dragon prince appeared at Caisteal Solais's doors. We didn't have a way to warn you without making Prince Pyralis suspicious."

Fair. I hadn't been here long, and a lot had happened since I'd arrived. My focus was on Tavish. "I can't marry him—"

"Stop." She lifted a hand. "What you want or desire doesn't matter. The vow has been set, and there is no getting out of the agreement unless the dragons do something to negate it. It doesn't matter if you and the Unseelie night-fiend are fated mates. A contract trumps everything, and you *know* that." She dropped her hand, and a crease appeared between her eyes. "I swear we don't recognize you anymore."

I opened my mouth to respond, but a maid entered the dining room. I wanted to say a lot more, but that crease between Mother's eyes always appeared right before I got into an extreme amount of trouble. I couldn't risk them having me watched because then I'd risk not seeing Tavish.

The maid stopped. "Do you require anything while waiting on King Erdan?"

"The king won't be eating with us." Mother steepled her fingers. "It'll just be Lira and me. Please bring out the food."

"Yes, Your Majesty." The maid curtseyed, looking down as she fluttered out of the room.

"For the love of Fate." Mother pushed her long hair behind her shoulders. "Behave."

Again, I couldn't reconcile her with the woman I remembered. She'd been warm and loving.

I needed to bite my tongue if I wanted a chance to spend time with my mate.

The maids entered with various types of honey, bread, and fruit, and I settled in to eat. The less talking I did, the better.

Breakfast took forever, but as soon as Mother and I finished, I excused myself to find Eiric and practice my magic.

I'd expected Mother to complain, but she seemed rather relieved. She'd mentioned needing to oversee the preparations to transport the fruit back with Prince Pyralis. I didn't want to get in the way of helping him leave Gleann Solas as quickly as possible.

It didn't take long for me to locate Eiric, who was in the training room with Mom and Dad. As usual, Mom understood that I needed to get away and think, so she excused Eiric to spend the day with me so we could reconnect with our magic.

The waterfall was the perfect location. No one was there because everyone was working for the day. The clear water had my water magic pulsing while Eiric practiced sprouting flowers on the grassy embankment. I learned to make my magic pulse from my hand and even had the water falling up instead of down for a time.

After a couple of hours, Eiric and I returned to the castle, exhausted. I holed up in my room for the rest of the day, taking dinner alone in my chambers and spending the time checking in with Tavish. Between that and thinking about how to help him and Finnian escape, I couldn't distract the guards long enough so they wouldn't realize I'd taken the keys that would unlock the chains to Tavish's and Finnian's wings before I could make it down the secret passage.

Right at ten, I gave in to the temptation to enter the secret passage and see Tavish. I hadn't planned to visit him so soon, but after feeling his worry all day, I needed to check on him.

I locked my bedroom and bathroom doors like before and quickly opened the secret door. This time, the journey didn't feel quite as long, and I moved more quickly, taking the same path as the night before.

When I reached the door to the holding cell, I placed my ear against it to listen while linking, *Tavish, is it safe for me to come in there?*

Our bond expanded with relief, confirming I'd made the right decision.

Yes, the guards left a few minutes ago.

I pricked my finger, and the door slid open to reveal Tavish chained to the wall. There were cuts down his wrists and wings, proving he'd been trying to get free. No doubt because of me.

I hurried to him and threw my arms around his neck, and then we were kissing passionately. The buzz sprang to life between us, and his tongue slid greedily into my mouth. I pressed my body to his, and his hands cupped my face.

The last thing I want to do is end this, but Finnian needs your help, he linked, pulling back slowly. His stormy gray eyes swirled as he looked over my shoulder across the cell.

A lump formed in my throat as I spun around to see Finnian unconscious. His eyes were swollen shut, and he had bruises down his arms and a fat, bloodied lip.

He hasn't said more than a few words the entire day. Tavish bit his bottom lip. *Can you heal him some, but not completely? I hate to ask, but we need to be ready to escape, especially with the dragon prince here. I can't leave Finnian behind. But I don't want him to learn about your powers because the knowledge would put him more at risk, so...*

You don't even have to ask, and I understand. True healing was a form of magic the fae had lost a long time ago. No one knew why. Select Earth fae had taken on the task of healing since they understood plants and their properties. I wasn't on Earth, yet I could heal people on the brink of death. People would covet that sort of magic.

I tiptoed to Finnian and squatted next to him.

My vision blurred, and my chest constricted. He seemed nothing like the charismatic fae I'd come to know. I reached out and touched his hand, and I could feel the icky sensation of jealousy flow from Tavish, but he didn't say a word.

I yanked at the warm, magical spot I now knew was associated with healing, and I felt it respond more easily than it had before. The warmth flowed through my chest to my arm and pushed into Finnian. Unlike with Tavish, my magic entering him didn't feel right, but I ignored the strange sensation and kept pushing more.

After a minute, his bruises began to fade, and then his lip became less swollen. Finnian groaned, and his eyes fluttered open.

"Lira?" he rasped.

I released his hand, not wanting him to know what I'd done, and lifted my finger to my lips. I mouthed, *Be quiet. Guards.*

He nodded and squeezed my arm gently, but his blue eyes darkened with questions.

He'll tell you, I replied and patted his arm. Then I stood and hurried back to Tavish, who buried his face in my hair and wrapped his arms around me.

He linked, *Today has been blasted hell between knowing the dragon prince was here and seeing Finnian like that.*

I kissed him again, needing to taste him. *I'm sorry. I think he went back tonight, though.*

Thank Fate. His arms tightened around me. *If he had touched you, I'd be forced to risk my life just so that I could kill him.* He growled menacingly.

"Right here," Finnian grumbled.

"Did you hear that?" a guard asked from the other side of the holding cell door.

I froze, and Tavish pulled back, placing his forehead against mine.

"It sounded like the injured one is awake." The other male guard snickered. "I want to see how much pain he's in. Don't you?"

Go. Tavish pecked my lips.

I didn't want to leave, but my heart hammered, knowing if I didn't, they'd find me in here. I spun around and took off toward the still-open door.

I stepped inside the secret passageway and pricked my finger. When the door moved, I helped push it along, causing it to make a noise. It shut just as the cell door opened. I pressed my ear to the door to listen.

"What was that?" the first male guard asked.

Finnian mimicked the sound as best he could, groaning similar to the *bang* of the door.

The second guard chuckled. "It's the Unseelie, moaning like the nightfiend he is."

"How bad are you hurting?" the first guard asked.

"Horribly," Finnian slurred, playing up his injuries.

Though the last thing I wanted to do was leave, I needed to get back to my room. Without wasting more time, I hurried back down the passage. *Is everything okay?*

They're just gloating. Nothing we can't handle, Tavish replied. The worry he'd been feeling all day was gone. *I just wish Finnian would've stayed quiet. I wasn't done kissing you.*

Was kissing all you wanted? I snickered as I opened the door to my bathroom.

No, but there's no way I'd do more with him awake and

conscious. I don't need him to see you on top of me. The way your eyes close and the way your face smooths as I fill you is for only me to know.

I shut the secret door and turned to find my bathroom door open and someone standing in the corner of my darkened room, watching me.

My mouth dried as I straightened and spread out my wings. Then I soared through the doorway into the bedroom, ready to fight whoever had caught me, needing them to keep their mouth shut about what they'd seen. As I flew over the bed, moonlight filled the room, revealing the identity of my observer.

I couldn't slow down my pace enough, and I slammed into a wide-eyed Eiric.

Her arms circled my waist, keeping me upright as her back hit the wall. I heard a sickening *thwack*, yet her arms still anchored me to her.

Sprite, what's the matter? Tavish's voice popped into my head.

Someone is in my room, but it's just Eiric, I replied as my heart leaped into my throat. I pushed back, breaking from Eiric's embrace, and rasped, "Dammit, E!"

"Don't *dammit* me." Eiric scowled and stood, rubbing the back of her head. "If anyone should be damned, it's *you*."

Fair, though I couldn't hide my smile. "You want me to go to hell now?"

"Like you'll ever die." Eiric stuck her tongue out. "Even if you weren't immortal, the amount of trouble you find yourself in will fuel you for eternity."

I snorted and moved to inspect the back of her head. I touched the spot where it had hit the wall, making her flinch. There was a huge bump, but with fae, it wouldn't result in a concussion. We weren't frail like humans, but that didn't mean it didn't hurt. "Eiric, I'm—"

"Don't you dare say what I think you might." Eiric glared at me. "You're a princess and shouldn't owe *anyone*, including me."

My chest warmed. "You protected me on Earth, even before your memories came back."

"I guess part of me always knew what my role was." She gestured to the bathroom. "Something I hadn't expected to be quite as difficult now that we're in Gleann Solas and in the castle... yet here we are."

She was fishing for answers, and I needed to be careful. The more she learned about the secret passages and my plan to leave with Tavish, the bigger the chance she'd catch hell for not informing anyone. "I was clearly in the bathroom." I bit my lip, fighting the urge to heal her injury. If it had been worse, I would've. No questions asked.

"You were *not*, Lira." Eiric pointed a finger in my face. "I went in there. Don't you realize both doors were open? Don't do this half-truth shit that they like doing around here. You said we were still sisters, so prove it."

Wait. Both doors would need to be unlocked for her to get in here. "How *did* you get in? The doors were locked." I scanned the room for answers. "Do you have a key?"

"I used my earth magic, manipulating the wood of the

door to work around the lock." She leaned back on her heels. "And, for your information, every guard on duty has keys to get in here in case you're ever harmed."

Blighted abyss. I hadn't realized every guard had keys to my room. "Well, that's not reassuring." The risk I'd taken to go see Tavish was even greater than I'd realized.

"Where were you?" She crossed her arms, leveling her gaze at me.

I couldn't lie to her, even if I was able to. We'd always been truthful with one another, and I didn't want to taint the relationship. She was too damn important to me. I sighed, crossing my fingers that she'd humor me. "Can we just let this go and forget it happened?"

"No." She lifted her chin. "If you don't tell me what you were doing, I'll be forced to inform Mom and Dad. Which, to be clear, doesn't mean I won't, depending on your answer."

Something indignant rose inside me, making my blood boil. "If I command you not to say anything, you'd be betraying a royal." As soon as the words left my mouth, I clamped my hands over it, wanting to take them back.

But the damage was done.

Her jaw dropped, and her arms hung at her sides. "I see. Is this how it's going to be every time I say or do something you don't like? Or if you want me to do something I don't want to?"

Regret hung heavy on my shoulders, and I swallowed. "No. I don't even know why I said that. I didn't—" My words cut off, preventing me from lying.

"You didn't what?" she asked sweetly, but her face twisted in pain.

Instead of making things better, I was digging myself into a hole. I was certain I didn't need to even dig it. Eiric would bend the earth to do it for me just so it could happen faster. "I meant it in the moment, but not now."

"Because that makes it better." She shook her head and moved to the door. "I'm tired. I need to head to bed."

I didn't want her to leave this way. "E, wait."

She opened the door, so I reached for her hand.

"Don't go. Not like this." I wished I could go back in time and change that moment. I'd been foolish to say that to her. She was my equal and family, not someone I ever wanted to order around.

"Don't fret, Your Highness." She removed her hand and curtseyed. "I'll obey." She then fluttered off down the hallway.

That hadn't been what I meant, but she was already halfway down the hall, flying past Sorcha.

Sorcha tapped a finger to her lips. She was already suspicious of me, and Eiric leaving like that added more questions.

Lovely.

Chasing Eiric down and forcing her to talk when she didn't want to was the worst thing I could do, but part of me wanted to do that. After all, she was a child of guards. Who was she to turn her back on *me*?

I stepped back into my bedroom and shut the door, shaking my head. I needed to get these foreign thoughts out. Something strange was coming over me, and none of it was good. It was as if the memories of my fae childhood were rising inside me and creating two versions of myself that I had to reconcile, which sounded crazy.

I'd never hidden anything from Eiric before. I couldn't let this former piece of myself change me... not like that. Everyone was worthy of respect unless they weren't good people... like Eldrin.

Surely Caelan had found the wildling by now and placed him back in prison.

Is everything okay? Did Eiric see you come out of the secret passage? Tavish connected.

I'd give anything for the bond to warm like it did when he wasn't in chains. I needed the extra comfort. *She didn't see how I got inside the bathroom, but she knew I wasn't there before.*

Is she going to tell anyone?

No. I threatened to command her not to. I hung my wings as I paced in front of my bed. *She said she wouldn't.*

That's good. Tavish's relief wafted through the bond.

Of course he'd think that, and I couldn't fault him. He didn't know any better. I did. *It's not. I changed the dynamics of our relationship by doing that. The relationship you have with Finnian and Caelan is what I had with Eiric, if not closer. I grew up with her, and we shared parents on Earth. She's not a guard to me. She's my family.* My heart panged as I realized how much I had hurt her. I'd never said anything like that to her in the past, and it would come out here in this realm.

I didn't think of it like that. Caelan and Finnian are both high fae, which is one reason we formed a friendship before the Seelie attack. But you wouldn't remember any of that information on Earth once your memories were lost. You care for her, and I was foolish not to see it before. You care for everyone, even your competitors in the gauntlet. That's one of the things that makes you so different and why some of the Unseelie weren't thrilled when you were severely injured.

The fact that he wasn't chastising me like my biological parents proved he was my other half. He'd been raised the same way, had lost his kingdom and parents, and had been forced to become harder, yet he wanted to understand me. *I really messed up.*

Love, there's no doubt that she loves you. Who wouldn't? Everyone makes mistakes. Look at the unforgivable things I did to you, yet you forgave me. She must feel threatened by the change in your relationship. Imagine if you came back to another world and the person you viewed as your sister was a princess and you were a guard assigned to protect her.

I hadn't thought about it like that, which made me feel worse. I hadn't considered the struggles Eiric was going through because I'd been focused on Tavish and Finnian. I'd been a piss-poor friend, and I hated myself for it. *You're right. I should've realized that.*

You both need time to adjust, especially you, sprite. Don't be so hard on yourself. Things will work out. You'll see. If you could want to be with me after all the things I did and allowed to be done to you, then I have no doubt you and Eiric can get past this.

Some of the heaviness lifted from my shoulders. Here Tavish was, injured and chained, with Finnian severely injured, yet he was comforting me. I'd never imagined that we would be like this together. And I wouldn't change a thing—except for him being a prisoner. *I love you, yet those words don't come close to conveying what I feel for you.*

You're the water that nourishes me. Something I can't and won't live without.

A tear rolled down my cheek, and I smiled.

Get some sleep. The first opportunity we have to escape, we need to take it, especially now that the dragons know you're back. We need to return to my people to ensure Eldrin has been caught and there isn't an uprising. With my magic bound, they'll believe that I died.

He was right. His magic was tamped down, and his

people had seen him wounded. Even my parents' guards had believed that Tavish had died and were surprised when he arrived here. *I'll figure out a way tomorrow.* I just needed to make sure I spoke with Eiric first. I couldn't leave with our relationship broken like this.

I crawled into bed, hating the way my body relaxed and sank into it. The fact that I lay comfortably in bed while Tavish and Finnian were chained to the floor and Eiric was hurt should have been a crime. Still, there wasn't anything I could do about it tonight.

Turning toward the window, I noticed thick clouds in the sky. No wonder the room had been so dark. A cloud moved over the full moon, blocking its light.

At least Eiric hadn't been able to determine the exact location I'd come from, though if my parents heard about it, they'd know without a doubt.

I could only hope that Eiric wouldn't tell, as she'd vowed.

My eyes closed, and I sighed, fatigued from the day's adventures. At least Eiric and I had spent time together before our falling out. I clung to my connection with Tavish as I slipped into darkness.

The next morning, I woke up not wanting to attend breakfast. I wasn't up for another round of criticism from my parents. I wasn't the little girl they remembered anymore.

Instead, I opted to fly around the castle and the land to get more familiar with the area through adult eyes and not the memories of a child. The castle was ginormous, even bigger than the Unseelie one, and about halfway around the castle, I stumbled upon a garden that opened up to the cliff overlooking a village below.

The garden itself was half the size of the castle, with the most gorgeous flowers. The grounds were covered in whisperweeds, which resembled grass back on Earth, with clusters of pink petals reminding me of the radiant pink of sunrise. The flowers ranged from dawnblossoms, to mystveil irises with deep-purple petals that seemed almost black, to the bright orange and yellow petals of the sunspark tulips, to the delicate, feather-like leaves of the fayleaves, which tinkled like tiny bells.

Between the flowers stood silathair trees that could easily pass for cherry blossom on Earth. The silvery bark and leaves of the starwood trees sparkled under the sun with their long, elegant branches. Deep, emerald-green leaves of the whispering willows swayed even without wind, and the tall, imposing trunks and branches of the ironbark sentinels, which appeared to be made of metal, with rich, rust-colored leaves.

The garden called to me. It was a place I'd enjoyed frequenting as a child, so I flew down and landed gently, settling underneath one of the silathair trees. I hadn't noticed that the dress I wore matched the silver of the starwood trees, and even better, today, I hadn't been forced to hide the fated-mate markings that connected me with Tavish.

I closed my eyes to center myself while hiding from my parents.

The scents of the gardens soothed my anxiety as the sun warmed my face. My wings stretched out behind me, allowing my back to sink more into the trunk, making me feel completely alone.

"They said I might find you here when you didn't show

up for breakfast." Prince Pyralis's voice came from right behind the tree.

My stomach clenched. He wasn't supposed to be here. How had I not heard him arrive?

Eyes popping open, I saw the dragon prince step around the trunk. His gaze landed on me, and he froze midstep, his pupils slanting as he took in the fated-mate marks across my chest and down both arms.

He flushed, the ruddy color the same as a human's blush, indicating his blood was red, but then faint scales patched over his skin. "Did you glamour those markings on you? They weren't there yesterday."

I might have allowed Gaelle to hide them yesterday to prevent the dragon prince from noticing, but I refused to deny that I had a fated mate and had completed the bond. After all, no one owned me, and I wanted to make my own damn choices. "The maid hid them from you yesterday. These aren't glamoured. They're real."

Smoke trickled from his nose as he towered over me.

That didn't sit well with me, so I fluttered my wings and stood, though he still had almost three feet on me.

"Another thing your parents failed to inform me about." Prince Pyralis's jaw clenched. He wrapped an arm around my waist, pulling me flush against his chest.

Lira, are you in danger? Tavish linked.

My heart hammered, and I tried to push him away, unable to focus on answering my mate.

Pyralis lifted me up and slung me over his shoulder, throwing a heavy arm around my waist.

Oh *hell* no. This wasn't happening.

Unsure what else I could do, I pressed my face into his back, ignoring the roughness of his golden shirt, opened my mouth wide, and bit into a chunk of his skin. He groaned and dragged me down his front, and I elbowed him in his ear. Hard.

He snarled, sounding more animal than man, and ripped me away from his body, holding me in front of him.

Blighted abyss. Are you okay? Tavish linked again.

All my years of training kicked in, and self-defense came naturally to me. I lifted both legs while flapping my wings, using the heels of my shoes to kick him hard in the chest.

The heels broke, and I flapped, ready to pull away.

But instead of his grasp relaxing, he held on tighter, refusing to let me go.

Out of the corner of my eye, I noticed a sheath with a hilt. I needed to reach it. *I'm fighting the dragon prince.*

"Stop fighting me, princess," he growled. "You're annoying me more than anything."

I gritted my teeth, his words pissing me off as terror filled the bond from Tavish. I didn't need his emotions affecting me, so I used the one thing I could access.

I tapped into my magic.

I tapped into the cool, refreshing spot in my chest and allowed the magic to pulse through my body and into my hands. I lifted them and sprayed water in the prince's face with as much force as I could bear.

He stumbled back as his hold relaxed, and I flew away from him. I continued to spray water from my hands as I flew away from the garden and him.

When I got twenty feet in the air, I pulled back my magic. The clear water thinned until it completely disappeared, my magic settling back deep inside me.

Prince Pyralis stood there, face scarlet as he breathed heavily. Faint patches of scales covered his skin, and his pupils were elongated, but the smoke that should have been trickling from his nose wasn't there.

I smirked, unable to stop myself. After manhandling me the way he had, he deserved what I'd done.

My parents had to learn what he'd done to me. There was no way they'd be all right with the way the dragon prince had handled me. We weren't in Tìr na Dràgon—not that it would've mattered to me anyway. I would've done the same thing there because no one would mishandle me ever again.

Turning my back to him, I flew off toward my bedroom. If he tried to find me there, I wouldn't let him inside. I was tired of all these people believing they had a say over what I did and how I lived my life. In fact, they more than believed it... they felt it was their *right*.

My wings moved faster, my agitation damn near taking control.

Pain pulsed through my connection with Tavish. Pain that wasn't my own.

Now I was the one who felt helpless, not knowing what was happening on his end. *Tavish, I'm coming.* Fuck my parents, Pyralis, and everyone else. I didn't give a damn if my parents and I lost our magic from not completing the agreement of my marrying the dragon prince as long as I saved Tavish from whatever they were inflicting upon him.

You are not. I'll find a way to get out of this and kill the ashbreath for whatever he was doing to you, Tavish replied, hot anger wafting through our bond. *Is he still hurting you?*

No, I got away from him. I swallowed, thankful when my room's large window appeared. I headed toward the break in the glistening white stone of the castle, feeling as if I would be somewhat safe once more. *I'm flying back into my room. Alone.*

When his anger didn't lessen, I realized my mistake before he even asked the question.

Did he touch you? Even in my head, his words were low and full of anger.

He did, but Tavish, it doesn't matter. I licked my lips, trying to help him regain control. *He saw our fated-mate markings. He knows I completed the bond.*

Blast. Icy tendrils of fear seeped through the bond, stabbing me. *That's not good, Lira.*

How is it not? I'd expected him to be thrilled that the dragon prince knew I was taken. My heart grew heavy. Had he reconsidered wanting to be with me? Surely not.

Because he'll be more determined than ever to make sure nothing interferes with the vow the dragons and the Seelie made with each other.

The pain from his side ebbed but didn't dissipate completely.

I landed in my room, preparing to head to the secret door. *I left him in the garden, soaking wet.*

Humor shot through the connection, easing the tension in my body.

You, sprite, never fail to surprise me. I suspect that will never change.

The warmth of his love spread throughout my chest, and I couldn't help but smile. His approval of my unpredictability was something I needed right now. He saw and appreciated me for who I was.

The warmth remained, but the fear crept back into the bond. He replied, *He won't want to leave you, which means we have to get out of here. Tonight. No matter what. We had a little flexibility before, but not anymore.*

I hated that he was right. We needed to get away from this land. If Pyralis was going to become more territorial over me, I had to escape while I could. *Okay. I'll figure something out.* Which was going to be a pickle in and of itself.

Someone pounded on my door, and I froze. I wanted to pretend I wasn't here, but a key slid into the lock and clicked before I could turn around and leave. The staff usually waited for me to tell them to come in.

The door was flung open, and Mom entered. Her lips were pressed into a firm line, and she shook her head. "Your parents are angry, Lira."

I placed my hands on my hips, refusing to back down. "He manhandled me. I don't regret defending myself."

She smirked. "I'm not saying you should." She touched my shoulders. "But in this realm, things are viewed differently. Even though I secretly approve of what you did, things are different for you here, especially as heir to the throne."

"Meaning I have no freedom to decide things on my own." I exhaled, my shoulders sagging. "I refuse to live like that."

Her face softened, and she brushed a piece of hair behind my ear. "I know, Lira. We'll figure something out. Things are tense between you and your parents because they expected you to come back the same as when you left and not tied to their biggest enemy. In time, they'll come around, and the three of you can figure out what sort of relationship you can have."

"I don't want a relationship with them," I muttered. "Besides, I have you and Dad." Then my lungs seized. "Right?" Maybe they didn't view me as their daughter anymore now that their memories had returned. I wasn't their blood, after all. Our magic bound us, but I couldn't prevent the insecurities from flittering within.

"Of course, little sprout." She kissed my cheek and pulled back. "Brenin and I love you as much as Eiric. On Earth, we became family, and nothing will ever change how we feel about you. But King Erdan and Queen Sylphia are your parents too, and the rulers of our land. You'll never be able to completely break free from them. Their royal magic runs through your veins just as much as it does theirs."

I hated that she was right. Father was the royal blood heir, and Mother was high fae. On their wedding day, their hands had been cut so that his blood mixed with hers, giving her some of the royal magic and anointing her as queen more so than the crown she wore. I sighed, knowing what she'd say next.

"You've been summoned to the royal office, and we've already taken too much time." Her wings spread out, and fire danced on her fingertips. "And if the ashbreath tries anything in front of me, you won't have to defend yourself because I'll do it for you."

The fact that she sounded like the same person I'd known on Earth eased some of the churning in my stomach. She'd vowed to always be on my side, no matter what, and it was clear she meant it here too.

Trusting her, I managed to swallow. "You should have seen him standing there, scaly and soaking wet."

Mom laughed. The sound was so carefree and infectious that I found my cheeks lifting from a smile.

"Okay, no more of that right now." She lifted a brow. "If you want to have a say in your future, it's in your best interests to play more by your parents' rules and not be so ornery. You and your father are too similar for your own good, and you're both being stubborn. Since you have more at stake, it'd be wise for you to bend first."

I flinched. I hated feeling so powerless, especially since I planned on leaving tonight, but she had a point. I didn't want to be an enemy to the Seelie, and I did care for my parents. "You're right."

"Oh, sprout. I love it when you say those words to me." She winked and marched to the doorway, waving me out. "The only person they sound better coming from is your daddy."

I rolled my eyes but breezed past her.

We flew side by side toward Father's study. I had no doubt that Mother and Pyralis would be there as well, and I'd be walking into a situation where, even though I'd been protecting myself, I'd be the person in the wrong.

As we turned left to head to the study, I saw Eiric out of the corner of my eye. My head turned toward her, and our gazes locked as I passed by. She neither smiled nor frowned at me, making a chill run down my spine.

I couldn't read her, which had never happened before.

"You're not the only one struggling with changes, dear," Mom said, brushing a hand down my arm. "But don't fret. The four of us are strong, and we'll sync our wings together eventually."

"I said some things last night..." I trailed off, unable to finish that sentence. I descended closer to the smooth white floor as my wings drooped with shame. "It popped out of my mouth without me thinking through the words. I'm not sure E will ever forgive me."

"You two are inseparable." Mom winked at me as we reached the door to the royal study. "Trust me." She paused, waiting for me to enter the room first.

I inhaled deeply, ready to enter, when Father said, "The markings are an illusion placed on her by the Unseelie king. It's nothing to be concerned about."

I straightened my shoulders, and Mom touched my arm gently and whispered, "Remember what we just spoke about. Don't allow your emotions to guide you."

She didn't have to add *like usual*. We both knew that I reacted on instinct, unlike Mom, Dad, and Eiric. They were more controlled and even-tempered, which made sense now that I knew they were guards.

Trusting her, I stepped into the study, wanting to make

my presence known. I dug my fingernails into my palms, embracing the agony so I had something to focus on other than Father's ignorant words.

This is driving me mad, feeling all your emotions and knowing that the ashbreath is here, Tavish linked.

The study was exactly the same as I remembered. Four dark-blue couches sat in a square with a wooden table in the center. There was enough legroom for even the tallest of fae to have space. However, no one was sitting.

The dragon prince stood in front of the large wall of windows that overlooked the waterfall. Worse, he was no longer dripping water, probably courtesy of Mother. Evidence of her wind magic showed by the way the couch cushions were askew, along with Pyralis's and Father's hair.

I've been summoned to the royal study, but Mom promised not to let the dragon prince touch me.

Your Earth mother? Tavish asked.

Yes.

He replied, *I like her more than the queen already.*

Father stood behind his desk with Mother at his side, framed by huge bookcases.

As soon as I entered, all three sets of eyes focused on me.

"If it was an illusion, then how are they still on her body?" Prince Pyralis arched a brow. "Unseelie can't enter Gleann Solas, which means any remnants of their magic shouldn't work here either. Unless there's something you need to tell me. You are rather excellent at excluding my family from important knowledge."

I lifted my head, refusing to cower. Still, I held my tongue, not wanting to say anything and risk exposing additional information that my father would rather he not know.

"Nothing we've done has affected the vow of Lira's

hand to you in marriage in the slightest." Father rubbed a hand along his earth-brown tunic. "We made decisions for our kingdom that didn't impact the dragons at all."

"Sending my betrothed to Earth should have been a decision we all made together." Prince Pyralis flicked his hand at me and wrinkled his nose. "If you didn't feel that you could adequately protect her, then she should have come to live with us."

The memory of how Father and Mother had rushed me away the morning after Tavish's escape resurfaced, and I wondered if this might have been the exact reason why.

"She was *ten*." Mother laughed forcefully, trying not to sound angry. "Way too young to *live* with her one-hundred-year-old betrothed." The way she spat the last sentence made her feelings clear.

Some of my anger toward them thawed. They'd tried to protect me in the best way they'd known.

"And now she's returned with the very nightfiend you tried to hide her from." Prince Pyralis's face twisted in disgust. "And she has fated-mate marks all over her body. I must say your decisions haven't been the wisest."

Father's face flushed yellow.

"Yet, it was their decision to make." I expanded my wings to ensure I didn't look timid. "I'm sure you haven't made poor choices, like grabbing me and trying to force me to go with you."

Dad stepped into view from the far-left corner of the room. I hadn't noticed him until now, but the way he glared at the dragon prince told me that Pyralis hadn't informed them of why I'd reacted the way I had.

"He thorn-clutched you?" Father's jaw dropped.

I didn't look away from Pyralis as I answered, wanting

him to feel all my anger for him. "That's why he came in here soaked and angry."

The corners of Father's lips turned up before he puffed out his chest and focused back on the dragon prince. "She's not yours to force into anything, even when she becomes your bride. Do you understand?"

Some of the walls I'd placed around my heart when it came to my parents began to crumble. Mom was right. They did care for me.

Feeling Tavish's worry, I linked, *Father and Mother are taking my side this time. They're not happy with the dragon prince.*

That's good. We need them upset with him in order to keep the dragon prince from you.

Pyralis nodded. "I let my anger get the best of me. That won't happen again, but everywhere I turn, you are keeping something from us." He moved toward me with both hands raised. "Which is not your fault, and I should never have taken that out on you, Lira. I vow to you that isn't how I will treat my bride, nor is it how my father treats my mother. From this moment on, you'll be treated like the most precious treasure. One I would kill for."

Treasure.

Dragons were obsessive and protective of anything they felt was of value. For me to be his most precious treasure wasn't a blessing... it was a curse.

In a matter of days, I had two men promising to kill people for me. With Tavish, it made me feel loved and cherished because I felt the same way about him. If another woman touched him with any sort of perverted intent, I'd murder her without remorse. But with Pyralis, the idea of meaning that much to him sickened me and made me want to get far, far away from him.

"Good." Mother placed a hand on her chest. "That's a relief. No princess should be treated with such disrespect."

"I'm glad I could ease your mind." He bowed ever so slightly. "Now that this is settled, I see no reason to remain here."

My knees almost gave out. Tavish had made it sound like Pyralis would be more determined to keep watch over me, but he was going back to his lands—something I was even more eager for because I couldn't stand being near him.

"We shall gather the fruits in satchels so you can carry them home with you in beast form." Father gestured to Mom, who had stayed behind in the hallway. "Hestia, please go handle that."

"And gather Princess Lira's things," Prince Pyralis added.

My heart stopped.

"Why would she need to do that?" Dad rasped.

"Because the princess will be returning home with me," the dragon prince replied easily and smirked.

I took a step back and prepared to fight.

I'd rather die than leave with Prince Pyralis. If I had to resort to kicking him in the balls to get away, I would. I didn't give a damn if my parents got upset with me.

Please tell me that dragon prince isn't causing your anger right now. Tavish's voice popped into my head.

Not wanting to be distracted, I opened my mouth to tell Pyralis where he could go, but my father cut me off.

"She will *not* be leaving with you." Father slammed a hand down on his desk. "Our agreement is that you will marry on her twenty-fifth birthday. We have over two and a half years before that happens, and she will remain here with *us* until then."

"Unacceptable," Prince Pyralis snarled. "In the last twelve years, while she's remained under your *protection*, my betrothed grew up on Earth, was kidnapped by an Unseelie wildling, and returned to Gleann Solas—and we weren't informed of her return—with fated-mate *markings* all over her, which can't be hidden. I fear what else will happen if she remains under your *care*."

Father's nostrils flared. "How dare you come into my

kingdom and castle and insult me in such a way? She is my *daughter*, and I'm the best person to protect her. If she remained with you, I suspect she'd be dead with how much disregard you've given her until this moment."

This whole time, I thought my parents were the worst people to watch after me, but I could only imagine what would've happened if I'd somehow gotten stuck with the dragons. A shiver ran down my spine at the horrible thought. *The dragon prince is demanding that I leave with him, but Father is telling him no.* At least there was that.

"I *disrespected* you?" He laughed bitterly, smoke puffing from his mouth. "Ever since our alliance was sealed, you've pretended we shouldn't have a say in the princess's protection—something I should've been involved with, but you didn't bestow that consideration on me. She's old enough to wed, and I can ensure she remains protected and unharmed. She is the woman who will bear my children and future heirs to the throne, and I refuse for that plan to change."

Chest heaving, Father gritted out, "Are you insinuating that I would try to find a way out of the agreement?"

"Not insinuating." Prince Pyralis lifted his head and stood with his feet shoulder-width apart, clearly wanting to intimidate. "I believe I'm being clear. You have no control over her and are struggling with what needs to be done to get her to behave the way a princess should."

Laughter choked me, and I sputtered, "That doesn't sound like treating someone as if they're your treasure." I lobbed his words back at him, and they left a sour, bitter taste in my mouth. I didn't want to be *anything* to the dragon prince, especially not his treasure.

He shook his head. "Treasures must be polished,

treated, and, at times, molded to ensure they retain their value or increase in worth."

My stomach roiled. I wasn't a person to him. I was property that he planned to use as he pleased. A shudder ran through me. "Clearly, you don't know me very well." I wouldn't change for anyone.

"Courtesy of your parents' subpar upbringing." His jaw clenched. "Had you remained in Gleann Solas, I would've had that privilege."

Ew. The idea of him hanging around when I was a child had a sour taste filling my mouth.

"That's enough," Mother spat as a breeze swirled in the room. "Everyone, stop fighting because Prince Pyralis is right about one thing."

Father's head jerked in her direction as my heart stopped.

"*He* should be leaving." Mother pointed right at the dragon prince to ensure everyone knew exactly who she meant. "But not with Lira. Lira stays here. We haven't agreed to modify the timeline of the promise, nor will we. The way you're trying to change the terms isn't how agreements are modified, and you know that better than anyone."

"I didn't say I would marry her ahead of schedule." Prince Pyralis glowered. "The only agreement we came to is when we'd wed, not where she'd live. As a child, she would obviously stay with her parents, but you handed her off to guards and sent her to Earth. Now that she's returned as a woman, there is no reason she can't come with me, especially since her future is set by my side."

Agony shot through the bond, indicating that Tavish had gotten injured. Between the pain, rage, and fear emanating from him, I had no doubt he was trying to escape from his chains.

I won't leave with him. I'd rather die than go anywhere with that scaly ashbreath, I connected, wanting Tavish to understand my resolve.

Neither of those options works for me, sprite, he growled through our connection, his anger boiling hotter than ever before.

"Hestia and Brenin," Father commanded. "Prince Pyralis has overstayed his welcome. Please escort him from Gleann Solas."

I inhaled sharply. I hadn't expected Father to do this. I would've bet he'd hand me over in fear of angering the dragons. If we went to war with them, I wasn't certain we would win. Their population was slightly smaller, but in beast form, they were fifteen times bigger than in human form, had razor-sharp talons, and could breathe fire for miles.

Still, Pyralis didn't have a choice since he was the only dragon here.

The dragon prince fisted his hands. "If you force me to go, I will return with larger numbers."

Father pivoted around the desk toward the prince and extended his wings at his sides. "I wouldn't expect anything less, but this conversation is over. You need time to cool off, and I want to spend more time with my daughter. As you pointed out, she's been gone for the last twelve years, and I want to use these two and a half years to get to know her again before she leaves for Tìr na Dràgon."

If the moment hadn't been so tense, I'd have run over and hugged Father. Everything he'd done to piss me off since I arrived vanished. *Father is forcing the dragon prince to leave without me. He just commanded the guards to escort him to the kingdom's edge.*

The uncontrollable rage mellowed, but Tavish's fear held on strong.

Thank Fates, but this is a temporary reprieve. He'll be back with his own guards, hoping your father won't risk a battle with them within his kingdom.

That made sense, and Prince Pyralis had already stated as much. *At least the imminent threat has passed.*

Despite the deep scowl, the prince bowed his head. "You're right. I must be on my way." If I hadn't seen the expression on his face, I wouldn't have known there was a threatening edge to the words. But between the flush and the faint scales thickening his skin, there was no doubt he wanted to eat us all.

Wings fluttered behind me, and I glanced over my shoulder to find Eiric standing next to Mom. Eiric's head tilted back as she took in the dragon prince.

I wasn't sure if she'd ever seen a dragon in person. Seeing one like this, on the verge of a shift, was almost more fear-inducing than seeing one in full dragon form. The merge had the hair on the nape of my neck rising with uncertainty about what the prince's next move would be.

She needed to get away from this and find safety.

"Eiric, call the most experienced guards. We need them to line the halls," Mom whispered, and Eiric looked from the prince to Mom.

After a second, Eiric nodded and rushed off toward the prison, where most of the guards were stationed with Tavish and Finnian there.

I watched the dragon prince stroll from his spot in front of the window toward me. I sidestepped, allowing him access to the door, not wanting to slow his exit in the slightest.

Yet he paused at my side.

"Until we see each other again, my gem," Prince Pyralis said with a toothy smile.

I gritted my teeth, fighting the urge to step away. Bile inched up my throat, but if enduring his patronizing gaze prevented him from becoming angrier, I'd do it. His scowl vanished, and his brows furrowed.

Good. My nonreaction caught him off guard. I needed to not flinch at his proximity to help reduce the urgency of my needing to relocate to his kingdom.

"Hestia, please remain here with the royals," Dad said and kissed Mom on the cheek. "I'll get a few other guards to go with me."

I mashed my lips to prevent myself from smiling. Mom hated Dad telling her what to do, but when she moved to stand next to me without arguing, I realized there was something more going on.

"After you, Your Highness." Dad bowed to the prince and gestured to the hall.

Prince Pyralis's back tensed, and my pulse pounded against my skin as I wondered what the dragon might do.

After a few tense moments, the prince exited the room. His footsteps were slow and steady, and he and Dad disappeared from sight.

Mother, Father, Mom, and I kept our gazes on the door as if the dragon prince might reappear, but after several minutes, I couldn't hear the footsteps anymore, and Mom shut the door.

"Are you all right, Lira?" Mother asked, flying over the desk to me. "I can't believe he treated you so poorly."

None of the disgust and criticism I'd seen since I'd returned was present in her eyes, and they softened as she examined me.

"I'm fine." I placed my hands on her shoulders to reassure her. "He tried to manhandle me, but I didn't let him."

Father tilted his head. "Manhandle? Did the prince

believe you were a man? Did he check to see if you had a penis?"

I blinked, processing if I'd heard what I thought I had.

"She meant thornclutched." Mom chuckled and patted my shoulder. "Despite forgetting our fae heritage, Brenin and I took protection jobs on Earth and trained Eiric and Lira on such measures. Now that things are getting settled, we can begin training Lira with a sword again."

Little did she know I'd already been brought back up to speed with a sword, but I suspected informing them of that and why would make things worse for Tavish. Instead, I focused on something of much more importance. "How long until he comes back with his parents and other dragons?"

"It'll take two days for him to travel back to his land, and then he'll need to rest and inform his father, so about a week." Mother nibbled on her bottom lip. "His desire to take you before your wedding is completely preposterous. He should know that we don't want you to leave our side until then."

"He doesn't believe we'll follow through on the agreement. You heard the beast." Father crossed his arms and frowned. "In the meantime, I want guards on watch at all hours. He could return, hoping that we won't expect him. The dragons are not to enter our kingdom until I invite them. I won't tolerate the disrespect of them showing up at our door again without notice, which brings us back to the larger problem—the veil is partially down due to the Unseelie presence here because we didn't feel the dragon's arrival."

I took a slight step back. "The dragons were blocked from coming here too?"

"No, but we included magic in the veil so that if a

dragon crosses into our land, we'll be alerted. That didn't happen, which is why Pyralis showing up at Caisteal Solais's door surprised us." Father rubbed his temples like he had a headache coming on. "We'll need to do something with the nightfiends if their presence is impacting the veil that much."

"But we can't kill Tavish." Mother placed a hand to her mouth. "Otherwise, Ardanos magic will become unbalanced—unless he's borne an heir since the Unseelie's exile?"

My anger and resentment toward them slammed back into place. "He doesn't have an heir. After waking up to find that his parents had been *murdered* by Seelie and he'd been kicked out of their home, he's been trying to prove himself to his people and help them survive."

"Murdered by Seelie?" Father scoffed. "Is that what he's told you? That we're the evil ones who killed his parents? How absurd."

Here we were again, playing with words to evade the truth. Did he truly believe I was ignorant enough not to have caught on, or was it second nature, and he wasn't aware of what he was doing?

"Not only that, dear, but he's got you believing you have a fated-mate bond with him. I doubt he'd be honest about an heir. Did you ask him directly about that?"

I wanted to stomp my foot, but the impact wouldn't be strong, seeing as I'd already broken both heels. "When he and I completed our bond, he told me he was a virgin. He said those exact words."

"Then we need to determine an alternative. We don't want to release him so he can regain the throne at the ruins. We need the Unseelie to stay disorganized." Father headed back to his desk and removed a map of Ardanos from the bookcase. "Hestia, go coordinate the patrols and guards while I determine another location to keep the nightfiend."

I swallowed, unsure what to do next.

"Lira, I need you to remain in your room until we know the ashbreath has officially left. I don't want you out in the kingdom until patrols are in place and we're certain it's secure." Father gestured to the door. "We won't have as many guards here, so I need you to stay in one place."

Even though I hated to be controlled, I didn't want to argue with him. In my room was exactly where I needed to be to get Tavish out before they moved him. With every breath I took, things got worse for us. But at least the guards' presence would be thin, allowing us an easier way to escape.

Father watched with an arched brow. He expected me to fight him.

"Of course, Father." I bowed slightly, listening to what Mom had recommended earlier. I needed to lull them into a false sense of security.

The corners of Father's lips rose, and he exhaled with relief.

"Aw, there's our little girl." Mother sighed and kissed my cheek. "Once your father and I are done strategizing, we'll make sure the three of us spend more time together. Just give us a day or two, and then we'll make sure to focus on you."

The last thing I wanted was their full attention. Still wanting to play along, I nodded. "I understand. I'll leave you to it."

I spun around, and Mom left the room with me.

At the intersection where she'd split off toward the prison and I'd go back to my room, she took my hand and said, "I was proud of you back there, Lira. I think all three of you need that time together your mother just spoke about."

"We probably do," I said, agreeing in the only way I knew how without lying. "Be safe. I don't want you getting harmed." Then I headed to my room to wait for the perfect time to escape with Finnian and Tavish.

I'd been going over my plan the entire afternoon and evening. Gaelle had brought my lunch and dinner to my room so I wouldn't leave, and I felt like a prisoner again, like when Tavish first brought me to Ardanos.

The only thing that kept my sanity in check was Tavish and me strategizing the entire time. From what he could tell, only one guard was watching them now. If I could distract the guard by giving him something that held his attention long enough to steal the key from him, I might be able to reach Tavish and Finnian before the guard noticed. As long as I could free them before the guard caught me, we should be able to take one guard down without alerting anyone else to our escape.

It wasn't a good plan, but it was the best option we had.

Because of that, I didn't eat the coveted sunberry tarts that only the highest of fae had the privilege of eating. Taking the sunny-yellow-filled pastry and wrapping it in a leaf, I headed to my door and opened it. No one was guarding my door or the hall. Right now, everyone was busy securing the kingdom, which worked to my advantage.

I flew down the hallway, heading straight to the prison. From what Gaelle had said, Mother and Father had locked themselves in the royal study to strategize, so I wasn't worried about running into them.

A guard stood with his back to me, facing the opening

that gave a clear view of the area west of the castle, searching for trouble.

I continued down the path.

When I found the lone guard in front of the holding cell, some of my worries passed.

He was leaning against the wall with his eyes closed. He didn't even hear me land right in front of him.

Good. All of the experienced guards were watching for the threat of dragons.

I cleared my throat, and his red eyes popped open almost comically.

He took in a quick breath. "Princess Lira. You're not supposed to be here."

"Oh, I only came to drop off this pastry." I held up the dessert. "Then I'm heading back to my room. With everyone gone, I thought you might like a snack."

He licked his thin lips. "Oh. That's nice."

A tingle on my neck made me feel as if I were being watched, so I glanced over my shoulder but didn't see anyone. Great, I could add paranoia to my list of growing problems.

"Here." I handed him the pastry, and when our hands touched, I held on to the sweet a little tighter than necessary.

He tried to take it from me, but some of the sunberry oozed down his armor.

"Oh, Fates!" I exclaimed, getting closer to his right pocket. I released the pastry and bent down, grabbing the edge of my gown as my left hand slipped into his pocket. When my fingers brushed the cold metal, I shifted my weight into him, lifting the key while raising my right hand to dab the sunberry off him with my dress. "I didn't mean to make a mess."

"It's armor, Your Highness." He smiled reassuringly. "It's easy to clean."

I clutched the key in my hand and placed it behind my back before I stopped dabbing his armor with the hem of my dress. "Right. How foolish of me." Sweat pooled in my armpits.

"The tart makes it worthwhile." He beamed.

"Good." I took a few steps back, angling my left side away from him. "I should get back to my room. I hope you enjoy it."

"I will." He lifted the tart and took a big bite.

Satisfied, I turned and flew back to my room. My wings wanted to move way too fast, but I forced them to flap at a reasonable speed as if I weren't in a rush. Still, I couldn't relax.

As I passed the intersection of the two hallways, someone grabbed my arm and yanked me toward them.

My body spun toward them, and I reared my arm back for a punch, but a familiar face appeared in front of me.

Eiric.

She wore the standard guard's armor, though I'd never seen her wear it before. From what I understood, she had to complete training before she qualified as a full guard. I pulled my punch, not wanting to cause more problems between us.

Her eyes darkened, and she hissed, "What the hell do you think you're doing, Lira?" Then she pointedly looked at my left hand.

Dammit. That hadn't been paranoia. Eiric had been watching me. She always sensed when I was up to something.

Did you get caught? Tavish asked, his trepidation swirling through our bond.

By Eiric, I replied, hoping there was a way to salvage this.

"You have one second, or—" she started.

"Can we go to my room?" I cut her off and whispered, "I'll tell you everything." Anything to get us out of the hallway so no one could see us like this. I glanced over my shoulder at the guard, who didn't seem to notice us. He was entirely focused on watching the area outside.

She pursed her lips, a sign that she was uncertain what she should do.

"Please, give me a chance to explain." I placed my free hand on her shoulder.

Closing her eyes, she exhaled and released her grip on my arm. "Fine, but once we get there, you have five minutes."

Blighted abyss. I didn't even have that long to convince her. I needed to get to Tavish and Finnian before the guard realized I'd swiped the key from him. If I didn't play along, she'd force me to hand it over, so I nodded. *I'm going to need to tell her everything.*

Is that wise? Tavish questioned, his concern constricting our bond in my chest.

Pivoting on my heels, I took off, rushing back to my bedroom. *If I don't risk it, our plan is over. She'll make me hand the key back.* I'd already wasted too much time, and I still had to allocate more to talk to her. My heart galloped as I darted back into my room.

Eiric stayed right on my wings.

Good. I needed to make up some of the time.

When I entered my room, I stopped at the door, and Eiric flew inside. I immediately shut and locked it to make sure we'd have a warning if someone tried to come inside.

She landed a few feet from my bed, folding her wings into her back. "Go on."

For once, I didn't need her prodding to encourage me to talk. "There's a reason I was acting irrationally last night." I swallowed, hoping my gut was correct about how to start this. "What I'm about to tell you is something Father and Mother made me swear to never share with anyone when I was a child. You questioning me had the old part of me surging forward, and it caught me off guard. Still, I never should have spoken to you that way because you're my best friend and sister. I'm still trying to reconcile who I was as a child and who I was on Earth with who I'm becoming now."

"You weren't the only one in the wrong." Eiric's expression smoothed, and she squeezed my hand gently. "I should've been more understanding."

Even though my guilt over how I'd treated her still weighed on me, some of the tension in my chest lightened. She and I would be all right after all.

I moved closer to her, lowering my voice. "I need you to swear you won't tell anyone... not even our parents. If you can't promise, then I can't share everything with you."

"And I thought you were trouble on Earth. You've never asked me to keep a secret before. And here you are, asking for the second time."

My mouth dried. I didn't like keeping things from Mom and Dad either, but unfortunately, I didn't have a choice. Not here in Ardanos, where everything was stacking against Tavish and me. "It's technically about the same thing." I forced a smile.

She rolled her eyes, but I watched her mash her lips together as if to hide a smile. "Fine. What's going on?"

"There's a secret, hidden passage that only royals know about." I pointed to the bathroom. "The hidden door is in there. That's why I suddenly appeared in the bathroom."

Her forehead creased. "What? Why would the exit be secret from the guards? And where does it take you?"

Good questions. The same ones I'd had as a little girl.

"Father said it's best if the guards don't learn of it, so if we're attacked inside the castle, the enemies can't learn how we escaped. We could hide in the passage and wait for them to give up searching for us or leave completely."

Eiric scowled as if she didn't like that answer.

I didn't blame her. If we were attacked like that, there was no blazing way I wouldn't bring as many guards as possible with me if it was clear we were going to lose against our attackers. "It leads to two exits—the gardens out back and the corner of the castle that opens to the cliff, so we can drop out and fly low and not be detected in the middle of the night."

"But why would you need to sneak out now?" She tilted her head, trying to put all the information together. "You're the princess, and we aren't under attack. You can go anywhere in Gleann Solas."

"Not the holding cell." I paused, allowing her to connect the dots.

Her jaw dropped. "You've been visiting *him*? You could've gotten caught!"

"We're fated mates. When he was hurt, I had to go see him. Then he was upset about the dragon prince being here, and I couldn't hide out in my room, knowing he needed comfort." I'd thought telling her everything would make me feel better, but it didn't. Instead, a lump formed in my throat, and the walls closed in on me. She had the power to inform both sets of my parents if she thought it was in my best interest. And I could tell she didn't like my answers.

"Are you planning to help Tavish and Finnian escape tonight?" she asked and gestured at my left hand, which held the key.

I could say yes and leave out the part about me going

with them, but she needed to realize where my loyalties lay. "Not just them."

"*What?*" she whisper-shouted and shook her head. "No way."

"I can't be away from Tavish." My heart stung at the thought. "And his people think he's dead, just like we did before he came here to find me. He needs to get back. His cousin could still be hiding, and the dragon prince will be back soon, determined to take me with him to his lands. Not only that, but Father and Mother are talking about what to do with Tavish. They don't want him to return to his people, so there's no telling what sordid plan they'll come up with. I can't let him be tortured!" Even though I tried to keep my tone calm, I couldn't help how my voice rose in tandem with my desperation.

Eiric exhaled loudly and twirled a piece of her hair around one finger as she strolled to the silathair tree. She wanted to analyze the situation, but we didn't have time for that.

"The guard will notice the key is gone, and I need to remove their chains before that happens." I lifted my hand with my palm facing up and opened my fingers. The moonlight streamed in, glinting off the golden metal, emphasizing my point. With a heavy heart, I spread my wings, readying to head to the bathroom. I'd wasted too much time, and I had to move; otherwise, this would have all been for naught. "Are you going to stop me?" I needed to know where her loyalties would fall, so I had an idea of what the three of us were up against.

Her wings fluttered, and she rolled her shoulders. Exhaling, she murmured, "No. I won't."

My wings suddenly felt lighter. Confiding in her had been the best thing I could've done, and I was thankful that this moment proved it. "Thank God." I darted into the bath-room, squatted next to the edge of the sink, and pricked my finger on the spike. *I'm on my way. Eiric said she won't inform anyone about what we're doing.*

The door opened, and I stood, grabbing the lantern I'd left for this moment and stepping inside. I turned around to shut the door, only for Eiric to step into the passage with me.

I froze. "What are you doing?"

"Coming with you." She rocked back on her heels and glared at me. "I thought that was pretty obvious."

Out of every possible scenario, I hadn't expected that. "You should stay here where it's safe and not get involved. I don't want anything coming between you and your parents."

"Girl, if Mom and Dad find out I knew about your crazy-ass plan and I didn't go with you, they'd chain my wings up and never let me out of their sight again."

I snorted then clamped my mouth shut. She was right. Even though I suspected that both sets of parents would be upset with me, I trusted that Mom and Dad would see reason once everything was settled. They always insisted that the only thing they wanted was for Eiric and me to be happy. Being with Tavish was that for me. "Are you sure? Because if you feel pressured—"

She lifted a hand. "You're my sister, and I don't think you should be forced to marry some sexy dragon prince if you don't want to. If Tavish makes you happy, then I want to be there to protect you and help find a way for you to get out of the arrangement with ashbreath."

My brows shot up, and I blinked. "You think Prince Pyralis is *sexy*?"

"That's what you want to talk about?" Her face flushed a faint yellow.

Right. We needed to move, and I didn't have time to argue with her about staying behind. In truth, selfishly, I wanted her to go with us.

I stepped past her and leaned down to hit the lever on this side of the wall to close the door.

"Okay, step where I do and be quiet. There are some areas where the walls are thinner, and someone could overhear us." I moved past her, holding up the light so we could see the floor in front of us.

"Got it," she replied, and the two of us were off.

I'm on my way, I connected with Tavish. *Has the guard realized I have the key yet?*

No, but he could at any moment, so try to be as fast as possible while remaining safe. He paused for a moment, and his surprise floated into me. *Eiric didn't stop you?*

I had to tell her everything, but she understands that I want to be with you and the risks that we face. I didn't know how to broach the topic of her coming with us, so I figured being straightforward was the best way to go. *And she's coming with us.*

The emotions coming from Tavish weren't easy to read.

Even though Eiric hadn't been in the secret passage before, she didn't slow me down. We had to be halfway to the prison cells when Tavish finally responded.

Are you sure she can be trusted? Do you think she'll tell the guard when you get here?

My chest constricted. I hadn't considered that. *Does it really matter? Either way, she could warn the guards. What's the benefit of her coming through the passage to get there? She swore she wouldn't inform anyone about this passage.*

She'd be doing just that if she called for the guard once I got inside with you.

Technically, she wouldn't be informing. No words would be coming out of her mouth.

No. I couldn't believe Eiric would do something like that to me, but convincing her to let me go had been easier than I'd expected. My certainty about her coming with us suddenly didn't feel so certain. But there wasn't anything I could do about it now, so I had to trust my initial instinct. *Well, I can't change anything now. We're almost there.*

As long as you unchain me first, I can make it harder for them to catch us.

The fact that he was certain that Eiric would betray us had my head dizzying.

The castle was quieter than I ever remembered it being, and after the chaos earlier, it put me even more on edge. Still, the silence made sense because half the guards had left to watch over the borders, providing another challenge we'd have to face once we got outside the walls of Caisteal Solais.

We were closing in on the door to the holding cell, and my heart pounded in my ears. This was the moment that counted. Once I entered the holding cell and unchained Tavish, there was no turning back.

I raised a hand, informing Eiric to stop. When she paused, I went to the door, pricked my finger, and pressed the lever, opening it.

Raising the lantern, I stepped inside the dark cell, and my eyes homed in on Tavish.

My stomach dropped. Dried blood covered his wrists around the handcuffs, and the chains had cut into his onyx wings, coating them with even blacker blood.

Without meaning to, I hurried to him, not being as quiet as I should.

I'm fine, sprite. Tavish's irises lightened from stormy gray to almost silver. *Especially now that you're here with me.*

All I wanted to do was heal him and kiss him, but that would have to come later. *Can you fly?*

He nodded, but then his irises darkened again when he glanced over my shoulder at Eiric.

After setting the lantern down, I held out the key to unlock his chains. My hands shook, making sliding the key into the hole more challenging. Just as I was about to slip the end into the slot, the key fell from my fingers and hit the hard floor with a *ping.*

My lungs seized, and the world tilted.

"What's going on in there?" the guard asked, confirming I'd been too loud.

I scooped up the key, gritting my teeth as I slid it into the lock and turned. The handcuffs came off, and as I moved to the lock at the base of Tavish's wings, the moment I'd been dreading happened.

"My key. Where did it go?" the guard gasped.

As I unlocked the chains, Eiric hurried to the prison door. I watched in horror as she removed a guard key from her pocket and put it in the keyhole on this side of the door.

"They're going to escape if we don't work together and hurry," Eiric said, opening the door and ripping my heart apart.

The chains from Tavish's wings fell to the floor as he took the key and flew to Finnian.

Still, I couldn't believe Tavish had been right. It was as if my chest had been ripped open. "How could you?"

"This is for your own good, Princess Lira," she said and opened the door.

"How did you two get in here?" the guard asked, his

mouth dropping open. Then his eyes landed on the open hidden door in the wall. "You brought me the tart to swipe the key from me." His wide, horror-filled eyes glared at me.

I lifted my chin, refusing to feel guilty about it.

The damage was done. Now Tavish and Finnian had to get out of here.

"Foolish sunscorched." Finnian chuckled as if he didn't have a care in the world. "Did you really believe the princess would randomly bring you a high fae treat just for the blast of it?"

Lira, run, Tavish linked. *Finnian and I will be right behind you.*

You don't know the way out through the secret passage.

The guard removed his sword. "Nightfiends, get to the side of the wall, or I'll gut you."

When Eiric removed her own sword, the betrayal sat heavy on my shoulders. I couldn't believe, after all we'd gone through together, that she'd do this.

Knowing they wouldn't kill me, I hurried over, blocking Finnian and Tavish. "To hurt them, you'll have to go through me first."

Lira, no, Tavish linked, and I felt him move closer to me, the air between us thrumming with static as the warmth of our bond surged back to life.

"Princess Lira, move." Eiric nodded to the side.

Instead, I stood tall. "No. They haven't done anything wrong."

"Get the princess out of the way, and I'll get the Unseel-ie," the guard commanded Eiric as Tavish placed his hands on my shoulders.

I allowed my healing magic to surge into him. The only way we were getting out of here was if he had his own magic. I remembered the way I'd felt when my chains had come off.

"You've always been difficult," Eiric gritted out, and she moved next to the guard. "Sometimes, I wish you'd just listen." She glanced at the guard. "You ready?"

"Let's move," he said, and then they moved forward, right at me, as Tavish yanked me behind him, ready to fight.

17

TAVISH

Though malnourishment during my time in the holding cell was making the room spin, I refused to let my mate get injured by her own people.

I blocked Lira and Finnian, trying to tap into the cool magic of darkness to blanket us. However, I couldn't access my magic, and I could feel the cold's frigid grasp on my mate through our bond.

Without my sword or magic, I had no protection, but that didn't matter. Better they hurt me than Lira and Finnian.

Finnian removed the chains from his wings as strong, warm hands touched my shoulders—no doubt Lira.

"Don't—" she commanded behind me as I hunkered forward, ready to fight Eiric and the guard as Eiric removed a dagger sheathed at her waist and raised it high.

Lira yanked me back hard. I stumbled. *Lira,* I growled, needing her to not only feel my displeasure but hear it as well. But considering how weak I'd become, I couldn't regain my footing and fell onto my blasted butt behind her.

Finnian's chains dropped to the floor, and he straightened and prepared to defend my mate, but then I couldn't believe what I saw.

Eiric slammed the hilt of her dagger into the center of the guard's head, and his eyes rolled back. He swayed on his feet.

As I regained my feet, the guard lost consciousness and dropped forward onto Finnian.

Being as malnourished as me, Finnian fell to his knees and grunted, trying to hold up the guard and himself.

Pivoting toward him, Lira lifted some of the guard's weight, and Finnian lost his balance completely. Now his butt hit the ground.

The fated-mate connection warmed as Lira's relief exploded through it and untangled the tightness in my chest now that the sting of betrayal had subsided.

Thank the Fates her sister hadn't betrayed her.

With her usual compassion, Lira laid the guard on the floor, taking care not to injure him further. I had thought it was a weakness, but now I wasn't so sure. It took a strong person to have that sort of compassion, and I didn't understand it. I was certain it was something I'd never achieve.

"E? What have you done?" Lira rasped, squatting next to the guard. "You'll get in trouble for this. Father and Mother won't be understanding if they find out."

"I'm not complaining and am selfishly glad E came to our rescue," Finnian grumbled, getting slowly back to his feet.

Lira glared at him over her shoulder and snapped, "No one asked you, and even though it's hard for you to keep your mouth shut, now's the time to exercise some restraint."

"And my name is *Eiric* to *you*." Eiric sneered at him.

"Whoa." Finnian lifted his hands, but I could see mirth dancing in his eyes.

I wanted to smack him, but that would require me to expend more energy. Unfortunately, I wasn't strong and needed to save my strength. "I shall be happy to remove the tongue from your mouth to make that possible."

Finnian rolled his eyes. Despite his attitude, he was tense, and he attempted to defuse situations with humor. Normally, I'd ignore him, but we were in an extremely dire situation.

Nose wrinkling, Eiric grimaced at me before turning her attention back to Lira. "They behave like this when we're in danger."

My back straightened, but I bit my tongue. Even though I hated to be spoken to that way, especially by a sunscorched, we deserved her criticism... and most important, this was Lira's sister in all the ways that mattered to her. I wanted to retrieve my sword, but due to the circumstances, I'd have to strategize how later. "We should leave before someone else checks on us. I suspect Fate won't bless us like that again."

Lira nodded, turning so she could see all three of us. "You're right. We need to leave before they begin tracking us." She headed to the cell door, shut it, and locked it. No one would be able to see the unconscious guard, though someone would suspect something was amiss when they noticed the guard wasn't right outside the door.

As if summoned by my thoughts, footsteps sounded outside the door, and the four of us descended into silence. After a moment, Lira raced toward the open secret door and waved for us to follow.

Knowing she'd refuse to leave if all three of us didn't

make a move, I gestured to Eiric and Finnian to go first. I could communicate with Lira through our mind link, so the other two needed to be between us in case she needed to explain something to everyone.

Eiric gestured for me to go ahead of her, making me believe I could possibly not despise her after all. Her actions stemmed from her loyalty to Lira, despite her dislike of Finnian and me.

Crossing his arms, Finnian confirmed he wouldn't move unless I did. Both of them were determined to protect the two people they cared for.

The footsteps grew louder, so I didn't dawdle. I raced to the spot behind Lira with Finnian and Eiric on my wings. As soon as the four of us had crammed through the opening, Lira bent down and pressed her finger to something at the foot of the door.

"Blighted abyss," a woman grumbled outside the cell just as the secret door began closing. A key slid into the lock, and there was a click just as the secret door shut completely, casting us in complete darkness.

A *bang* came from the other side of the wall, followed by a loud gasp. "Greason," the woman half screamed, half rasped.

There went any hope of us getting out of the castle before someone realized we'd escaped. *We need to move.*

I left the lantern in the cell, Lira replied, her frustration burning my chest. *I can't see a damn thing.*

Damn? I had no clue what that meant, but there was no time to dwell on that. *Heal me a little with your magic. I can fix this.* I hated to ask her to do it, but we didn't have time for the four of us to stumble over each other.

The moment her hands touched my arms, I wanted to moan at the comforting jolt that thrummed through us.

Though we hadn't been apart for long, she was meant to be by my side *always*. While I'd been chained with nothing but time to think, all I could focus on was how much I needed and missed her.

She leaned toward me, her lips finding mine as she raised her hands and cupped my face. She kissed me, and I folded, completely at her mercy. Maybe I should've said no, but I couldn't stop. Her tongue slipped into my mouth, and I swallowed the groan that almost left me, mainly because I didn't want to risk any guards hearing me. When her warm, refreshing magic pulsed inside me, I nearly came undone.

Between the feel of her, the way my chest felt like it could implode from her love, and the way her magic synced with mine, I forgot where we were and what we were doing. The only thing better would have been burying my cock inside her and giving her even a portion of the pleasure she had me feeling.

Slowly, my magic sparked to life, and the wounds I'd gotten from trying to claw my way out of my chains closed, the skin tightening as they faded away.

White-hot rage warmed my usually frozen blood as I thought of the flamer who was the biggest threat standing in my and Lira's way. He'd die painfully by my hands in a matter of time, eliminating the threat he posed to Lira and me. I would not tolerate *anyone* coming between us.

Am I hurting you? Lira asked, her concern bringing me back to the present.

No. I was merely contemplating all the things we have against us and how I'll bring each one to its knees.

The two of us together, she vowed, making me fall more in love with this perfect-for-me woman.

You've done enough. Even though I wanted to continue

to focus on the moment, having a future with her was more important.

The cell door slammed shut, and the woman yelled, "Someone get the king and queen *now!*"

Lira tensed.

"Are we ever going to make our exit?" Finnian muttered. "I get that you two have been apart, but now isn't the time for romance. I can hear you, and the guard just rushed out of the room."

"I can't see a fucking thing," Eiric whispered. "How the hell are we supposed to get out of here?"

Even though I didn't understand every word she'd said, I comprehended the meaning. I flicked my wrist, allowing the inky feel of my illusion magic to take root and emanate light around us.

It lit up the entire passageway, and I permitted only the four of us to see it, eliminating the risk of anyone else spotting it through cracks or holes in the walls.

"What the—" Eiric's jaw dropped. She then recovered. "I thought you were the king of darkness, frost, and nightmares. How are you wielding light?"

I didn't want to waste time answering such juvenile questions, but she was important to Lira and had helped us escape. So I gritted my teeth and responded as politely as possible. "My nightmare magic includes powerful illusions. I'm allowing you to see light, but I'm not actually wielding it."

The entire way appeared like the underground portion of the rightful Unseelie castle Dunscaith in Cuil Dorcha, which had scared me as a young boy. *Lira, you lead, and I'll stay at the back since we can communicate this way.*

She frowned but, thankfully, didn't argue and moved to the front.

When she slid past Finnian, he tried to smirk at me, but with all the bruising around his face and eyes, his arrogance fell short. His attempt to get under my skin at least proved that the Seelie hadn't come close to dampening his spirits.

Still, as her body brushed his, the urge to punch him took hold. I clenched my free hand to keep myself in check.

As soon as she moved past him, rationality returned to my head. Thankfully, the urge to hurt Eiric wasn't there when Lira moved past her.

"Everyone, keep up with me. Once my parents are alerted, they'll know how we escaped and will come looking for us." Walking faster, Lira led us down the hidden passage, taking us toward the dungeon.

Eiric had no issues keeping up, but Finnian struggled, stumbling over his feet. I'd have been doing the same if Lira hadn't partially healed me, though my legs and body remained sluggish because I needed to eat and drink. *Sprite, you need to slow down. I know we're in a hurry, but Finnian and I haven't eaten anything since we've been here.* I could already feel my magic draining, but I kept that to myself. I didn't need her worrying about something she couldn't control.

Her shock pierced the bond. *Father and Mother didn't feed you? Why didn't you tell me? I would've brought you both something.*

Despite the horrible situation, I felt my cheeks lift because of how innocent she truly was. *I didn't need you sneaking food or water to us and tipping off anyone who might have been watching. Besides, you would've been upset and confronted your parents, which I suspect would've changed them from ignoring me to punishing me physically, which would make this escape more difficult. It was better for you to not know.*

The entire goal of the Seelie royals had been to prove I wasn't important by never visiting or feeding us. I wasn't even worthy of torture. Little did they know that I didn't care if they found me important or not. All I cared about was retrieving Lira and taking her home. Their opinions didn't matter because they meant *nothing* to me.

That was still something I should've known. You were keeping information from me. Her hurt struck my chest and heart.

Love, have you not protected me by withholding information of your own? Do you not remember that a certain cousin of mine attacked you in the bathroom?

Her upset changed to anger, heating my blood. *If you remember, thorn, at the time, we weren't together. You were still declaring you'd kill me and all that jazz. Not a good comparison, and frankly, you just pissed me off more.*

From somewhere far behind me, the king's voice echoed down the passage. "She used the blazing tunnels—if we don't find them before the guards do, it won't matter. We'll deal with her when they catch them."

We've got to move faster, Lira linked. *You and Finnian have to keep up.* She quickened her pace, and this time, Finnian didn't struggle.

It had to be due to adrenaline because, suddenly, I wasn't struggling so much either.

Each time we twisted and turned, I expected us to come to an exit but was disappointed. It was as if Caisteal Solais was never-ending. My heart pounded quicker than my feet moved, and I tried to keep the edge of hysteria away, knowing it wouldn't help.

When we took the next turn, the passage ended in a wall of concrete.

Lira's shoulders heaved as she bent down and searched

for the lever to open the door. However, she kept running her hand around the bottom.

I... I can't find it, she linked as her fear strangled me. *We're going to get caught.*

I took a deep, steadying breath. Then I felt our connection latch on to my calm and push it toward her. I linked, *Sprite, how can I help?*

Excitement leaped through the bond. *You just did.* Her hand stopped moving, and she pressed her finger into a very small slit. And just like the other door, this one slid right open, revealing the worst exit we could have.

The opening revealed a cliff that would require Finnian and me to fly down or get flattened. Even though we were immortal, that didn't mean we could withstand a four-hundred-foot drop. I tucked my illusion magic safely back inside me, not wanting to drain myself any further.

Lira and Eiric didn't hesitate, flapping their wings with no issue.

However, malnourished as we were, Finnian and I struggled to walk, let alone put all our weight on wings that had been bound for days. Maybe I'd been foolish after all, not getting Lira to bring us something to eat, but I hadn't wanted to put her more at risk.

She turned to me, eyebrows raised, waiting for Finnian and me to follow.

Go back to Caelan and let him protect you, I linked. *I'll find a way out of here, but go help the Unseelie. They need one of us right now.*

She shook her head. *I'm not leaving without you.* Then she touched Eiric's arms. "Can you help Finnian fly while I help Tavish? They've been starved and bound and fear trying to fly."

"I don't fear *flying*," Finnian scoffed. "I fear falling.

There is a huge difference, and I wouldn't hesitate if I were at my best."

"Oh god." Eiric snorted and quickly removed the smile from her face. "You sound like Lira." She landed beside him and placed an arm around his waist. "Time your wings with mine so we don't get tangled."

He sighed. "Got it."

The two of them stepped off the cliff, and thankfully, they worked well together, hovering a few feet away from us. Eiric's forehead lined with strain, but other than that, her hold on him was steady.

Then Lira flew to me.

Go, I'll slow you down. I—

"Stop it," she snarled at me. "I won't leave you. We're in this together. So do you want to get out of here or waste time moaning like a little thornling?"

"Lira, he didn't say anything," Eiric gritted out, revealing her strain.

"Oh, they can speak to each other through their minds," Finnian answered. "The fated-mate link is peculiar and also mind-melding."

"I hear them!" the king shouted. He was closing in on us.

Knowing she was as stubborn as the night was long, I wrapped an arm around Lira as she did me, and we took off.

As soon as we stepped off the ledge, we dropped several feet, but Eiric and Finnian moved beside us as we descended toward the ground.

Sweet, fresh air rushed past us, smelling nothing like the ash and brimstone of the land the Unseelie had been forced to live on.

"There they are! Make sure the princess remains unharmed," a male shouted above us.

I turned my head to see ten royal guards charging after us.

There was no way we'd lose them unless I used the magic of darkness to hide us, but when I tugged on my magic, it didn't respond.

18

LIRA

For some asinine reason, after the close call with Eiric and the guard, I'd expected that we'd come out of this unscathed. I should've known that, with my luck, something else would happen. I figured Fate would give us a break. Boy, had I been wrong.

I could use water against the guards, but at least one, if not more, would have the same affinity as me. We'd wind up canceling out each other's magic, and I'd be wasting time and slowing us down.

I assume you don't have the power to cloak us in darkness? I asked Tavish. If we could move close enough to the cliff's edge, we might have a chance of blending in with the surrounding darkness.

The *whooshing* of the guards' wings drew closer. They wouldn't risk harming me or Eiric, which was our only salvation because I was certain that at least one archer was part of their party.

Tavish's guilt and disgust with himself made our connection feel icky. *I'm trying, but I can barely feel it. Your healing helped, but I drained everything I had with my light illusion.*

That's when it hit me. *Why did everyone believe you were dead when you arrived?*

I should've been. I could feel his confusion as he answered. *But our fated-mate bond flared to life, and I felt something coming through it...* He trailed off, and warmth replaced the horrible sensations. *You shared your strength and magic with me.*

Exactly. I wasn't sure if he'd initiated it or I had, but if he could use my strength, I'd gladly let him. We had to get away, and his magic was the best option. *We need to try.*

"They're going to be on us in less than a minute," Eiric gritted out. "If anyone has a plan, now would be the time. Until then, we need to fall as far as possible."

She was right. Though stopping ourselves in time from that sort of drop was risky, we had to buy time. "Fall halfway, then pull back," I whispered, hoping the fast drop would prevent the guards from hearing our plan. "We can't risk splatting on the ground."

"I don't know what splatting is, but I'm pretty sure I don't want to learn," Finnian added as Eiric and I nodded at each other.

We stopped flying and let our bodies drop.

The air blew past and lifted my blonde hair like some sort of blanket, making us easier to spot in the night.

Tavish yanked on our bond, opening it wide. Our emotions mixed, though our souls didn't come close to merging like they did when we had sex and orgasmed as one. Still, I could read his emotions more easily, including his panic.

I didn't know what to do, but I wanted to help, especially since we were close to pulling back. I tugged at my healing and water magic and pushed them toward our connection.

Tavish's breathing became labored, and nothing happened.

Then something pulled on my magic, and a siphoning sensation slithered through me, draining my strength.

"Pull back," Eiric muttered.

I flapped my wings, and my body and Tavish's jerked from the sudden change of momentum. I gritted my teeth, his weight heavier than it had been seconds ago, but maybe that had to do with him using my magic. He flew in tandem with me as I glanced over my shoulder to see how close the guards were.

We were still twenty feet from the ground, and they were right on our wings. We'd only kept the same distance between us and them, and they were quickly descending.

We were at the edge of a village, out in the open. The trees were thirty feet away, and the guards would be on us by the time our feet touched the ground, despite Eiric and me angling our escape as close to the trees as we could.

My magic is responding, Tavish revealed with some relief, and some of the weight fell from my wings and shoulders... but we still weren't hidden.

"What's the plan?" Finnian croaked. "I'm assuming Tavish can't access his magic anymore, and I almost don't feel the pulse of my own. I'm blasting worthless."

Then, the cold, tingly feeling of Tavish's magic brushed my skin, covering me whole.

"Blighted abyss!" the deepest-voiced male guard exclaimed. "It's like they disappeared right before our eyes. I thought he couldn't use his magic within the veil."

Tavish's magic also affected me, making it appear as if I were in a dark hole. If not for his comforting arm around my waist, I'd have been hysterical. Even through my panic, I kept my wings steady, and before I understood what was happening, my feet touched the ground.

Suddenly, I could see through the shadows as if we'd been freed from the darkness, the only indication we were still covered in the comforting chill.

We need to move. They know where we landed, Tavish connected, intertwining our fingers and tugging me toward the village instead of the tree line.

Eiric's eyes widened, and I watched as Finnian placed a finger in front of his lips, telling her to be quiet. He took her hand, and they followed on our heels.

My breath caught. *Shouldn't we go into the trees? You might not have to use your magic for as long.*

Feet hit the ground where we'd been, and I glanced over my shoulder to see a guard less than ten feet from us. All four of us somehow moved quicker, adrenaline pushing us harder than before.

"Even though we can't see them, we can still catch them," a male guard with a high-pitched voice said behind us. "They aren't invisible, and they'll be heading for the trees. It's the fastest route to leave Gleann Solas. Pay attention to anything that feels strange."

That's why we aren't going toward the trees. We need to gain distance before they can home in on my Unseelie magic and use it to track us. His lips pressed into a firm line. *It won't take long for them to realize that.*

Eiric's jaw clenched as she continued to keep pace with us, but I could see from the way she held her arms close to her sides that she didn't like not being in charge.

We passed by four stucco cottages when a female voice called out, "I sense strange magic."

"It must be the king of the nightfiends," the deeper-voiced man spat. "We'll follow your lead until we can all sense it for ourselves."

I pumped my hands at my sides to move faster. Flying would be ideal, but there was no way Finnian and Tavish could handle that.

The four of us were halfway through the village when the deeper-voiced man said, "Where are you leading us? I thought you were following the essence of his magic."

"I *am*," the woman gritted out. "And it's leading toward the village."

"Impossible," the deeper-voiced guard responded. "They wouldn't risk staying in the open longer than they needed to. The Unseelie can't hold on to his magic for long, not after being bound and neglected."

Of course a male wouldn't trust a woman's senses. Why would they be different here than on Earth? In this moment, though, I appreciated the sexism.

My side ached, reminding me I far preferred swimming to running. Eiric and I had a lot in common, but she didn't find swimming as enjoyable and much preferred to pound the ground with her feet. Maybe that had something to do with the affinities of our magic.

Tavish and Finnian were slowing as well. I could feel my mate's exertion, and I wished there was something more I could do for him.

"Unless they wanted to hide behind a cottage while we went into the woods," the woman countered. "Because they know we'd expect them to head for the trees."

Even though our gait had slowed, the end of the village was in sight. Luckily, most of the lights were off, blanketing us in complete darkness. Most of Gleann Solas was asleep for the night, and this village wasn't on the edge of the kingdom, so no guards had been allocated here to watch for the dragon prince to circle back.

"She has a point," the higher-voiced male countered. "And they'll get away if we continue to argue amongst ourselves."

We were near the woods on the other side of the village. My heart hammered. Us reaching the trees didn't mean shit. I knew better than to believe that Fate would bless us with a reprieve.

My magic was running low, making me move slower. I wouldn't let Tavish know, or he'd beat himself up for draining me. He needed to be focused and not riddled with guilt.

As we stepped through the tree line, I waited for the next obstacle we'd be forced to face together.

The guards had slowed as they carefully tracked our movements, allowing us to get deeper into the woods. Their voices faded, indicating we were gaining distance from them. But there was no telling for how long.

The tingling of the darkness vanished from my skin, leaving me exposed, and the funneling of my magic stopped.

No.

Had Tavish realized I was growing fatigued? *What are you doing?*

Before he could answer, the woman exclaimed, "I lost his magic."

Now that we're deep enough, I don't need to hide us, which will make following us far more difficult, he replied.

I glanced over to see that Eiric hadn't noticed that the magic was gone and was continuing forward. Her breathing wasn't labored at all, while I felt sweat beading on my brow.

We continued our trek with Eiric in the lead. My legs

became heavy, and I struggled to lift my feet. I bit the inside of my cheek and closed the connection between Tavish and me so he couldn't sense my fatigue. It covered me like a weighted blanket, and the ground felt a little off-center like I was on a rocking boat.

The guards' voices got farther away as we continued deeper into the woods. Still, none of us risked speaking. I had no doubt that guards were rushing throughout the kingdom to alert everyone that Tavish and Finnian had escaped.

After what felt like hours but had only been minutes, we slowed. Finnian blanched and hunched over. There was no way we could make it off the island, not with Tavish, Finnian, and me drained. We needed rest.

Nonetheless, we couldn't risk staying here. The guards would be searching for us in this area.

"Let's find a place to hide so the two of them can eat and rest." Eiric ran a hand through her curly hair, which bounced when she removed it. "They can't fly for long, and we can't bear that much weight for hours."

I hated that she was right, but worse, I was now part of that equation. I sighed as the trees closed in on me. "Where do we go?" Everywhere I could think of meant my parents would think of it too, and they'd find us. Eiric would be in the same boat as me. We were at a clear disadvantage.

Again.

"I have an idea." Tavish inhaled deeply. "If we can get there."

Eiric grimaced, but my heart leaped with hope. Neither set of our parents would know Tavish's habits, and he'd spent time in Aetherglen, the kingdom's name when both Unseelie and Seelie had occupied the lands here.

"Let's go," I said, taking Tavish's hand. Eiric wasn't

likely to argue against him if I agreed. "We'll follow your lead."

He nodded. "We shall travel slowly and steadily because it's a ways away."

Of course it was, and I noticed Eiric flinched at that as well.

Finnian used the bottom of his tattered, soiled tunic to wipe the sweat from his brow. "Let's go, or I may fall over. Slowing down makes my body want to rest."

With no disagreements, Tavish headed south, away from the castle and guards.

The moon rose high, the light shining down on us. Thankfully, it illuminated the ground, so we didn't struggle with the path or require additional lighting to move fast.

I struggled not to let my feet drag over the ground and make more noise, and I wasn't sure how much longer I could go on. I suspected I'd done too much when I funneled my magic and strength into Tavish.

Something tugged at our connection, opening it back up to its normal state. Tavish jerked his head toward me, a deep scowl on his face.

You're exhausted, and you didn't tell me. Tavish's eyes darkened to the storm-cloud gray that conveyed his anger or annoyance. *What happened? I didn't see or hear anything.*

I swallowed, hating the way his betrayal rolled into me. *It was when you were using my magic. Our bond tugged, and I pushed everything I could through it.* I added the last part, not wanting him to blame himself. *I didn't know what I was doing.*

He bit his bottom lip, and anger pulsed through him. *I should've known better. I thought it felt too easy, and now you're more exhausted than I am. You were angry because I kept the fact that Finnian and I hadn't eaten or drunk anything from you, and you do this?*

I winced, hating that he was right.

"What's going on?" Finnian huffed. "We've slowed down, and if we stop, I may not be able to get moving again."

Several pairs of flapping wings sounded overhead.

I froze.

That had to be the guards searching for us. We'd been walking for four hours, and the moon was setting. We had to get out of here before they located us.

"Get down and hide in the brush," Tavish whispered.

We obeyed, and my legs dragged along the fallen leaves, making a sound. But no matter what I did, I couldn't get the noise to stop. My heart clamored, making my actions more erratic.

Tavish gripped my arm, pulling me behind him, his face turning purple from strain. I was putting a strain on both of us. Eiric came over to help, and we got under the thick purple brush that would hide us from above. The brush indicated we were close to the Unseelie side of the kingdom.

Eiric flanked me with Tavish on my other side.

"Did you hear that?" a guard asked from above us.

There was a pause, and I held my breath.

"Probably an animal, but we should investigate," a woman replied.

Between exhaustion, fear, and a lack of oxygen, I grew dizzy.

I took a deep breath, trying to be as quiet as I could, but the damage was done. My vision blackened, and I linked, *I'm passing out.* Then my body gave out, and darkness took me.

My head throbbed. I reached up to rub it, and the memory of what had happened flooded into me.

The guards.

I must have alerted them to our location.

My eyes popped open, and I saw a smooth silver ceiling overhead that I'd never seen before.

We'd gotten caught. I had to find Tavish.

I sat up, and the room spun. A wooden table sat across from the bed I was on, and several candles were lit, casting warm light inside the sparse room. There were no windows, which made me think I could be in a cell. But the frosty-blue sheets, dark-gray fuzzy blanket, and cloudlike pillows and mattress contradicted that thought.

Sprite, are you okay? Tavish connected, his concern hovering heavier than the covers over me.

A door opened, and I jerked my head to see Tavish enter with a lantern in his hand.

My breath caught. Somehow, he appeared more handsome than ever.

His skin was almost as pale as snow, but it had a healthy gleam that hadn't been there in far too long. He hurried over and dropped onto the bed next to me, examining me with stormy eyes that held hints of starbursts that I hadn't seen since he was a young boy.

"Where did the guards take us?" I croaked while trying to make sense of it all.

He set the lantern on a table next to the bed and pulled me into his arms.

A jolt of electricity shot between us, but there was no pain... just pleasure.

"They didn't catch us." He kissed the top of my forehead, holding me tightly. *We're safe.*

Relief crashed through me, and I relaxed and burrowed my head into his chest, feeling the hard curves of his muscles against my cheek.

How? I swallowed, my throat dry and achy. *They were right on us.*

We reached the divide of the Seelie and Unseelie lands, though you couldn't tell anymore. The Seelie have grown plants and warmed up the area since they forced us from our homes. But that didn't matter because Unseelie magic is still tied to the earth. It rejuvenated Finnian and me enough for us to assist Eiric in handling the guards... though that's now a point of contention between your sister and us. His displeasure flowed into me. *She isn't thrilled that we killed the guards, but we couldn't risk them informing the others that we had traveled onto Unseelie soil. They'd have known we hadn't left the island and would've sent more guards to search the area, making it more difficult for us to leave.*

My stomach roiled. Even though I understood that Tavish and Finnian had felt it was necessary, the thought of some of my people dying at their hands rubbed me wrong. *Killing people isn't always the right way to handle things, especially if we want to bridge the gap between the Unseelie and Seelie so we can have a future together.*

He sighed. *They were trying to kill Finnian and capture me. What did you expect us to do? Let them? This is the same conversation we've been having with Eiric.*

I coughed and winced, the dryness of my throat hurting more than I anticipated. *I need water.* My magic still hadn't recovered. *How long have I been out?*

We just got settled about ten minutes ago, so not long. You didn't get a good rest because we had to carry you, so I'm not surprised you still feel unwell, he answered, releasing me to stand. *I'll fetch you something to eat and drink. We need to be at full health when we leave here.*

I'll go with you. If Eiric was upset with them, I needed to help de-escalate the conversation. Eiric already struggled with my allegiance with Tavish; the worst thing that could happen was for her to feel alone and uncomfortable. I pushed the covers off me as Tavish frowned.

You aren't well. You shouldn't—

Don't. I climbed to my feet and tried to stand upright without swaying, though the ground wobbled. *I need to go out there for E.* I had no doubt she was worried about my current state as well, and seeing me would mean more than Tavish relaying the message that I was awake.

His forehead creased with worry, and he rushed around the bed to wrap an arm around my waist and steady me. The jolts of electricity thrummed between us. Though his arms were strong, he exhaled and said, "I despise that I can't carry you. Despite my magic strengthening here, my body hasn't fully recovered."

My heart expanded with warmth from how much love I had for him. *This is more than perfect.*

We headed toward the white door he'd entered through. I noticed a closet full of clothes and a door to the left that led to a massive bathroom. *Where are we?* This place was nice, but it also reminded me of a basement back on Earth.

He opened the door and led me into a long, narrow

hallway with four doors on each side. The room we'd come out of was at the end of the hallway. The other end opened into a sizable room. Lanterns hung between each door, lighting the area for us.

This is the Unseelie secret underground living quarters, created in case we needed to hide from an unprompted attack or have our guards use the passage to attack the Seelie without warning. He flinched. *Sort of like your secret passageway behind the walls of your castle.*

Even though I hated that they'd had a way to attack us without warning, I was happy that Tavish was so forthcoming with me, especially since I could feel his guilt. *I appreciate your honesty.* I squeezed him, my legs becoming a little steadier. *But I'm confused. If you had this, why couldn't you hide when the Seelie attacked twelve years ago?*

We moved down the stark white hall.

The entrance is outside the castle, in the royal garden. We'd been expecting a visit from the Seelie royals, including their guards, to discuss the future. We assumed it was to make official the agreement that the two of us would wed and unite Aetherglen as one kingdom once again. We weren't alarmed until guards kept entering with no sign of you or your parents. When we understood it was an actual attack, it was too late. We didn't have time to escape and hide here. Your parents used the goodwill established during years of meetings to skin our wings and take everything from us.

My heart ached. I hated that my parents had done that to his, but something must have prompted it. I'd been so focused on the wrong actions they'd been taking against Tavish that I hadn't asked why they'd attacked the Unseelie and relocated them twelve years ago. If I could go back, I'd ask for their side of the story. *Tavish... I—*

You have nothing to feel bad about. A sad smile flitted

across his face, and he kissed the top of my head. *You saved my life and helped me escape. None of this is your fault.*

Even though he was right, I felt as if I had somehow attacked him along with my parents. But that was preposterous. Still, my father's words repeated in my head—*People are responsible for the decisions their royals make.* I'd argued with him about that, but here I was, feeling like I was to blame just as much as them. Why was my mind beginning to change, especially since I truly believed that Tavish shouldn't be held accountable for his parents' actions?

We reached the end of the hallway and stepped into the gigantic room. There were four oversized dark-gray oval couches and a huge silver chandelier with twenty candles on the intricately thorned vines that spiraled around it. A large table that seated twenty stood behind it, and Finnian and Eiric sat across from each other in the middle, a bowl of sunburst fruit, bread, and water in a clear pitcher placed between them. My stomach grumbled, and my tongue felt like sandpaper in my mouth.

I picked up my pace, untangling from Tavish, desperately needing water. I fell into the seat next to Finnian and snatched his blue crystal glass from his hand.

When the first drop of water landed on my tongue, I immediately felt better, but it wasn't close to being enough. I downed the entire thing and set the empty glass back on the table just as Tavish sat beside me.

"Better?" Finnian quirked a brow.

Tavish reached for the pitcher and refilled the glass while I wiped my mouth with the back of my hand.

"A little." This time, when I responded, I sounded like my normal self and not like a frog back on Earth. "I didn't realize how dehydrated I was."

"We were walking in the woods for hours." Eiric took a

bite of fruit. "We were all dehydrated, especially after Finnian's stunt with the Seelie guards." She leveled a deep, hateful glare at him, the type I'd seen from her only once before.

It'd been right after her parents had adopted me, and we'd gone to school. I'd struggled to fit in, and a boy had asked me if I was from this planet. Eiric had torn into him in a way that had made me petrified of her, but it hadn't taken me long to realize she was protective of her family. And the guards were part of her family because she was training to be one of them, and they were Seelie.

My stomach dropped. Her eating wasn't necessarily a good sign. She liked to eat her emotions more than I did.

Tavish placed the glass of water back in front of me, and I didn't hesitate to drain it. He swiped a sunburst fruit that reminded me of a lemon but was twice the size, along with a piece of brown bread. As soon as I put the glass down, he handed me the food and refilled my glass.

Chuckling, Finnian leaned back in his seat, placing his hands behind his head. "It's nice to see Tavish serving others. When we get back to the castle, maybe he can cut down on his servants since he now has such capable hands."

As soon as Tavish placed the glass back in front of me, Finnian yawned and said, "Can you hand me another piece of bread?"

"Go fly in a volcano," Tavish sneered. "The only person I tend to is my mate."

My heart skipped a beat. I loved when Tavish made it clear that he did certain things only for me. He made me feel special.

When I took a bite of cold bread, a sweet honey taste hit my tongue. "Where did you find this?"

"It was in the ice chambers here." Tavish smiled. "My

parents ensured that our food would survive here for hundreds of years if necessary."

Eiric scowled, chomping on her bread.

"I'm just glad to see our little featherling has healed." Finnian winked. "I've missed all the trouble she causes."

I snorted. "We just escaped a castle and were chased by guards. I think we can all use a rest before the next adventure."

"Amen to that." Eiric lifted her water up at me.

"A men?" Tavish tilted his head. "That doesn't make any sense. A is singular and men are plural."

"Unless the man has multiple penises." Finnian stroked the beard that had grown during his time in captivity. "Would that work to make it plural? Does the penis make a man singular or the actual head?"

Tavish rubbed his temple. "Is that a relevant question?"

"Wait." Eiric inhaled sharply. "There are men here who have more than one penis?"

I didn't know if I was exhausted or just having a hard time following the conversation. Either way, I wanted it over. "She just meant she agreed with me. Amen is something humans sometimes say when they agree with someone. It has religious ties that don't translate here in Ardanos."

"That's a strange word for people to use, then." Finnian pursed his lips. "And, sunscorched, if men could have multiple penises, I'd definitely be one of them. Alas, we only have one here. Do some humans have more than one?"

Eiric crossed her arms. "With how arrogant you are, you have to be compensating for something. I bet it's rather small."

Finnian's jaw dropped. "It is quite large." He stood and readied to drop his pants.

Tavish snarled, "You'd better not do what I suspect you're doing. Friend or not, I will kill you if you expose yourself to my mate."

"It would've been nice if you'd threatened him like that when he killed the three Seelie guards." Eiric wrinkled her nose.

"They were trying to *kill* me." Finnian rocked back on his heels. "What would you do if an Unseelie guard attacked you?"

She bared her teeth. "Kill them like I want to do you."

Wow. I figured there was tension, but nothing like this. I should've known better, and they were putting me in the middle, even if they didn't mean to. "Which is why all *three* of you are in the wrong."

"What?" Eiric dropped her hands into her lap as her eyes widened. "How am I wrong when they *killed* some of our people?"

"Because I view both Unseelie *and* Seelie as my people now." I straightened my back.

Our fated-mate connection expanded as Tavish's love flowed through. He leaned toward me, a faint smile on his face.

"Which means we should learn to live harmoniously. Neither side should be killing the other unless it's inevitable." I took the time to look at Tavish, then Eiric, stopping with Finnian.

Finnian nodded. "Exactly. The guards tried to kill me, and I merely defended myself."

"Someone has to make the first move toward peace between us." I lifted my chin in challenge. "Why can't it be you? After all, you claim you have a big penis. Prove it."

A deep, menacing growl came from Tavish, followed by

rage flooding our bond. "I'm not kidding, sprite. I will kill him if—"

"For crying out loud, it's a saying." Eiric rolled her eyes. "She didn't mean for him to actually show her his dick. She meant for him to prove he's brave by taking the first step and not killing guards."

"Then the others would know we're still here." Finnian bit his bottom lip. "I did that to protect us so we could get out of there."

And that was why, even though I was disappointed in them and wished they hadn't killed anyone, I wasn't mad. Peace between Unseelie and Seelie wouldn't be an easy change, and I was asking a lot of them. "But maybe next time, just knock them out. It's not like they can locate us in a hidden spot underground. The other guards know you were injured—they could assume we still haven't left."

"They did see us in Unseelie territory." Tavish scratched the thick scruff on his face. "They could narrow down the search area. Right now, they're probably searching the woods where they lost track of us."

Eiric slammed a hand down on the table. "They're still our people, and your father started the feud, so quit pretending you're innocent."

"My father?" Tavish straightened and bared his teeth. "He didn't do *anything*. The Seelie came into our kingdom and randomly attacked us!"

"Is that the story you've convinced yourself to believe?" Eiric barked out a hard laugh. "That's pathetic."

Of all the times for Eiric to decide to be the mouthy one, it'd be now. Normally, I was the one who impulsively spoke without thought, but for the first time, I could see both sides. "He can't lie, E." My appetite had vanished, and I turned to face my clueless fated mate.

No wonder he held such hatred toward the Seelie.

"Is that the story Eldrin told you?" His cousin had retrieved him from the Seelie and perverted the situation to make Tavish believe he'd saved his life. I had no doubt he'd played additional mind games with him. After all, Tavish had been such a young boy... not even yet a man, though the responsibility of ruling had fallen to him.

"Why would he lie about that?" Tavish shook his head. "Neither my father nor any of his guards had left Unseelie land in weeks. There is no way anything they did could've been mistaken as a threat. He'd gotten sick weeks before, and he recovered but continued to act strangely. None of us could figure out what was the matter."

Eiric gestured to the room. "He could've used this place to go to Seelie lands, and you wouldn't have been aware of it. You just told us that."

"Mother wouldn't leave his side for long, and I was learning to handle the business of the kingdom while he recovered. I had control of the guards with Eldrin assisting me." Tavish's determination flowed into me, confirming he believed every word. "There was nothing we did to even hint at war. Even then, I was planning on a future with Lira by my side. I would never have risked the peace within our grasp."

"If that's the case, why were Gleann Solas and Tìr na Dràgon's skies covered in darkness?" Eiric leaned forward, watching Tavish's every move.

Tavish spat, "Is that what your king and queen led you to believe? Did you not see the sun each day rebuking their claims? They had to be masterful with their words in order for you to not believe what you saw."

My heart stopped because I could feel the truth in his words through our bond. He didn't believe his father had done anything. I didn't want to tell him and change his perception of the man he loved. I feared what that might do to him. He loved and cherished his parents, but I thought he knew what they'd done.

He felt the change in our bond, and his gaze landed on me. He whispered, "What are you hiding from me?"

M y throat thickened, and I couldn't answer. The words wouldn't form, and I knew why. I wanted to protect him from the truth... the one he didn't know. In his mind, it was easy to view the dragons and the Seelie as the enemy. That was the reason he'd been able to push forward with his life and become the man he was today. If I took that from him, I didn't know what might happen to him.

He blanched, turning the same color as the snow he covered his lands in as he stared deep into my eyes.

"Great Fates, Lira." Eiric rubbed a hand down her face. "Just tell him. He won't believe me."

"You believe this too?" His face crumpled, and a sense of betrayal wafted through our bond.

The damage was already done, so I had to get past my fear. Still, I grimaced as I started, "I more than believe it, thorn. I saw it. Everyone in Gleann Solas and Tír na Dragon did. That's what brought my parents and the dragons into their alliance. I even flew around the country because Father feared leaving Mother and me behind at the castle with all the royal guards gone. Everything was blanketed in darkness, hiding the sun and even the moon and stars. Our crops and flowers were dying."

"Maybe the dragons did something to cause it." Tavish placed both hands on the table. "Because nothing else makes sense to me."

Eiric crossed her legs and leaned back. "How is it out of the realm of possibility that your father did that?"

For once, Finnian was uncharacteristically quiet, which I didn't know how to take. If he jumped in to agree with Tavish, it could make the situation more dramatic.

"Because using enough magic to blanket the entire realm would require more magic than he possessed... more magic than I possess, even being on Unseelie soil once again." Tavish karate-chopped the air in front of him. "It's not possible that he could cover the entire realm. The Seelie and dragon magic would have been constantly fighting against him."

"The dragons can't control darkness, and no Seelie could manage something like that either... so what do you propose happened?" I bit the inside of my cheek, weighing my words and tone carefully. It wasn't that I didn't believe Tavish. I did. But nothing else made sense.

"I... I don't know." Tavish ran a hand through his hair, messing it up in the best of ways. "I have no idea how anyone could have accomplished that."

"Tav, I hate to bring this up." Finnian cleared his throat and leaned forward so he could look around me and meet Tavish's gaze. "But you said the king had been acting strange for a few weeks before the attack. Could his peculiarities be linked to it?"

"He would've been completely drained to even attempt that." Tavish shook his head. "When he came back from his last trip to Seelie three weeks before that, he seemed excited but secretive. Mother and I assumed that King Erdan and Queen Sylphia had announced they would be coming to visit to formally announce the merging of the two royal families."

Something in his story didn't add up. "But I thought you said your mother was worried about him and staying with him all the time."

"She was, but not when he first came back from the visit. It was a few days later, when on top of remaining secretive, he began doing strange things, like pacing the castle, having a shorter temper with everyone, hovering over me in my room while I slept, and discussing how things would change when he ruled more than just the Unseelie."

"Sounds like he had a plan." Eiric lifted her hands from her sides. "Which he was clearly implementing."

Tavish's frustration grated through our bond, along with the sickening feeling of doubt. "Maybe, but that doesn't negate that what you're proposing he did was physically impossible."

"We're missing something." Finnian rubbed his hands together. "Something that would make sense of everything."

Tavish's confusion and guilt gnawed at me, and I could feel his exhaustion. I glanced at Eiric to find dark circles under her eyes, and Finnian's shoulders were hunched like he was too weak to sit up tall. Even though I felt better after taking a few bites of food and drinking water, I struggled to keep my eyes open.

"Which we won't figure out right now." I placed my hand on Tavish's and squeezed it comfortingly. "We all need rest because we need to head back to the second Cuil Dorcha as soon as we're mended. Sitting here and debating what happened twelve years ago while we're exhausted won't get us anywhere." Not only that, but Tavish needed time to process what he'd learned, and so did Eiric and I. No one had considered the amount of magic needed to pull that off. Everyone had reacted to save our land and people, and the darkness had gone away after the king's death.

"Excellent suggestion." Finnian yawned. "I'm struggling to keep my eyes open, let alone stay engaged in the conversation. Even though my magic has resurfaced, my body needs to rest on something softer than a holding cell floor."

Eiric frowned, and I suspected she regretted helping us, especially after three of our guards had died in front of her. I couldn't blame her, but the decision had been made and the damage done.

"And she's still angry with me." Finnian raised his hands in surrender. "Just so you know, I didn't relish killing those guards. They weren't the ones who harmed us during our captivity—they merely found themselves in the wrong time and place."

She jumped to her feet, pushing back her chair. "Oh. You didn't *relish* it? That makes it *all* better." Sarcasm dripped from every word.

Finnian beamed. "I thought you'd see it differently. See, things don't have to continue to be as—"

"Well, when we relocated the Unseelie, I didn't smile about it," she interrupted with a raised brow. "I wasn't upset because, frankly, I didn't care. So I hope that makes you like me more."

She was goading him, and though I couldn't blame her because his comment had been callous, he was trying to mend things between them. I'd seen a lot of Unseelie take pleasure in others' deaths and pain, but Eiric hadn't. She didn't understand that was his way of showing remorse. I interjected, "Because we weren't in Ardanos when it happened." I didn't want another argument to start. "Can we please not say another word until we get some rest?"

Tavish stood and helped me up. "Lira is right. Let's retire to our bedchambers and talk further when we have more sleep. Arguing amongst ourselves won't rectify anything. It'll just make our tempers more frigid."

I watched as Eiric tried to hide her yawn, her jaw clenching. "Fine. Where do I rest?"

"You can take the first bedroom on the right," Tavish answered. "Finnian can take any of the others."

"That's fine with me." Finnian rolled his shoulders back as if he didn't have a care in the world... as if Eiric's comment hadn't bothered him.

The four of us headed back toward the bedrooms. I felt better after eating, but I still needed rest to recharge my body and magic.

Silence descended, and when Eiric peeled off to the first room on the right, some of the tension eased from within. I'd been afraid that she and Finnian would start arguing again, and I wasn't sure I had the energy to break it up.

As soon as Eiric's door closed, Finnian went to the door right across from hers. He whispered, "I'm staying here in case she decides to wreak havoc. Your sister is feisty and determined. She's more of a challenge than the women I'm used to dealing with."

"Because her sister is already royalty," Tavish shot back while smirking.

"Oh, go jump in a volcano." Finnian wrinkled his nose. "Women find me charming."

I rolled my eyes but enjoyed the moment, which felt somewhat normal. Well, as normal as anything was here in

Ardanos. "You must be losing your touch. Maybe sleep will help you."

"Don't fret, Lira." Finnian opened his door. "Your sister will be thawed in my hands by the time you wake up."

I was certain he'd never met anyone like Eiric, but I played along. "We'll see."

Tavish tugged me back to our door, his emotions all over the place. I couldn't decipher what I sensed before he moved on to another.

My heart hammered. I wasn't sure what to expect once we were alone. I hoped our revelations hadn't changed anything between us, but the fact that I'd confirmed Eiric's statement might have forced him to change his perception of the Seelie. Not that what we'd done was right, but at least we'd had a reason. Most situations weren't clearly wrong or right.

We entered the bedroom, and I moved to the side as he closed the door. When the door clicked and he turned the lock, my knees almost gave out.

He turned to face me and tilted his head, asking, *Are you feeling all right?*

I wondered if he was deflecting his own feelings by forcing me to address why I was a bundle of nerves. I lifted my head, not wanting to come off as timid. I needed to be direct and make sure nothing changed the way he felt about me. "I'm worried. Your emotions are all over the place. I just hope you aren't upset with me for confirming what E had to say."

"Why would I be upset with you or Eiric for speaking the truth? I'd wondered why the Seelie attacked and allied with the flamers. Now I have an answer. I just don't know how *anyone*, including Father, could blanket the realm in darkness. That part doesn't make sense. Father was strong, but nothing like that." He took my hands, turning so we stood in front of one another. "But I don't want to think about that anymore. I have a place to take a bath and lie in a soft bed with the most important person in my world next to me. Right now, before we have to leave safety, I just want to focus on that."

My body warmed, enjoying the sound of that. "Sounds like an excellent plan."

"I'm glad you're agreeable." His emotions leveled out, and warmth and tenderness emanated from him once more. "You're tired. Why don't you go back to bed while I clean up? I haven't bathed in days."

The thought of him naked and wet had need unfurling in my stomach. We'd never bathed together, and suddenly, some of my fatigue vanished. *Mind if I join you?* I wasn't sure how large the tub was, but I didn't care. The smaller it was, the more our bodies would be pressed together.

His breath caught. *As long as you're able. If you need rest—*

Instead of letting him finish that thought, I covered his mouth with mine. His hands snaked around my waist, pulling me against him as our tongues intertwined. I hadn't expected this overwhelming need to surge through me, but knowing we were together with nothing threatening us had me desperately needing him. We'd been so close to death and capture—I *needed* to connect with him again.

He stumbled back toward the bathroom, but he didn't keep his fingers from digging into my sides. He paused at the door, detangling himself from me to snag a lantern on the large table. "Follow me."

He led me into the bathroom, hanging the lantern on a hook in the white wall. The walls reminded me of cement, and there was a large, dark-gray circular tub in the center of the floor. Tavish turned the handle, and the gorgeous sparkling blue water of the realm began filling the tub. He grinned at me and reached around my body toward the sink on my right.

I waited for him to capture me in his arms, but he bent and opened a drawer, then removed a sharp knife. If he'd done that when we first met him, I'd have been certain he intended to kill me.

But not anymore.

"Aw, sprite," he cooed then ran his tongue across my lips. "You don't fear me anymore."

I stepped toward him, pressing my breasts against his chest. "Disappointed?"

He moved the knife, brushing it along my arm, but it didn't nick me. Desire flooded me like never before. "Never. I'd *never* hurt you. I know now that I never could have hurt you before, even if I'd tried."

Moving the knife, he placed it at the neckline of my gown and cut slowly downward until the garment was falling off me. My chest heaved as the material fell from my body onto the floor, leaving me completely naked in front of him.

Those storm-colored eyes lightened, and his pupils dilated as he slowly took in every inch of me. He murmured, "So blasting gorgeous."

Not having the patience that he did, I gripped the bottom of his ruined tunic and ripped it in half. I pushed the material from his body, enjoying the curves of his muscles as they flexed to let the shirt drop. When I reached his six-pack, I followed the trail of hair that took me closer to what I desired.

I ran my fingers over his cool skin, tracing his abs, and

slowly made it to his waistband. Then I pulled down his pants.

He growled, kicking them off as he bent down and grabbed a container with a bottle inside. Before I could ask what it was, he pulled my body against his. He then walked backward until his legs hit the edge of the tub. He let me go, bent down to turn the water off, then stepped into the tub. I followed him, enjoying the refreshing tingle of the water over my skin.

As I sat in front of him, Tavish set the knife in the container with the bottle on the side of the tub and then went under to get clean. I followed suit, and when we resurfaced, I didn't waste any more time. I wanted him inside me, and now.

He smirked. "I'm not ready. I want to shave first so I can feel your skin against mine everywhere." He set the bottle and knife on the side of the tub and dunked the container in the water before putting it alongside the other things. The urge to take care of him took hold.

"Let me?" I held out my hands, wondering if he'd let me do it.

Affection swirled through our bond. "Sure."

My pulse quickened. I enjoyed that he trusted me as he moved to sit against the back of the tub. I followed him, and he snagged my hips and lifted me, so I straddled him. His hardness pressed against me, proving he already wanted me.

Use the oil in the bottle to coat my face so that cutting the hairs will be easier and prevent the scruff from falling into the tub, he instructed.

I nodded, picking up the white container and dumping some oil into my hand. The liquid was cool and smelled of winter dew. I rubbed my hands together then gently spread it over his chin, neck, and mustache.

His breathing quickened, and his eyes fluttered shut as I made sure to coat every surface. Then I set it back on the side and rinsed off my hands, not wanting the knife to slip. The oil vanished, and with steady hands, I pressed the knife to the base of his neck and lifted upward, slowly shaving the scruff from his face. I dunked the knife into the pitcher and watched as the hair disappeared. I then went back to work, taking my time.

Sprite, this is killing me, he groaned. *I didn't know you shaving me would make me want you even more. I love you taking care of me.*

I understood what he meant, and when I dunked the knife back into the water to start again, I kissed him. He tried to deepen the kiss, but I pulled away, my head growing lighter from the lack of oxygen, my desire, and having to retain control. *Nope. You said we couldn't do anything until after you'd shaved. Don't distract me.*

I'm regretting that decision. He moved so his cock brushed my clit.

I sucked in a breath but shifted away, determined to finish the first job I'd started. I worked slowly and carefully, not wanting to nick him, and with each break I took, he either rubbed against me or slipped fingers inside me, pushing me closer to the edge.

I managed to focus and remove all the hair from his face. *Done.*

Thank Fate, he replied, taking the knife from my hand and tossing it over the side of the tub. Immediately, he captured my nipple in his mouth and caressed it with his tongue. He moved to slip his fingers inside me again, but I'd had enough.

I needed him.

Moaning, I caught his hand and lifted my hips, then

sank down onto him. He thrust his hips upward, filling me to the point I thought I'd burst. Then he wrapped his arm around me and flipped us over so that my back was now pressed against the tub and he was hovering over me.

The entire time, he somehow remained inside me.

You've always been on top. He moved back and thrust into me again. *It's my turn to be in control.*

My back slipped against the tub with each stroke, and I wrapped my legs around his waist, wanting more. He slid one hand down my waist and between my folds, and his fingers circled as he continued to move deeper inside me.

My vision blurred as the tingles of the water heightened the electricity jolting between us and the friction that knotted deep inside me. I opened myself up to him through the bond, wanting him to know how much I loved him... more than anything in the world.

He responded, and there was no doubt we both felt the same.

This time, when he filled me, he paused, rubbing a little bit harder. The orgasm exploded through me.

His body quivered in response, and his release was a mere second behind mine. We got lost in each other, our souls connecting even more deeply. Even my magic seemed to return to its normal level as everything within us mingled with the other.

After moments, minutes, or hours, I wasn't sure which, we came down from our high. Our bodies were completely satiated, and exhaustion set in. I wasn't even sure how I would get out of the tub.

Tavish helped me to my feet and removed two fluffy, frosty-blue towels from under the sink, and we dried off. Then he took my hand and led me straight to the bed, not bothering with clothes.

As he pulled me into his arms, he kissed the back of my head and connected, *I love you, sprite. I've never been this happy before.*

I love you too, thorn. I enjoyed the way my skin tingled everywhere we touched. *You complete me.*

We drifted off to sleep in each other's arms, feeling warm and safe.

A crash had my eyes popping open. For a moment, I couldn't remember where we were, but when I felt the electricity thrumming, I remembered everything.

Just as my breathing leveled out, there was a loud *clang*, like two swords hitting.

"You could've beheaded me!" Eiric shouted.

"Almost doesn't count," Finnian chuckled. "Wait until next time."

Oh fuck. I spun around, shoving Tavish hard. *Wake up. Finnian and E are trying to kill each other.*

TAVISH

Fear strangled me, waking me from the most comforting sleep I'd had in days. My skin was still jolting from having Lira's body next to mine, and I felt completely satiated from making love and then holding her all night long despite feeling slightly sluggish from my time in imprisonment. Yet, my magic flowed at full strength inside me, thanks to being back in the lands that held the essence of Unseelie power.

The mattress shifted, informing me that Lira had gotten up from the bed, and then the words she'd spoken through our mind-melding in the haze of slumber replayed in my head.

I sat up and watched her hurry to the closet, completely naked, and need tightened in my stomach and made my dick harden again.

I swear, if Finnian harms her, I'll cut off one of his testicles, she connected, disappearing into the closet for all of one second to come out with a gray tunic and leather pants for me and a snow-white gown for herself.

She had dark circles under her gorgeous blue eyes—

proof that sharing her magic with me was impacting her—but she stood steadily on her feet, whereas she hadn't the night before.

Right. Finnian and Eiric were fighting. We needed to stop that, but all I wanted to do was admire my mate's body. However, I knew better. Even though Lira was threatening Finnian, she'd be equally upset if Eiric harmed him. She cared about both of them dearly, which meant breaking up the fight was as much a priority for me as for her.

I couldn't tolerate her being hurt again.

Snagging my pants, I threw the covers off and slid the material on. Not bothering with the shirt, I flew across the room, unlocked the door, and barreled toward the main room.

Lira followed close behind me, the tips of my wings brushing her body a few times. The intimate sensation made me struggle to keep my mind on the task, but I managed.

We turned the corner as Eiric swung her sword at Finnian, who blocked the attack at the last second.

He grinned. "Good. Your eyes didn't telegraph your attack."

When I realized they weren't actually trying to slice the scales from each other's wings, the tension drained from my body. I dropped to my feet behind a couch, and Lira landed beside me.

Her concern morphed into frustration as her face turned a faint golden hue. "What the *hell*?"

Finnian and Eiric lowered their swords and turned to us. He rubbed a hand over his new beard and asked, "I don't understand. What is this 'hell,' and what does it have to do with us?"

"I thought you'd be happy that we were training together." Eiric sheathed her sword and placed her hands on her hips. "Why are you upset?"

"So hell means she's upset..." Finnian nodded. "That's a strange saying."

Even though I agreed, I was more concerned with her being upset than with Earth's vocabulary. I wanted to smack Finnian since he wasn't focused on what mattered. I opened my mouth to defend Eiric, but I didn't have to.

"I'm glad you two are amicable enough to train with each other, but a heads-up would have been nice." Lira lifted her chin, staring down the woman she'd claimed as a sister. "Instead, I'm woken by the sound of you almost being beheaded. I thought you two were actually fighting."

"I didn't want to risk knocking on your door and hearing you and the Unseelie fiend fucking, or waking you up if you were actually sleeping." Eiric shivered. "I was being considerate."

Lira's anger vanished, and relief lightened our connection. "I know. After the way last night ended, I just got freaked out when I heard you almost got injured. If something happened to either of you..." She trailed off.

I placed an arm around her shoulders and pulled her to my side, our wings touching. I didn't understand how Lira could be that angry and then calm down so fast. She'd never been that way with me. I needed to learn Eiric's trick for managing that.

"We woke up an hour ago and had some bread and sunbursts. We came to an understanding. One that will allow us to work together more easily." Eiric strolled to the table and drank from a glass of water.

Now I couldn't deny being intrigued. "And what exactly is this agreement?"

Finnian beamed. "I won't kill another Seelie unless

there's absolutely no other way, and she'll be cordial to the Unseelie when we arrive back at the castle and remember she can't go around killing our people either."

Hands dropping from her waist, Eiric scowled. "Damn nightfiends."

"It was eye-opening when she put herself in our wings and thought about arriving in a kingdom full of Unseelie who will want to kill her." Finnian bumped his shoulder into Eiric's. "She hadn't thought that far ahead, especially with her wearing a guard's uniform."

He was right. I'd been so consumed with Lira and her well-being that I hadn't thought about what might happen to Eiric once we returned to my people.

"There should be an outfit here she can change into." Lira nibbled on her bottom lip, burrowing deeper against my side. "God, I hate that you got yourself into this situation. They'll know you're Seelie. You should've stayed at Gleann Solas and pretended not to know anything."

Eiric's face softened, and she came toward us.

I tensed. A Seelie being this close to me had the hair rising on the nape of my neck. My gut reaction was to yank Lira and myself back, but I fought the instinct for *her*.

"What did we promise each other?" Eiric arched a brow as she took Lira's hands in hers.

The tingles of affection shot through our connection, warming my naturally icy chest more than normal.

"That was on Earth." Lira smiled tenderly, moving from my side closer to her. "You aren't bound by it here."

Eiric rocked back on her heels. "It might as well have been made here because I always keep my promises, even those not bound by Ardanos and Seelie magic."

"Oh... what was this vow?" Finnian shuffled forward, expanding his wings in excitement.

The urge to punch him nearly overwhelmed me.

"That we would stand beside each other, no matter what." Lira mashed her lips together. "But I didn't expect you to go rogue against the king and queen on my behalf."

"Whether I like it or not, you chose to complete the mate bond with an Unseelie, and you swear he makes you happy." Eiric winked and shrugged. "So I didn't really have a choice. Besides, you're a pain in the ass to keep in line, so I figure Tavish will need help keeping you out of trouble."

I laughed, and Lira cut her eyes at me. Somehow, that made me smile even wider. "She's not wrong."

"That's one of Lira's best attributes, in my humble opinion." Finnian clasped his hands, holding them toward Lira. "She finds trouble where there shouldn't be any. She even tamed a cù-sìth, which has never been done before."

Lira tried to frown, but the corners of her lips tipped upward. "I don't like the three of you teaming up against me. Maybe I want you fighting each other again."

"No, you don't." Eiric snorted, pulling her into a hug. "The three of us know better than that."

I could feel the happiness wafting from Lira, and the last thing I wanted to do was ruin that moment, though several threats were hovering over us. We needed to return to—

My thoughts cut off because, after returning here to the real Cuil Dorcha, I couldn't call the ruined dragon lands by that name anymore.

Some of the joy ebbed, and Lira pulled away from Eiric. I had no doubt she felt the guilt of what came next weighing me down. Even though I cherished our fated-mate connection, sometimes I wished I could protect her from my feelings so they didn't spoil her happiness.

"Let's eat some breakfast and then find something for

Eiric to wear that doesn't scream *Seelie guard*." Lira ran a hand over the stomach of her gown. "We should probably head back to Cuil Dorcha before the dragons join my father in retrieving me."

My stomach soured as if I'd eaten rotten fish. Even though she spoke the truth, I hadn't determined a way to keep her safe. I couldn't abandon my people, but Lira remaining there with me wasn't an effective strategy either. The only solution I could see was to kill the dragon prince, thus ending the demented agreement their parents had arranged between them.

"How does one's outfit scream?" Finnian lifted his hands. "This conversation has yielded so many questions about hell, God, and why someone would want to look upward when two people are getting along when they haven't been. The Earth language is quite fascinating—it sounds so illogical."

Of course, the thornling would be more concerned about Earth's vernacular than a huge war brewing. Nonetheless, we needed to return to prepare my people for battle. The one benefit we had was that Finnian and I had been recharged by our true lands, and I hoped neither the Seelie nor the dragons expected that. "Now isn't the time, Finnian."

"If not now, when?" Finnian pouted like I'd stolen the last bit of spirits of the night.

Eiric pivoted back toward him and said, "I'll tell you all about it once we're crossing the ocean and not at risk of being found by the Seelie."

"I guess I can wait," he teased, heading back to the table and grabbing a piece of bread. "But everyone should note that I'm on my best behavior."

"Oh, it's noted, all right." Lira crossed her arms and

stepped in front of me. *Now that everything is calm, why don't you put on your tunic before we eat? I love E, but you're my mate, and if she glances at you for a moment too long, I might lose my rationale and slit her throat.*

Hot desire shot straight to my dick. *Are you threatening to kill the person you consider family for merely looking at me?* She was usually so empathetic and kind—for her to threaten violence like that made me want to throw her against the wall and bury myself inside her.

She looked over her shoulder at me. *I am, and I feel awful, so do something about it. Because at this point, if she does, it'll be your fault. You're aware of the threat.*

Something was wrong with me. That threat only made my hands itch to follow through on the very naughty thoughts running through my head. I smirked as I turned toward the hallway, spreading out my wings so Eiric couldn't see me. If we were at the castle and safe, I'd be dragging Lira with me, and the only thing holding me back was needing a future with her.

I had to determine how to kill the dragon prince, freeing Lira to always be with me. That was the only thing that mattered.

Two hours later, the four of us left the hiding spot, and I cloaked us in darkness. The magic came easily now; it didn't drain me while I used it, and we left the kingdom behind without issue.

Finally, Fate had blessed us. The first sign that maybe things would turn for the better.

We waited to leave until the moon was rising and the faint shadows of darkness shrouded the land, knowing the

Seelie would expect us to make our move while the moon was higher in the sky. We flew over the water, and the strength of my magic slipped as we left our true kingdom behind.

Finnian and Eiric flanked Lira and me, with Finnian on my left and Eiric on Lira's right. Our wings beat in a similar rhythm as we flew high in the sky. I kept the darkness close to us, not wanting to risk the dragons locating us with their keen eyesight.

Every so often, Eiric tugged at the long, dark-green dress she and Lira had found. She'd demanded to keep her sheath and sword, which I'd agreed with. Whether Eiric was in Seelie guard attire or not, she'd need to protect herself once we were back on land. Lira was competent with a sword as well, and I'd be giving her one too. She needed a sword to protect herself in case we got separated if Eldrin attacked us on our return to the ruined lands.

After an hour of flight with no danger, Eiric and Finnian began having the Earth conversation she'd offered to have. I learned a lot of pointless vocabulary that only Eiric, Lira, and her parents would ever know. I tried to focus on the conversation, seeing the way Lira enjoyed Finnian's foolish questions and interpretations, but each moment we came closer to returning to my people, the problems I'd left behind reared in my head. I hoped Eldrin was still alive so I could kill him. After all his deceptions, I needed to be the one to use my sword and stab him in the heart.

Lira's wings brushed mine as she reached for my hand. The jolt sparked between us, easing some of my turmoil and tiredness from the physical exertion.

Are you thinking about Eldrin? She squeezed my hand comfortingly.

Of course she'd know. She was the other half of my

soul and could sense my feelings the same way I could hers. *I hope Caelan found him and wasn't forced to kill him.* I hated that I'd hinted he had my permission if needed. That I'd wanted him dead but didn't think I could do it myself without risking my magic over the debt I owed him.

Not anymore. I wouldn't feel complete unless I was the one who punished him.

I won't lie. Her gorgeous emerald eyes hardened. *I'd love to see the wildling die at your hands, especially after what he's done to us.* Her disgust made our bond feel like grainy sand.

I didn't have to know what she was remembering. Though the scar had faded from her healing magic, I remembered exactly how it had looked, especially on the night she'd received it and she'd refused to tell me what had happened.

Eldrin had threatened her Earth family if she told anyone he'd attacked her while she was bathing. The first thing I'd do to him was cut his eyes out for laying them on Lira like that. Then I'd chop off his hands for touching her before stabbing him in the heart. That would be the minimum, but based on whatever he said, I might draw out the torture in front of my people so they could see what happened to anyone who dared to hurt my mate in any way, even if it made her uncomfortable.

Don't fret. If he's alive, we'll make sure he dies a fitting death for what he's done to us, I replied. She would have a say in the ways he was punished if she desired.

The steep, jagged, ruined spikes of the land we'd been forced to relocate to broke through the skyline in the distance. Living here had been difficult for all of us, and after returning to the Unseelie land and feeling the strength it provided, the land before me didn't feel remotely like home.

I didn't notice before because I didn't have my memories, but... why do you call the places on this island the same names as the ones back in your actual home? Lira connected.

My heart grew heavy, but with Lira by my side, there was no doubt I'd be fine. At that moment, I realized she was my actual home. It was her presence. *When we relocated here, I wanted to make this place feel familiar. As a fourteen-year-old boy, I decided that using the same names would make things easier.* I'd been so young and foolish, but I'd tried.

Did it? Lira tilted her head, a few wispy pieces of her blonde hair flying into her face.

Not really, but no one questioned me. I inhaled, smelling the brimstone of the dead land we were approaching. *We were all looking for something to cling to.*

You're truly amazing. Awe swelled through the connection. *I doubt I could've done half as well as you at fourteen.*

I smirked, the tenderness of her affection and words nearly choking me. *You didn't have magic and wings, and you survived the gauntlet. I have no doubt that at ten, you would've been a better royal than me.*

"This is the land you've been living on?" Eiric gasped.

"It's amazingly awful, isn't it?" Finnian chuckled. "But yes, this has been our living quarters since your people forced us to leave our true kingdom behind."

The island was five hundred yards in front of us. The dark castle seemed to hover in the sky, and the village came into focus down below. Everywhere else was dirt and rock, proof that the dragons had killed the land before moving on.

"It's something." Eiric's voice deepened with what

sounded like pity. "I can't believe this is where they sent you."

Normally, that would have angered me, but instead, it endeared her to me a little more. She seemed to care, similar to Lira.

Concern swirled from Lira. "Tavish, when did you begin recloaking the island in shadows?"

I lifted my brows as something sank inside me. "I haven't." I was so used to it being hidden in darkness that it hadn't hit me that I wasn't the one doing it.

"Can Caelan do that?" Lira's eyes widened.

We were upon the island, but my heart stopped beating. "No. Only members of the royal line can do that."

Eldrin.

But what did this mean?

Suddenly, Eiric screamed.

Cold fear stabbed me in the chest, halting my wings. My body dropped an inch as I spun around to see Eiric straightening her body and fluttering in the same spot.

"I know our kingdom isn't pretty or nice, but do we need the theatrics?" Finnian pursed his lips, cocking a brow at her.

Eiric glared. "I *ran* into something and bounced off. It had *nothing* to do with this awful place."

Dread filled the mate bond, and between all my nerves and distractions, I noticed a faint cold tickle over my skin. *Something is brushing my skin that wasn't there before. Do you feel it?* The sensation was similar to Tavish's magic but held a distinctive edge that made my skin crawl, emphasizing that mine was only at half strength.

No, I don't, he replied, pulling me to his side, his wings moving and blocking my view of my sister. He scanned the kingdom in front of us. "Stop speaking so loudly. We don't need to reveal our presence—" He cut off abruptly as the castle doors creaked open.

I faced forward to see Eldrin flying out the front doors

with guards flanking him and more behind him. His white hair blew back in the breeze, and his dark wings flapped furiously. He wore dark armor and a dark, thorny crown on his head, contrasting with his snowy skin.

"I hope you have a plan, Tavish." Finnian's face looked strained. "Because out of every possibility, I didn't expect to return to *this*."

"Neither did I, but *he's* not the rightful king. *I* am," Tavish rasped, his wings flapping viciously. "Whatever he did doesn't matter. I am of the rightful royal blood. Everyone must follow me. I hold the strongest magic."

That wasn't how things *had* to work, but I wasn't sure I wanted to explain that to Tavish. In Earth's history, a change in leadership occurred often, and part of the time, it was due to the people revolting and wanting a new leader. Surely, that wasn't the case here; Tavish had sacrificed so much for his people... even if he'd been misguided, in my opinion.

"It's kind of hard to fly and face him when Eiric can't get in here." Finnian exhaled. "Go on, and I'll stay with her."

"No need," Eiric said and appeared at my side. "I got through." She shrugged. "It was the oddest thing."

Eldrin was only fifty yards away from us, and at least half the Unseelie people were standing in the stone streets, their eyes wide with surprise, while the remainder watched from their windows, gesturing at Tavish.

Eldrin puffed out his chest and spoke loudly, "We know the Seelie wildling is here even though we can't see her, which means my traitor of a nephew is using darkness to hide her. The small veil I put up to alert me to her return could only be triggered by a Seelie."

He was baiting Tavish. I connected with him just as I

felt the chill of his magic leaving my body, exposing us to Eldrin.

Tavish, don't.

But it was too late. Eldrin's smirk turned into a beaming smile.

Eiric and Finnian inched closer to us, our wings moving in tandem as if we were one.

There is no reason to hide, Lira. Tavish squeezed my hand, making sure everyone saw the gesture. He pushed his calm toward me with certainty. *These are my people, and the Unseelie always follow the heir of the late king. They must believe that I died, and Eldrin capitalized on that as my father's nephew. It made him the logical next king, though the magic wouldn't pass to him.*

"Why are you wearing the Unseelie crown, Eldrin?" Tavish's voice boomed, amplified by his magic so that everyone could hear.

I wished he hadn't exposed us like this. I feared that, for the first time in fae history, things wouldn't go according to expectation. Maybe I was letting my human knowledge affect me in a way that wasn't relevant here. I had to bank on that.

"When I learned you were injured, despite you turning your wings against me for a Seelie, I came to assist in mending you back to health. To my surprise, I learned you weren't anywhere in the castle and had abandoned us after two Seelies disguised themselves as our own. When your magic didn't return to cover the land, I assumed you had died in your callous attempt to free the sunscorched, and thus, I had to become the Unseelie king." Eldrin reached us and stopped as the guards lined up behind him. "I thought this would be rather clear."

I'm going to enjoy killing him, Tavish linked, rage

boiling within him. *I'll make sure he feels every bit of anger, hurt, betrayal, and vulnerability he made us feel.*

Finnian tapped the top of his head. "The crown is too large for you. Maybe you should hand it back to Tavish before you lose it."

The crown did look as if it might fall over his face at any second.

Knowing I needed to play the part of his dutiful fated mate, I laughed. "Anyone can wear a crown that doesn't belong to them, and Finnian is right. It's clear it wasn't intended for you." I smiled, noting the pale-blue-haired guard to his right.

Lorne.

The fae I'd saved and had been paired with during the gauntlet and who'd assisted in saving my life a couple of times. I thought we'd worked out some mutual respect between us, but clearly, I'd been wrong.

A sour taste filled my mouth. His loyalty to Eldrin stung like betrayal.

"You should've never come back." Eldrin bared his teeth. "And Tavish should've allowed you to die in the gauntlet."

Out of the corner of my eye, I noticed Eiric's brows furrow. She had questions, but she knew better than to ask now.

"I should've never allowed her to enter into it in the first place." Tavish tensed even more. "Lira is my fated mate, and subjecting her to any sort of mistreatment, especially the gauntlet, was the biggest mistake of all time."

A few Unseelie gasped like they hadn't expected to hear Tavish say that. A lump formed in my throat, so large I couldn't swallow. Eldrin was leading the conversation to get Tavish to say everything he needed the Unseelie to hear.

I love you for everything you're saying and doing, but your people need to know what you've done for them. Not what you wish you would've done for me.

My people need to know how important you are to me; otherwise, they'll continue to despise you. They need to see that I won't tolerate any negative or harmful actions toward you. He lifted his chin, ready to fight everyone on my behalf.

The stark change in circumstances from coming back to Unseelie territory with him this time versus last time would have been inconceivable if I hadn't been involved both times. He was the same person, but his actions were the exact opposite toward me. *Thorn, trust me. The Unseelie need to view me differently through my actions and words, not through your threats of violence.*

I could feel his turmoil. He wanted to respect my wishes like the caring mate he was, but his possessive and protective side wanted to bulldoze anyone who threatened me. I loved both sides equally, but if I wanted the Unseelies' true respect, I had to earn it.

I was my own person.

"The people saw Tavish receive a fatal blow from *Seelie* glamoured to look like us." Eldrin flicked his wrist. "This could be another Seelie trick to confuse our people."

Dread sat heavy in my stomach. Eldrin had allowed people to believe that Tavish was dead. No wonder they hadn't fought against him stepping into power, and he was using that to manipulate them now. Not surprising, but I could easily turn that back around on him. "That alone is telling."

Eldrin's neck corded. "What do you mean?"

"Tavish felt my Seelie power when it came back, and my father immediately identified Tavish upon his arrival in

Gleann Solas. Yet, you can't confirm this is your cousin. I find it interesting. Is your power so much weaker than theirs, or are you lying?" I batted my eyelashes to come off innocent.

Finnian laughed freely. "I hadn't considered that, but you're correct. Which one is it, Eldrin? Though I suspect the real answer is both."

Frowning, Eldrin took in a ragged breath.

"Allow me to ease everyone's minds." Tavish held out his hands. The sky darkened to the color it'd been before the Seelie attack. Dark clouds gathered and snow fell, landing on the dry, dark ground.

"It *is* King Tavish!" a female exclaimed from below. "He's not dead after all."

"That changes *nothing*," Eldrin spat. "He will ruin all of us if you continue to follow him. Remember the reason for the gauntlet. *She* escaped and had the cù-sìth assist her in killing some of your own people." Eldrin's mouth dropped in fake horror, and he clutched his chest. "Those actions led all the prisoners into the gauntlet, and now our resources are more scarce because the prisoners we lost were working the lands to keep up our food resources."

When Eldrin's malicious gaze landed on me, a shiver ran down my spine, and the horror of him attacking me while I was naked in the tub flashed through my memory. I hated how weak and vulnerable he'd made me feel and, worse, how it still affected me.

Tavish edged in front of me, blocking part of me from Eldrin's view, and I knew he was sensing the emotions that raged through me. His own fury spiked.

"That may be true, but I know Lira, and she would never attack anyone unprovoked." Finnian straightened his shoulders, showing not only his support for Tavish but for me as well. "If anyone attacked her, she deserved to defend herself, the same as anyone here."

My chest expanded uncomfortably. Even though Finnian liked to give people hell, he'd be receiving a hug from me later.

"And *you* orchestrated the games and the rules this time." Tavish karate-chopped the air. "I didn't interfere. At your request."

Eldrin laughed bitterly. "But you did interfere multiple times, even ending the last game before she died."

"Even though I understand you'd never favor me in any situation because I'm Seelie, there is a more prominent reason that you wanted to ensure I died as quickly as possible." Not wanting to be seen as a coward, I flew around and hovered beside Tavish. "Something both Tavish and I might have found rather interesting if I'd regained my memories before I perished."

His face blanched, and I clenched my hands to prevent myself from raising my fist upward in celebration.

"Guards, capture them and take them to the prison cell." Eldrin gestured at Tavish and me, making sure the guards understood exactly who he meant. "Do not kill any of them. We need fresh prisoners to man the lands since all the others died during the gauntlet."

When none of the guards moved, some of the cold tendrils of fear loosened within me. I'd expected them to obey Eldrin, but their inaction validated what Tavish knew: the Unseelie would follow him. My doubt had been unwarranted.

Silence blanketed the entire kingdom, and Eiric placed her right hand on the hilt of her sword, preparing for an attack.

Face flushing gray, Eldrin snarled, "*Now!* And if anyone

doesn't move, they'll be locked in the prison alongside them."

Lorne moved first, flying toward us, with the next handful of guards following his lead.

Some of my hope died, and each breath felt like a struggle. This was what I'd feared.

"Do *not* obey him. I *am* the rightful king and heir. He's committing treason." Tavish's irises turned the stormy gray that warned anyone of his temper who rose against him. "If you go against me, I will be forced to kill each one of you for your betrayal. You won't get a chance to sit in a prison cell."

The guards paused, glancing back and forth between the two of them.

"Are you listening to *him* when he is protecting a *Seelie royal* over his own people? If my father hadn't died when he had, there would be no questioning my order." Eldrin glared at each guard and then glanced down at the rest of the Unseelie.

My chest tightened. He was pleading with the masses. *Tavish, end this before it goes too far.*

"He killed two guards on the first day she arrived before ever claiming her as his fated mate." Eldrin held out his hands. "He allowed you to believe he had died when, clearly, he's alive and standing before you now. And why did he allow you to believe he perished? So he could abandon you without consequences while retrieving the Seelie princess. By going there and bringing her back with him, he's declared war with the Seelie. A war we cannot win in our current state. The safest thing to do—until we can rise again—is to lock him up and give the princess back when the Seelie king comes for her. Tavish ruined our chance of taking our rightful lands back."

"Do not listen to him." Tavish had the snow falling

harder, and the temperature had dropped fifty degrees within the last minute. "He's been conspiring against *me* and *us* since my father died. He claims he saved my life, but he didn't. Lira is the one who tended to my wounds and kept me alive. All Eldrin did was retrieve me from the holding cell. Nothing more than that."

The way the guards' heads went back and forth between Eldrin and Tavish reminded me of watching a Ping-Pong game. They still hadn't come to detain us, which counted for something.

"I *did* save your life and our people." Eldrin clenched his hands. "What sort of life would we have with our ruler captured and under the Seelie's control? *None.* We'd have wound up working for them and doing everything at their will. By rescuing you from the castle, I ensured we had the royal power back."

"That is not the life obligation you had me believe." Tavish's face twisted in anger and betrayal, the sting overwhelming me through our bond. "And maybe we could have bridged the divide between us and the Seelie if I'd remained with them after I healed for a short while. Maybe they wouldn't have exiled all of our people in this awful land, afraid of my thirst for revenge, and we'd still have direct access to our Unseelie magic."

"I did what I believed was right." Eldrin clenched his hands. "Which I've continued to do every day since coming here. I've advised you and always put our people first while you threw everything away for a sunscorched princess."

"Long live King Eldrin," a few Unseelie chanted from below, making my heart stop.

Shock pulsed from Tavish, followed by a crushing sense of anguish.

More and more chimed in while Eldrin's grin stretched into a gigantic smile.

Even though numerous fae didn't chant and instead frowned, they remained quiet as the majority showed support for Eldrin.

"We need to *leave* before we're imprisoned," Eiric growled from beside me.

I hated that she was right.

"No. They can't turn on me." Tavish breathed raggedly. "I'm their king."

"Tav, she's right," Finnian agreed.

I understood his issue—leaving would make him look weak. *We leave and regroup. Then we'll come back and kill Eldrin. If we get caught, it'll be harder—*

"Seize them!" Eldrin shouted again.

This time, the guards obeyed, yielding to the masses.

"We're not going anywhere," Tavish seethed as fury shot through him and into our bond.

A moment later, magic pulsed through our connection from *him*, which had never happened before. His magic felt sludgy and heavy, resembling the nightmares I used to have when he would watch me through my dreams.

Eldrin grunted, and the smile dropped from his face, his expression changing into one of discontent that eventually crumpled his features into pure terror.

People on the street screamed, and I understood what Tavish was doing.

He was using his illusion magic.

A few guards jerked back as if something they feared stood right before them.

"Thank god we're on his side," Eiric muttered, watching the chaos unfold in front of us.

Tavish released my hand and removed a dagger from his

sheath, his sights on Eldrin.

He had to die, and I wouldn't stop Tavish... not after this.

"Death to the sunscorched wildling!" a woman a few feet below shouted near the edge of the houses closest to us.

A whistling noise filled the air, and something sharp pierced my wing and lodged into the other. Agony coursed through me, stealing my breath. Worse, my wings stopped moving correctly, like air was flying through them, and I dropped.

Lira, Tavish linked, his magic leaving our bond and terror replacing his wrath. He followed me, swooping below me to gather me in his arms. When he caught me and moved forward, two guards appeared at his sides and threw chains around his arms, cutting off his magic. They gripped his biceps, the chains biting through his skin and drawing blood. The pressure forced him to release me.

No! Tavish shouted as my body rushed toward the water again.

Unfortunately, my magic struggled to come through, and I couldn't make the water yield to my power. Like something blocked it. My wings tried catching the air, but they weren't working well, merely stopping my fall. The wound where the weapon had lodged into my wing burned and pulsed, and I bit my tongue to stop from crying out.

The sounds of blades clashing had me glancing up. Eiric was fighting three Unseelie guards and Finnian was fighting five. Each set had chains to capture them, but I didn't have time to focus on that. I had to watch the woman below as she readied to shoot at me again.

Pale blue flashed, and strong arms wrapped around me. It wasn't Tavish but Lorne. He didn't hurt me, though he flew back upward toward Eldrin.

"Don't hurt the Seelie anymore." Eldrin rolled his eyes, though he gave the command too late. "Due to Tavish's poor decisions, we will have to use them to keep the Seelie from obliterating us. It's a means to survival."

When I glanced up, Tavish had a dagger held to his neck by a third guard as two guards held his arms back. Eiric and Finnian had been detained too, and Eldrin's eyes twinkled with glee.

Acid burned my throat over seeing my mate like that. The snow no longer came down, emphasizing his power was completely bound.

Lira, I'm so sorry, he linked, sounding broken.

It's not your fault. I didn't need him to fall apart. *Stay strong. We'll find a way through this.*

"Take all of them to the prison cells." Eldrin crossed his arms as he sneered at us. "We may have to use them as leverage over the Seelie, but they'll live a prisoner's life here."

Lorne nodded. "As you wish," he said gruffly, and his arms tightened painfully around me.

The guards dragged us toward the castle with Tavish, Finnian, and Eiric bound by chains, suppressing their magic.

We flew in through one of the sizable windows near the back by the prison cells. The dark tile and stone that had once felt like home now felt like a trap.

The guards took us through the hallways' twists and turns, and soon the cells came into view, accompanied by the scents of piss and feces.

And my gaze landed on something that made me sicker. Something that had my heart shattering into smaller pieces than I ever could have expected.

My heart hammered as I took in a crumpled Caelan who lay next to a beaten Nightbane. The cù-sìth's snout had a large gash as if someone had struck it with the end of a blade, and dark blood covered the green ends of his fur.

I suspected Caelan wouldn't appear any better.

Worse, there were no mattresses in the cell, which forced them to lie on the stone floor with no blankets or pillows.

Lorne pushed me more gently than I'd expected, but my wing jerked, and pain sliced through me again. The pain was worse than being stabbed in the arm and shoulder.

"I should've killed you at the close of the gauntlet," Tavish seethed. "Of course, at the first opportunity to harm my mate, you'd inflict misery upon her. Everyone who lays hands on her will die at the end of my sword or by my magic. I vow to each and every one of you." His concern for me swirled within me, but the connection between us had cooled since he didn't have access to his magic.

The door to the small cell that held Nightbane and

Caelan opened, and Lorne pushed me inside. My back muscles jerked, causing my wings to spasm, and I could feel the skin of the wing with the arrow lodged in it rip further.

Tavish's, Eiric's, and Finnian's guards kept them in place at the door as Lorne walked toward a wall where more chains for wings hung. My stomach dropped as he picked up three, but then I paused. He'd forgotten about one of us.

Nightbane's eyes opened and flashed a lime green as he jumped to his feet. He snarled, but the sound was broken as if they'd injured his throat. He limped to his spot beside me.

"Do you need to learn your lesson again, death beast?" asked the dark-brown-haired woman who held Finnian hostage. "The only reason you're alive is because of the bad luck bestowed upon the race that kills your kind."

My heart heavied and my mouth dried. I needed to know everything they'd done to this poor animal. Nightbane was fierce, but only to those who mistreated him... Tavish included. To me, he was the most loyal friend in the palace.

"Don't antagonize them." Lorne sighed as he placed the chains on Tavish's wings first.

Tavish tried to break free from the guards, flapping his wings and attempting to force the chains off him, but Lorne secured the lock in seconds.

Lorne continued as if Tavish hadn't fought him at all. "Not until we have everyone secured in the cell."

The bond pulsed in tune with his rapid heartbeat, and our connection clenched from his panic. I remembered my panic the day I'd had my wings restrained, and I'd had them back for only a day. Tavish had used his wings his entire life and didn't know anything without them.

The navy-blue-haired guard mashed his lips together,

and the dark-brown-haired guard shoved Tavish inside the cell toward me, causing him to trip over Nightbane.

Nightbane whimpered, and I bent to help my mate. My wings moved again, and more pain shot through me as my wing ripped even more. Tavish dropped to his knees while Nightbane dropped to the cold stone floor.

Tears burned my eyes, but I blinked them back, refusing to cry in front of the guards. I turned to help Tavish and pushed my agony away. *Are you hurt?*

I'm fine, Tavish replied. *Better than you are. The more you move, the worse your injury will be. I just bruised my knees.* As if to support his claim, Tavish quickly climbed to his feet and turned to face the guard who'd shoved him.

"You will pay for that, Ecoar." Tavish bared his teeth.

The guard snorted. "I don't fear you. Eldrin may keep you alive because of your blood, but that doesn't mean we view you as true royalty anymore. You picked a sunscorched over us." He spat on the ground, barely missing Tavish's black boots.

My blood boiled, and it had nothing to do with the insult he'd lobbed at me. The fae part of me that had been dormant for so long came rushing out. "I can't wait to slit your throat and replace that cocky grin with the knowledge that you're dying." This guard had gone too far. Turning on Tavish hadn't been enough. He'd had to belittle him, physically abuse him, and taunt him just to make himself feel better.

"You expect me to feel threatened by *you* when you mourned an Unseelie who tried to kill you during the games?" He rocked back on his feet, expanding his wings. "We all know you're weak."

"I'd rather be weak than use a horrible opportunity to pretend to have a big dick." My mouth was running again, and there was no stopping it. I almost felt like I had when I first got here. "I'd threaten to cut it off, but I doubt I could find it quickly enough. So I'll settle for your throat."

Finnian laughed as he was led in by his guards. Unlike Tavish, they weren't manhandling him, which I assumed was because Finnian had never had any say over them. They resented Tavish for so many reasons, and this was their first opportunity to act on it without immediate repercussions.

"Good point, Lira." Finnian smiled, but it didn't reach his eyes. "I've never heard anyone compliment his lovemaking. That has to be why."

Ecoar expanded his wings, which were below average in size. "Insult me again. I dare you."

"Well, if you insist—" Finnian started.

Not holding back, Ecoar threw a punch at Finnian's jaw, but Finnian ducked, and the guard caught air, further embarrassing himself.

"Enough," Lorne snapped, shuffling Eiric inside.

My sister's face turned a sickly yellow as her wings ruffled under the chains. Lorne didn't manhandle her, but that didn't lessen my sense of betrayal as he turned his back on me. I hadn't realized that I felt like we had forged some sort of mutual respect during the trial. If not for him, I'd be dead.

"We have priorities that require our full attention, like watching for the Seelie who could show up at any second." Lorne turned his back on us like we weren't a threat. "All of you are aware of the risks, and we need to speak to King Eldrin about that threat on the horizon."

Ecoar's wings lowered to his sides, though a vein bulged between his eyes.

Lorne stepped back into the hallway and locked the cell door.

"What about the princess?" the woman guard asked, gesturing to my wings.

My pulse galloped. I'd hoped that no one would notice I was unchained. If they didn't bind my wings, I could use my magic to heal myself, which I desperately needed to do if we were going to get out of this place... somehow.

"Let her suffer for a while longer. We'd have to remove the arrow to get the chains to sit properly on her. The others will try to help her, causing her pain and then feeling bad about it." Lorne looked over his shoulder at me and wrinkled his nose. "When I come back later to check on them, I'll put the chains on her. Her wings will be more raw and bloody."

Lorne was a vicious bastard. No wonder he'd been friends with Eldrin before getting placed in jail for rising against Tavish. His loyalties changed as often as Nightbane shed fur, which was daily.

A few of the guards chuckled as Lorne led them away.

He didn't glance back as they left the prison area.

"I vow to you, Lira. I will make everyone who turned against us suffer." Tavish moved beside me, touching my wing.

A sharp sting shot through my wing and a deep ache shot into my muscles. I was trying to keep them stationary to avoid further damage.

Nightbane tried to stand beside me again, but he whimpered and flopped back onto his stomach. I could only imagine the agony he'd been in as he'd tried to protect me when I entered the cell.

"Let me look," Eiric said, and she carefully stepped around Nightbane while not trampling Caelan.

The cell barely fit two people, but the guards had forced all four of us in here with Caelan and Nightbane. We wouldn't be able to sleep comfortably, but at least we were all together.

Let me change places so she can take a look at my wings. Eiric didn't have expert healing knowledge, but our parents had taught us basic first aid.

As I shifted my weight to walk around Tavish and not step on Nightbane, the muscles in my back moved, and the wound around the arrow stretched apart. A tear trailed down my cheek before I could stop it, and I groaned faintly.

We should never have come back here. Tavish's guilt weighed on our bond. *We should've stayed in the Unseelie underground house.*

I took his hands, enjoying the electric jolt that shot between us as I faced him. Eiric stepped into the opening in the corner, and Finnian hurried to Caelan. My wings were in Eiric's view, and my heart hammered.

We had to come back. Your people need you. I wanted him to realize that this was an opportunity for mercy and not fear. Fear didn't drive loyalty. He had to see things more clearly. *Besides, we'd be miserable living underground and never feeling the wind in our wings.*

"Did you see who shot you?" Eiric asked.

My breath caught. "Yes, but I'm not sure why that matters." The woman had done what she'd been taught to do, hate Seelie and kill them whenever she could.

"Because the bitch lodged that arrow perfectly, and I can't wait to repay the favor." Eiric huffed dramatically. "She hit your wings almost directly in the center, meaning each flap will cause further damage."

"We'll put her in chains and hoist her so every Unseelie can see her withering in pain with an arrow in the exact

spot as Lira while we let her starve and bleed to death."
Tavish's body tensed as he cupped my cheek and whispered, "So tell us, sprite. Who did this to you? Describe her
for me. I will get retribution for you."

I bit my bottom lip as warmth surged through me. I
cherished how much he loved me. "Don't encourage him,
Eiric." I tried to chastise him, but the words came out
breathless.

A deep, low groan came from Caelan. "Finn?" he asked
groggily. "Is that you?"

Thank Fate he was awake.

"We've returned." Finnian's forehead lined with worry.

"You need to leave..." Caelan opened his eyes, and he
clutched Finnian's hand. "Before—" His gaze landed on us,
and he stopped.

Caelan's loyalty made my heart expand, and I could feel
Tavish's relief from hearing his friend speak and knowing
he'd tried to warn us.

"You're too late for that warning." Finnian winked, but
his eyes didn't twinkle in their usual way.

I couldn't blame him. I didn't see a way for us to get out
of this situation. Eldrin had us right where he wanted us,
and he had the crown.

"We need to get this arrow out, or it could tear up her
entire wing." Eiric reached around my wings, placing a
hand on my arm. "It'll hurt."

"Don't sugarcoat it or anything," I tried to tease, but my
words fell flat.

Tavish's eyes darkened almost to onyx as his worry
choked me.

She chuckled, playing along. "I'll be blunter next time."

I turned to see her face, which twisted with concern.

"Did one of the Unseelie do that to her?" Caelan's

unswollen eye widened, and a cut on his bottom lip reopened. Black blood oozed down his chin.

"They won't be Unseelie for much longer," Tavish answered, stepping close to me.

"Finnian, I need your help," Eiric commanded. "Can you assist me?"

"Of course." Finnian helped Caelan prop himself against the stone wall and moved to stand next to Eiric. He winced as his eyes skimmed my injury.

Eiric rubbed her hands together. "I need you to hold down her wing there. It can't move when I break the arrow in the center. If it jerks, the arrow could rip through her wing."

I swallowed loudly. I wished they could speak telepathically so I didn't have to hear this.

"Understood." Finnian nodded sternly.

"Good." Eiric stared at Tavish and said, "I need you to calm her the best you can and make sure she faces you the entire time."

Not wanting this moment to drag out longer than it needed, I turned to face Tavish again. He lowered his forehead to mine, the tingling thrum between us, and placed his hands on my shoulders.

You're going to be fine. He kissed my lips. *We'll get through this.*

"On the count of three," Eiric said. She stepped between my wings and squatted. When she touched both sides of the arrow, the pressure made the throbbing deeper and more uncomfortable.

"One..."

Finnian stepped behind Eiric, getting into place. Though I couldn't see him, I felt his presence.

My ears rang from anticipation. I wasn't sure I could handle what came next.

"Two..."

Two large, strong hands gripped the top part of my wings, and the arrow jerked. A cracking sound split the air as agony ripped through me.

I tried leaping forward, but Tavish's hands secured me in place. And when Eiric yanked the arrow from my wing, I was certain this was what dying felt like. It hurt worse than when I'd actually died after the gauntlet.

I cried out, a sob racking my chest. I hated sounding so weak, but I couldn't contain the sound. I crumpled into Tavish's arms while Nightbane tossed his head back and howled heartbreakingly.

Sprite, I'm so sorry, Tavish linked, kissing my forehead as Finnian released my wings. *I never should've taken you from Earth.*

I couldn't stop my chest from heaving again. *Don't you dare say that. I wouldn't change a thing, even with all the chaos. You've made me the happiest I've ever been.*

I don't deserve you. I should've let you live and be happy. You wouldn't have known any differently.

Not true. I stepped toward him, staring at his blurry face. *I never found anyone interesting and always felt alone. I never dated anyone... kissed anyone... never wanted to until you showed up that night to bring me here. Even then, I felt a connection to you. There's no going back, and I wouldn't change it. You're my home now... not Gleann Solas, Cuil Dorcha, or Earth. Just you.*

He ran one hand through my hair and used the hem of his tunic to dry my eyes. When I could see clearly, what I found destroyed me.

Tears rolled down his own face. *We will get out of here and regain the throne, and if I have to burn this realm down to keep you safe, that's what I'll do. I will do anything for you.*

The warmth surged between us, and the truth behind his words had blood pumping through my body, making every cell come alive. I understood what he was saying. The past twelve years had been one hardship after another for him, and it needed to end. We deserved to be together and find joy and peace. We shouldn't have to face challenge after challenge. *I feel the same for you. I left Seelie to come here and be with you.*

"May I examine the arrow?" Caelan asked, bringing me back to the present.

"Sure," Eiric answered.

"Maybe we can use the arrow tip as a weapon?" Finnian shuffled backward.

Folding my wings in to give us more room made them feel as if they were being ripped apart again despite the arrow being removed. The damage was done and needed time to heal. Unable to fully close them, I pulled them back, and Tavish moved so we could face everyone and took my hand.

"It's two inches long." Tavish arched a brow. "And the guards know we have it... so what do you propose?"

Caelan held a piece of the broken arrow in his hands and lifted it to his nose.

"Maybe we can poke their eyes out." Finnian shrugged. "Or give it to Lira so she can stab Ecoar in the penis."

"No." Caelan dropped his hands. "This doesn't make sense."

Silence descended as we all stared at Caelan. What did he know?

Tavish went as still as a statue while my chest heaved, though I was still in torment from the injury to my wings.

"See." Finnian crossed his arms, shoving his hands under his armpits. "Even Caelan knows Ecoar's penis is too small to be found. A two-inch arrowhead would still be too large to remove it."

Forehead creasing, Eiric blinked. "I'm certain he wasn't referring to that particular comment."

Even Nightbane huffed at the end of Eiric's sentence, adding to her point.

When things settled, I'd have to heal the poor beast. He didn't deserve to be in misery. He'd become what Tavish and the others had forced him to be.

"It wasn't." Caelan frowned then grimaced. Blood dripped down his chin from the crack in his lip. "The wood here isn't the dried bark of the ruined lands. It's from the true Unseelie kingdom."

Shock and concern swirled through Tavish. "Only the

guards are supposed to use those weapons. How did a townsfae get hold of one?"

"Obviously someone provided it to her." Finnian pursed his lips. "But they would know that doing something like that is punishable by death."

"Death?" I choked. "That seems extreme for merely using an arrow from your homeland."

"Those arrows are more deadly because they're infused with Unseelie magic." Tavish lifted a hand. His wings flexed, but the chains held them in place. He tensed, and I could see the flash of stormy gray in his eyes from his anger. He exhaled and continued, "They are the strongest weapons we have, more so than our swords, and are to be used only in dire circumstances. The metal isn't as strong because it isn't forged solely from Unseelie metals. It's a mix of Seelie as well, which helped form the point the way we needed to."

"If she was attacked with Unseelie magic, shouldn't the damage be worse?" Eiric rolled her shoulders. "The cold out there alone had me turning into an icicle, and your magic wasn't even centered on me."

"I'm assuming it wasn't worse because our fated-mate bond is complete." Tavish took my hand. "I broke through the Seelie veil when Finnian couldn't, but then the guards took down the veil temporarily to pull him through, and when we returned here, Lira got through while you couldn't. Our fated-mate connection protected her, and the blood Eldrin stole from her must have created a veil strong enough to keep you out for a short time. Once it blocked you the first time, the veil came down because he didn't take enough to form anything stronger."

My gut lurched as if I'd been kicked. "Eldrin didn't scold anyone for harming me until after the arrow was shot." Had that been his intention? To damage my wings? But why? What was the point?

"She must have been aiming for the muscles at the base of your wing and missed." Caelan shifted around and grunted. "That would've caused each flap to rip your muscles more."

Finnian's blue eyes widened. "The actual base of your wings, leaving you unable to fly ever again. A Seelie princess that can only walk would make the Seelie appear weak, especially to the dragons."

That would be the only benefit. *I almost wish they'd succeeded. Then Prince Pyralis wouldn't be interested in me.*

Wait. That wasn't true. I enjoyed flying, and I refused to have another thing taken away. My parents and the dragons had already influenced my life too much.

Don't speak like that. Tavish's anger swirled within me. *The fact that you want to sacrifice something so precious makes my hatred for the ashbreath grow more.* His breathing quickened, and his jaw clenched. *It's bad enough that he touched you, but this makes it worse. I will kill him for even looking in your direction.*

"I'm hoping you know a way to get out of here." Eiric sighed. "Do you have a secret key or tunnel? Something no one knows about?"

Tavish shook his head. "I don't know of another way out, but we didn't build this castle. It belonged to the dragons. They lived on this island and ruined the lands before heading to the next island they now claim as their home."

Eyes widening, Eiric glanced around the dark cell. "The prince lived here at one time?"

"All the dragon royals." Caelan leaned his head against the wall. "Not just the prince."

"Right. Of course." She laughed breathily.

Nightbane lowered his head, a faint whimper coming from deep in his chest. Unable to handle it anymore, I released Tavish's hand and squatted next to him. When I touched his fur, my wings screamed in torment, but I ignored the pain. My friend required comfort.

I cringed when my hand touched the dried blood in his fur. I fought through the instinct to jerk my hand back, and Nightbane let out a contented sigh.

Realization washed over me. I knew we'd talked about keeping my healing ability a secret, but I trusted everyone here. I lifted my head to meet Tavish's gaze. Soon I would have chains on my wings, preventing me from tapping into my magic. I remembered the way I'd felt during the gauntlet when they'd chained my newly returned wings. Part of me had gone missing. I could only imagine what it would feel like now that I'd grown accustomed to them. *If I heal us enough that we regain some of our strength while still looking injured, we might have a better chance to get out of here.* I nibbled on my bottom lip, dreading Tavish's response.

He closed his eyes and pinched the bridge of his nose.

I pressed on, knowing his one weakness. *If I don't heal myself, I won't be able to fly if we get a chance soon. But if I heal myself, the others might notice and ask questions.*

The corners of his lips tipped upward, and when he opened his eyes, the irises had lightened marginally. *You're learning how to get your way with me, sprite. I'm not sure I like it.*

I crinkled my nose, trying not to return a smile. Even in a cramped jail cell, he made the world seem less bleak, if only for a moment. *That's not what your face is saying.*

You and Eiric speak so strangely still, even with your memories restored. He exhaled, allowing his shoulders to hunch. *I assume, since my face can't actually speak, you're suggesting I'm not upset that you know me so well, and you're right. I blasting love that you know you're my weakness. Your well-being and happiness surpass everything.*

Nightbane lifted his head and stared into my eyes. The light-green color pulled at my heart. I could ease his pain.

Eiric has proven she'll do whatever's needed to keep you safe, and I trust Finnian and Caelan. Since you're right and we're in a dire situation, I agree with you, especially about healing your wings.

Some of the weight lifted from my body, and the healing magic swirled deep within me, readying to release. My magic was weak, but I had enough to repair some of the damage.

My gaze dropped back to Nightbane, and I allowed the warm, healing magic to flow into my wings and through my hand.

The sharp pain in my wings faded. I couldn't heal us completely. The guards would come and place chains on my wings to restrain me, and I couldn't be back to normal health. But I could have the wounds scabbing over.

I allowed the magic to flow freely into Nightbane and watched as the cut on his nose slowly closed. His breathing became less labored, and he opened his large mouth, allowing his tongue to roll out.

Eiric sucked in a breath. "That dog's nose is healing. How is that possible? Is that part of his magic?"

"What?" Finnian yawned, and then he gasped. "No. Cù-sìth heal like normal fae."

"You two, calm down." Tavish turned his back toward me to address the others. "Don't alert anyone outside this cell. Lira is healing him, but that secret remains between us.

That's how I know Eldrin isn't the one who saved me. Lira came to me that night. She kept me from dying."

Caelan's head tilted back. "How long have you known this?"

"Since her memories came back while we were in Gleann Solas."

"That must be why she didn't die at the end of the gauntlet." Finnian clasped his hands together. "We all heard her heart stop. I'm so glad Lira is here. She's made our world so much more interesting. If she wasn't yours—"

A deep, threatening snarl came from Tavish's chest, and even though our bond was cool, the heat of his anger bled through.

"Finish that sentence and I shall kill you here with my bare hands." Tavish's words ended in a snarl. "And I won't have one ounce of regret for doing it."

"Just let me finish." Finnian smiled widely, showing his teeth. "You could be wrong."

Calean hung his head. "Finnian, this isn't the time to pester him. Do you value your own life?"

"We don't have time for any of this." Eiric's jaw dropped. "We shouldn't be expending energy. We should be saving it for later. And what is this gauntlet everyone keeps speaking of, and how did Lira almost die? Why weren't the king and queen informed of this?"

My chest tightened. She wouldn't like the answer about the gauntlet. "This is how Finnian copes with stress, and the gauntlet is in the past. None of that matters now. It's over." At times like this, I wondered how Tavish and Finnian had remained friends, but then I remembered how loyal Finnian was to us. He just enjoyed riling up Tavish. *If you ignored him, he wouldn't do it nearly as often. He won't say what you expect. Just let him finish so E doesn't kill him because she doesn't like jokes in situations like these.*

Nor do I, Tavish replied and clenched his hands at his sides.

My wings still ached, but the pain no longer stole my breath. I pulled my healing magic back in. Neither Nightbane nor I needed to be completely healed. Doing this much might already raise questions. Still... I couldn't allow my friend to suffer like that.

When I dropped my hands, Nightbane climbed to his feet and shook out his fur like he wanted to get the blood off. That would require water, and even though I could do that, I didn't want the guards to notice I was back here using magic.

"Let me get past you two," I murmured, knowing Caelan needed some of my magic.

As I stepped between Tavish and Finnian, I felt the toll that healing Nightbane and myself had taken on me. A decent amount of my magic had been used, and it thrummed inside me faintly. Healing Caelan even a little was better than nothing.

When I reached him, I touched his arm and pushed my magic toward him before it dried up.

"Lira's nonanswer is bad. That's her habit when she knows I'll be pissed," Eiric answered. "Someone better tell me what happened to my sister."

My stomach dropped. She wasn't letting this go, and I couldn't blame her. If I were in her wings, I'd want to know the same damn thing.

"She escaped and fought with some of our people," Tavish answered, causing a warning sensation to course down my back. My magic vanished, along with most of my energy. Dammit, I hadn't healed Caelan enough.

I spun around to find Tavish with his head lowered, staring at the floor. Normally, he was composed and confident, but at this moment, he appeared broken.

We wouldn't do the thing where he took the blame and let Eiric hate him, so I interjected, "When a prisoner goes against the rules, the punishment is to have all the prisoners fight each other. If Tavish hadn't called for it to happen, they would've killed me on the spot. At the end of the last game, Tavish interfered and saved my life, which is why I'm standing here today."

"You *bastard*." Eiric bared her teeth at him, and Nightbane growled.

He inched in front of Tavish, his eyes glowing as he stared at my sister.

"I'm not sure what 'bastard' means, but given the hate with which you said it, I agree." Tavish straightened, regret clinging to him like a second skin. "I should've done something before then, and I wish there was a way to go back and do it now."

I had no doubt he would let Eiric hurt him as punishment, but we wouldn't do that.

Pushing through so I stood between Eiric and Nightbane, I faced my sister. "I'm fine, and we need to focus on a way to get out of here. He's beaten himself up over it enough. Let's leave the past behind."

Eiric gritted her teeth. "Fine, but when this is over, this conversation isn't. Do you understand?" The way her emerald-green eyes hardened told me there was no negotiation. The question was merely a formality with one acceptable answer.

"Fine." I patted Nightbane's head.

A groan had me spinning around to find Caelan slowly climbing to his feet. His swollen eye had healed some, making it look an even deeper black, and his lip had a scab.

"I wish I could've done more." The injury to my wings had reversed any recovery I'd made since passing out in the woods. "But—"

Caelan raised a hand. "I'm a lot better. Believe me. It doesn't hurt to breathe anymore."

"What in blighted abyss happened when we left?" Finnian asked.

"A few hours after you left, the snow melted, and the sun came out fully. Eldrin flew in front of the castle doors, proclaiming he was the new ruler and that Tavish had died." Caelan sighed. "Me and the guards who knew tried to tell everyone you were alive, but Eldrin is convincing, and we had no way of knowing if you'd died while at Cuil Dorcha. Eldrin beat me to a pulp in front of everyone, proclaiming me a traitor, and had me thrown in here. I've been here since you left."

My chest constricted.

"They haven't been feeding me or giving me water, so I've been growing weak."

"The same blasted thing the Seelie did to us." Finnian's eyes narrowed.

Which meant they would be doing the same to the rest of us. That was why they'd crammed us in here together—to ensure we had no room to sleep comfortably.

Silence hung around us, and the tension could've been sliced with a knife. We were in a horrible situation, and I doubted we'd be getting out.

"Everyone, think." Tavish leaned against the cell wall. "There has to be something we can do."

No one spoke for a long time. My legs cramped from standing, but I didn't want to sit on that nasty floor. I had no clue how long we stood there, but it felt like hours. My only comfort was having Tavish's arm around my waist.

"Please tell me someone's figured out a strategy by now." Finnian sighed as the sound of footsteps headed our way.

I turned so my wings couldn't easily be seen, and I partly hid Eiric. She was Seelie too, and I didn't want her to be mistreated like I had been before.

The steps were slow and unhurried... like they were letting us know they were coming.

It had to be a scare tactic, and unfortunately, it impacted me, even if I didn't want it to.

Eldrin and Lorne rounded the corner, and Eldrin's heartless silver eyes focused on Tavish. "Dear cousin. I hope things aren't too cramped in that cell of yours." He grinned.

Tavish's face turned stony, but he didn't reply.

"Don't fret. I have plans for your pet." He nodded toward the door.

Lorne removed a key and slipped it into our cell lock.

There were two of them. This was the moment we could use to escape. Eldrin's arrogance would work in our favor.

Tavish shoved past me, preparing to fight to keep me here. Nightbane snarled at my side.

"Bran, handle the beast and Tavish," Eldrin commanded.

Bran? The twin brother of the woman I'd been forced to kill in the final round of the gauntlet. The strike from his sword was what had killed me... temporarily.

A guard stepped around the castle wall of the cell, green hair sticking out from under his helmet, confirming my fear. "It'll be my pleasure." And then his green eyes darkened, and Tavish, Nightbane, and the others crumpled in the cell. Everyone but me.

What's wrong?

He's using his illusion magic on us, making us feel pain and fear.

Bran had done that to me in the tournament. With Tavish's magic bound, he couldn't protect himself. I needed to protect them, but Lorne opened the door, grabbed my arm, and pulled me out. He led me away from the cell.

I heard a *click,* informing me they'd all been locked in again.

"Lira!" Tavish screamed.

My heart pounded in my ears, and I tried jerking out of Lorne's grasp.

"It won't work, Lira." Lorne tightened his grip on me.

He led me into another holding cell where several large bowls sat on the floor. Bile inched up my throat.

I had no doubt what this was about. The same reason Eldrin had attacked me in the tub.

He wanted my blood. He wanted to drain me.

I had to get out of here because there was no coming back from blood loss.

Lorne paused, but then his hand tightened on mine, and he pulled me inside the cell I'd stayed in the first night Tavish had brought me here.

The cot remained against the wall near the bowls. The cell could have been left untouched since the last time I'd been inside, except Malikor's blood and decimated wing had been removed and the bowls placed on the floor. Malikor, a guard, had been injured, courtesy of Tavish as a punishment for attempting to harm me.

Two pairs of footsteps headed my way, and my blood froze. Unfortunately, it had nothing to do with Tavish's magic and everything to do with the paralyzing fear Eldrin held over me. Ever since the attack in the bath, my palms became sweaty around him.

"Help me," I murmured, staring directly into Lorne's eyes. I swore I saw a flash of something reflecting back at me, but then his eyes turned back to an emotionless, blank gaze.

"Even with your wings and memories back, you're still weak." Eldrin breezed through the door, joining us in the cell. "Begging a former competitor to help you is quite pathetic. The fated-mate connection has to be the reason Tavish finds you appealing. You may be nice to admire from the shadows." He winked. "But that's the only pleasant thing about you."

I shivered, and he smirked. He wanted to remind me of the tub attack, and I'd given him the very thing he wanted, confirming he had power over me.

That ended now. I refused to inflate his ego any more. I stood tall, ignoring what Eldrin had in store for me. My magic remained depleted, but there was no way in hell I'd stand here and allow him to drain *me*. I had every intention of getting away. "You say I'm weak, but I'm one of the few prisoners who survived the gauntlet."

What's happening? Tavish connected.

I wasn't sure what to say. If I told him, he'd be more upset, but he couldn't do a thing about it. *Eldrin is just being himself. I'm getting him talking.* I'd distract him for as long as I could.

"You were meant to *die*." Eldrin's face strained with anger. "You only survived because of Tavish's interference. He was the king our people needed until he brought you back from Earth."

A lump lodged in my throat. No wonder Tavish had changed so much from twelve years ago. He'd believed his cousin had saved him, and he'd wanted Eldrin's approval. "If that's the case, why did Tavish have to stab you the first year he became king?"

His face darkened to the color of a bruise. "The day he stabbed me, I realized he had become vicious enough to lead our people in our trying times. I merely stood beside him and guided him until he grew weak once more."

"Do you think we're that stupid?" I spat, trying to get

the horrid taste from my mouth. "You've been preparing for this moment the entire time."

He shrugged, and all the tension eased from his face. "None of that matters. Now we strategize how to protect the Unseelie from the Seelie."

"Your Majesty, I thought you said we wouldn't kill her." Lorne sounded disinterested.

Eldrin arched a brow. "If I say I changed my mind, will you have a problem with that?"

"I would've worn something else. This is my best armor." He frowned. "If the Seelie attack, I'd rather know the blood I'm coated in came from warriors on their side and not mix it with such an easy kill."

All hope vanished. Lorne wouldn't aid me. I felt like a balloon that had lost all its air, but I refused to give up because that was what Eldrin wanted—to break me.

"We aren't going to kill her, but we do need a decent amount of her blood." Eldrin gestured to the bowls. "We can't handle a full Seelie attack yet, so we need enough to create a strong barrier like theirs. They used my uncle's blood to keep us from entering Ardanos, so we will use the Seelie princess's blood to keep them out."

There was one flaw in that logic. "How will that work with Seelie inside? Won't that negate the barrier?"

He rocked back on his heels. "Not if your magic is bound."

I swallowed. I hadn't considered the chains. Was that why Father had placed them on Tavish and Finnian so quickly, to rebalance the magical veil? I had to think more like a royal and consider everyone's actions. Maybe Eldrin had a point, which burned deep in my chest to admit.

Lorne yanked me closer and removed his sword. "Get down on your knees," he rasped.

Throwing his head back, Eldrin laughed. "I love the enthusiasm, but you don't get the privilege of making her bleed. I've bestowed that kindness on someone who deserves the right to do with her as he wishes."

He had to mean Bran. I'd killed his sister during the trials. She'd attacked me—it had been her life or mine, and part of me had reacted before I understood what I was doing. Bran didn't agree with that sentiment. All he knew was that my hands had held the blade that ended his sister, and I couldn't fault him. He was right.

"Enter, Malikor."

The walls closed in around me as the tall, muscular man with one white wing entered the cell with wing chains in his hand. His eyes were as white as his remaining wing, and a deep scar marred each cheek. Before he attacked me, he'd had only one scar. He'd attacked me in this holding cell, hoping to scar my face the same as his since the Seelie had given him the mark. Tavish had arrived seconds before he could stab me, and he had cut off Malikor's wing and given him the injury intended for me on his other cheek.

Even then, Tavish had protected me, though he'd insisted it was because he wanted to be the one to kill me. Looking back, I knew it was the fated-mate instinct that had driven him to those measures.

One corner of Malikor's mouth tilted upward as his freaky eyes focused on me.

I wanted to shudder, but I'd already allowed enough Unseelie to feel strong.

Lira— Tavish warned. *I need to know.*

Malikor is alive and here to make me bleed so they can strengthen the barrier. I couldn't hide that from him. He'd see me when they finished what they'd started.

Clanging metal echoed down the hallway. "Eldrin!

Don't you dare hurt her! I swear to Fate, if you or Malikor harm a hair on her body, your breaths will be limited."

Eldrin's brows shot up. "I always thought that mind-melding between fated mates was pure legend. However, for him to yell, that means you informed him of my plans. He hadn't been alerted to that because I wanted him to see you weak and broken."

I made sure my face remained indifferent because I was tired of being so easily read. "Maybe you aren't good at keeping secrets." I shrugged, ignoring the way Lorne's fingers dug into my skin. He'd tightened his hold slightly, and I had to accept that, even if I got away, he would be able to cut me and catch enough of my blood for their means. Still, I refused to give up fighting.

"Even in prison, the dethroned king is arrogant." Malikor removed a dagger from a sheath positioned behind his sword.

"If Malikor was alive, why wasn't he in the gaunt-let?" I managed to keep my voice level, but my heart galloped with fear. Eldrin might want to cause me pain, but he wouldn't want true revenge on me... unlike Malikor. Tavish protecting me had made Malikor's anger more personal. His goal wouldn't be to make me bleed—that would be the end result for Eldrin—but to make every cut hurt in the most painful way.

"That's none of your concern." Eldrin shook his head. "But enough talking—the Seelie could arrive at any moment. We need her blood to reinforce the veil."

Malikor strolled toward me and commanded, "Force her to the ground and hold her wing over the bowl. There's no point in starting slow since we're in a hurry."

My wings fluttered and my wounds ached.

"Her wing is already injured," Lorne said, pulling me a little against his side.

A malicious smirk spread across Malikor's face. "Even better."

My stomach roiled, and the banging on the cell door continued as Tavish yelled even louder. I couldn't make out the words with my pulse pounding in my ears.

Lorne turned me so my wings were over the bowl, and I swung my free hand, nailing him in the face. His head jerked back, though his grip didn't loosen, and Malikor leaped over some bowls with the dagger raised over his head.

Ignoring the way my scabs stretched and pain shot through them, I spread my wings out completely so they lay completely flat along my back. The dagger *whooshed* by, missing me. It was close enough that the air hit my back.

Lorne released me, stepping forward.

A deep, pain-filled grunt came from behind me, and I spun around to see Lorne's sword lodged through Malikor's neck. Malikor's eyes widened in shock as his black blood poured out.

"Here." Lorne handed me the keys. "Go. Only a few guards are here since the Seelie—"

Wings flapped, and Eldrin soared toward us. I squatted, knowing he would hit me, but Lorne flew over me, catching Eldrin head-on.

I stood as Eldrin landed on the bowls with Lorne on top of him, and I took off back toward the prison cell, the cold keys heavy in my hand.

"Lira!" Tavish screamed in agony as I darted toward them.

Get ready. We're getting out of here, I connected with

him as the cell came into view. I landed at the door, slid the key into the lock, and swung it open.

The sounds of Lorne and Eldrin's scuffle were faint, but it gave me enough hope that we would make it out. Then, complete agony filtered into me, forcing me to my knees.

Bran.

The keys dropped from my hands. Finnian scooped them up and stuttered, "Tav... turn...." His words trailed off as Bran's footsteps headed toward us.

No. I couldn't let him take control of the situation. Lorne was risking his life to free us, and we'd never get another chance like this.

Though my magic was weak, I tugged at it, calling for healing. If I could negate the pain enough by healing myself, maybe I could free Tavish. He was stronger than Bran.

My magic was a mere trickle, but it took the edge off. Though I didn't have a fresh injury, the magic healed my mind from thinking it did. I lifted my head. Finnian was hunched over with the key between his fingers and Night-bane whimpering at his feet.

Gritting my teeth, I stood and took the keys from him and stumbled the two steps to Tavish's chained wings. Tavish's chest heaved as he struggled without his magic protecting him.

Tears filled my eyes, and my hands shook as I tried sliding the correct key into the hole.

"Quit that!" Bran snapped. His footsteps got faster. He understood that I was a threat.

Just as he reached the door, I slipped the key into the lock and turned it. The click sounded magical, and Tavish grunted as he moved his wings, allowing the chains to clank to the floor.

Bran fisted the hair on the back of my head, yanking me away from Tavish. The ripping pain at my roots fizzled the last bit of my healing magic.

"You blasting sunscorched!" Bran yelled a moment before he started whimpering.

The chill of darkness brushed across me. Tavish was using his magic, and my fated mate reached for Bran and pulled back, holding Bran's sword.

"Don't," Bran squeaked, releasing his hold on me. I dropped to my knees in relief while snagging the keys which had fallen to the floor with the chains.

"Do you remember my warning?" Tavish seethed.

Nightbane rushed to his side, snarling. He wanted to teach Bran a lesson as well.

Turning to Finnian, I freed his wings as Bran whimpered, "I'm sorry."

My breath caught, and I jerked toward them. A fae never apologized or thanked anyone.

"Not good enough." Tavish swung the sword, the blade so sharp that it sliced clear through Bran's neck. Black blood squirted everywhere as his head dropped. His body continued to stand for a second longer before it followed suit.

Something wet slid down my cheek. I touched it and pulled my hand back to see smeared blood. "Really? You couldn't have just stabbed him?"

Tavish lowered the sword to his side and grinned. "I don't even feel bad. You wearing the blood of our enemy is blasting sexy."

My body warmed despite the dire situation, but my human side surged forward enough to make me feel guilty. I bit my bottom lip, conflicted, and turned to find Eiric's face all wrinkled as if she smelled something bad.

"Fate no." She shook her head and moved so I could reach her lock. "Never talk like that in front of me again."

When her wings were free, Finnian took the keys from me and said, "This is nothing. Just wait. He ruined a chessboard over me helping her before."

"She was practically naked." Tavish marched out into the hallway, but he stumbled before regaining his balance.

My chest tightened as I followed after him and linked, *Are you okay?* Usually, he was more graceful than me.

Just a little off balance between not being fully healed from my time in Seelie and having my wings chained. I'll be fine.

Nightbane raced to my side with Eiric, Finnian, and Caelan hurrying after us.

I wanted to push him for more because something didn't seem right, but the chill of Tavish's darkness covered us, hiding us from anyone who might look down the hall. The entire castle was blanketed in shadow, and even the flickering lanterns dimmed for those who didn't harness shadows to see. I didn't want to distract him, not when we needed to get out of here quickly.

No sounds of the battle in the holding cell reached us, and we all hurried there to find Lorne standing over Malikor, removing his sword from the dead man's neck. More worrisome was that Eldrin wasn't there.

Tensing, Tavish readied to attack. I caught his hand and connected, *Don't. He helped us. He turned against Eldrin to free me and all of you. He gave me the keys. He's our ally. He played along until he couldn't. You could use him on your side.*

I still don't like him, but I won't kill him... yet. Tavish pulled some of the darkness back and asked, "Where's Eldrin?"

Head jerking up, Lorne sighed. "He used the shadows and left. He has to be calling for reinforcements. You all need to leave and come back with the Seelie if you can. That's the only way you will take back the kingdom."

Anger swirled through Tavish. "Absolutely not. I will kill Eldrin and prove I can take back my kingdom on my own. Otherwise, the people will never respect me."

Lorne bowed his head slightly. "That's what I thought you would say. Then I would like to fight alongside you."

"Don't make me regret this." Tavish raised the sword. "Lira trusts you, but I don't."

Caelan exhaled. "We don't have time to bicker. Guards will be here any second if Eldrin went to get them."

"We should go outside so they can't find us as easily." Eiric pointed to the window we'd flown through. "I see about twenty heading our way right now."

Everyone turned toward the window, where Eldrin flew in front of several guards. He could sense Tavish's magic now that it was freed, so Eiric had a point.

"Let's move." Tavish waved his hands, indicating that Lorne should follow us.

"Nightbane," I rasped. I didn't want to leave him. Not after what I'd seen them do to him.

"Don't worry about the beast." Finnian placed a hand on my arm.

Tavish snarled, and he dropped it quickly, taking a few steps back. "I'm not touching her anymore, so don't turn feral on me." He lifted both hands like I was the wild animal. "Nightbane can teleport anywhere on the island without a leash as long as he leaves before someone uses their magic on him."

Good to know. Maybe that was how he'd located me when I tried to escape that night.

Eldrin and the guards were only fifty feet from us and flying quickly.

"I'm done waiting. I'll go." Eiric flew toward the window, and the rest of us followed.

As soon as she reached the window, something crashed into her.

TAVISH

M y throat constricted as a new guard, coming from a
different direction, flew through the window and
crashed into Eiric. The guard grunted, unable to see her
with my darkness surrounding us, but this momentum
pushed her backward. Lira prepared to catch her sister, but
I gripped Lira's waist and yanked her to the side as I moved
forward to keep Eiric from falling.

The world spun slightly. I was far more drained than I
wanted to admit. The injuries and the burst of magic I'd
used on our arrival had caught up to me, and I had not been
able to refuel during the past few hours with the chains
on me.

Still... I refused to allow Lira to be injured more than
she already was.

Tavish, no! Lira exclaimed as determination flashed
through our bond, but I ignored the sensation as I moved my
shoulder forward just as Eiric's body pressed into it.

Nightbane stepped in front of Lira, blocking her from
heading back toward the threat. I kept Eiric aloft, fighting
the momentum of the guard, and I connected, *You're*

injured. You'll wind up getting all of us hurt, because everyone here is determined to protect you, including Eiric and Nightbane.

Her displeasure pulsed between us, but Nightbane growled a warning at her. Knowing the beast would protect her and not allow her to interfere, I turned my attention to her sister. Eiric's wings flapped in my face, causing my skin to crawl. Wings were one of the most intimate parts of our bodies, and it felt wrong having hers all over me. This wasn't for pleasure but out of necessity.

Another guard rammed into the first one, and my feet slipped underneath me. I gritted my teeth, shoving forward and allowing my illusion magic to trickle out and swarm the guards. My magic quivered and stretched, but I didn't have the luxury of not using it. I had to remain strong.

Finnian gripped my shoulders to aid in our battle, and we shoved both guards out the window, hitting a third who had paused outside.

Continuing forward, I clutched Eiric's arms, keeping her from falling out with them. Then I pivoted to her and spoke in a faint whisper, "Go out another window *now*."

"Are the windows unlocked? Otherwise, we're going to get hurt," Eiric hissed under her breath.

"They're like the Seelie's," Lira replied. "They're all open air except for the royal chambers to protect the ruling king and queen. Everywhere else is wide open."

The sound of the three guards' beating wings helped cover my instruction, but a female guard yelled, "The former king is cloaking them and attacking us here!"

Excellent. Let them believe we'd remain here so we could find a better exit.

Our best chance to beat Eldrin was to get out of the castle so we'd be harder to locate. With the sky dark once more, we could easily hide in the ruined lands and sneak attack the guards. No one but a royal could sense my darkness magic, which meant disarming the guards and killing the ones who posed an actual threat to us should be easy.

The six of us flew down the hall toward my chambers as more guards flew in through the window. We needed weapons—another dilemma to rectify as blasting quickly as possible.

Caelan and Finnian led the charge as Lira waited for Eiric and me before flying alongside us. Of course, Nightbane remained glued to my mate's side, and I found myself feeling grateful for the beast I'd once tortured. I never would have believed that I'd feel indebted to a cù-sìth, but Lira had again changed my perception.

Lorne followed us with his sword in his hand, prepared to fight the guards who'd followed us. Yet another person I'd never dreamed of allying with because he'd led the rebellion against me twelve years ago.

After a few strokes of our wings, I felt a faint sting through my connection with Lira, as if she were hiding her pain from me.

Her wings.

Of course, they'd hurt if we flew. I hadn't considered that.

I turned to see a tear trailing down Lira's cheek, and my heart squeezed uncomfortably as the rigidness of my terror spread throughout my chest.

She'd fight me on it, but I needed to carry her. Her injury was worse than mine, and I couldn't stand to let her suffer any more than she already had.

"Wait," I said, louder than I wanted, but I needed Finnian and Caelan to hear me ahead.

Without question, the entire group stopped, searching for the threat.

The guards we'd left behind quieted too, and then I heard their feet shuffling in our direction.

Nightbane whimpered, staring at Lira, realizing the same thing I had. I wanted to scold the beast, but I'd already given away our location. I bent and lifted Lira in my arms like the princess she was, and her mouth formed an O of surprise.

What are you doing? she connected.

Since we were all cloaked in darkness, we could see each other, and I nodded as the guards flew toward us. We had to move before they reached us. We hadn't made it far.

"They must be heading toward the king's chambers!" a guard shouted.

We had been since I had weapons stowed there, but not any longer.

Our group took off again, and Lira squirmed against me. I let my aggravation leak through to her and mind-melded, *Sprite, it's clear that I'm carrying you. You're in agony, and you can't fly for long. You were already slowing us down. I need you to reserve your strength in case there's no choice but for you to fly on your own.* I'd do anything to ensure she got free. The Unseelie had done enough damage to her, mostly because of me. I'd do whatever was necessary to fix the huge list of mistakes I'd made against her.

I could feel her frustration brew between us, but before she could respond or fight me further, Eldrin snarled, "Let me through!"

I'd hoped that the chaos would've kept him occupied a little longer, but I should've realized that my wildling of a cousin would be more focused on locating me than checking on *his* people.

We pumped our wings harder to gain distance from the guards. They were moving cautiously, allowing us to move ahead undetected, but not for long.

Not with my cousin here to aid them.

Even though the guards couldn't see us, Eldrin could keep them right on the cusp of our wings until I drained my magic enough not to be able to hide us. Allowing the sky to light up would conserve my magic, but then we'd be easier to locate.

"They're almost at the turn in the hall," Eldrin rasped.

Numerous wings flapped. Most of the guards that had been following Eldrin had made it through the window and were now chasing us.

My pulse raced. Time was of the essence. Thankfully, my adrenaline spiked, allowing my strength to return fully, if only temporarily.

Eiric glanced over her shoulder, and the castle walls began to quake like they did before a volcano erupted on the island. Chunks of wall began to crumble between us and the guards, and thick pieces of the ceiling and walls crashed down, separating us from them.

Guards screamed, and someone shouted, "The other Seelie must have earth magic!"

We turned the corner toward the king's chambers as Eiric faced forward. She'd bought us more time, though the Unseelie would be on us shortly if we didn't get out of here.

Ten guards appeared through the window that Finnian and Caelan had been leading us to, and I funneled more darkness between us. Eiric readied herself to use her magic again, but Finnian and Caelan flew close to the side of the hallway. The ten guards moved slowly and warily, knowing we could be anywhere.

I wanted to attack them, but the risk of Eldrin locating us if we didn't leave the castle held me back.

Finnian darted in front of Caelan, preparing to attack.

No. That was the worst thing he could do.

Nightbane hunkered in front of me, but Caelan grabbed Finnian's shoulder and yanked him back against the wall. Caelan shook his head as Finnian fought against him, and the first guard held his sword in front of him. The guard glanced around, searching for anything out of the ordinary, and continued forward, breathing hard.

The guards following him moved much faster, no doubt knowing if they ran into us, the lead guard would get attacked first.

Selfish idiots, but that was the fae way.

After five passed us, the sound of the rubble being pushed aside had us all moving again. We moved alongside the wall toward the window, and the ten guards stopped to listen to the commotion ahead.

"Those who can, fly over it!" Eldrin exclaimed in frustration. "Those trapped inside can get out on their own. Our kingdom is under attack."

Disgust slithered through me, and Lira wrapped her arms around my neck. Our connection jolted where our skin touched.

He'll get what's coming to him, she vowed as Caelan darted out the window.

One by one, we took to the sky, and when I stepped onto the window ledge and readied to fly, Lira gasped.

Heart hammering against my ribs, I took flight. *Is it Eldrin?* Had he located us again so quickly? I braced myself for an attack, but I refused to spin around with Lira in my arms.

No. It's Nightbane, Lira replied. She pulled back, her cobalt eyes wide and twinkling. *He vanished.*

I smiled, loving that even with all her memories back, I still got to enjoy her wonder at new things. *We told you he could portal on the island.*

Hearing and seeing are two different things. She arched a brow, but then her face strained once more. *At least he'll be okay.*

I wanted to vow that she would be as well, but I couldn't even if I tried. We had so many stakes against us that it could very well be a lie. *I will do everything in my power to protect you. That is my priority.* My people had come second to her, but they were no longer on my list. They'd turned on me after everything I'd done for them, and the fact I was the rightful heir made their betrayal worse. They should've supported me over that alone, but I'd done everything for them, including changing, which made their turning their back on me hurt more than I ever imagined.

Lira cupped my face, and the wind blew a few wavy, blonde tendrils of hair in her face. She pressed her lips into a line and sighed. *I know that, but your safety is my priority as well. So if you do something stupid to protect me, just know I'll follow you right into the lion's den.*

Lion? Even with her memories back, she spoke like a human.

I scanned the area for guards around the city. They should be stationed along the perimeter of the island in case the Seelie tried to attack us. As expected, twenty-five guards were stationed on the mountain peaks.

The snow I'd summoned when I'd arrived here had melted while my magic was bound. The temperature was almost as warm as it had been back at Glean Solas, but thankfully, it was nighttime, so we were blanketed in darkness. Even if I'd wanted to, I couldn't have spared the extra magic to signify my power. I had to reserve it to cloak us.

We flew toward the center of town, which was vacant as most people had gone to bed. Every household slept with their weapons beside them in preparation for the Seelie's arrival. Our people yearned for the day when they could fight the Seelie once again, and my goal had been to ensure that day would end in our victory.

I was no longer sure that was possible.

Caelan, Finnian, Eiric, Lorne, and I flew close together. Lira had stopped fighting me and nestled into my chest. Her wings hung limply, and even though I no longer sensed her torment, I could tell they bothered her from the way she flinched any time they brushed my arm.

"What do we do?" Eiric arched a brow. "We need weapons. You can't use your darkness forever, and you need to kill Eldrin."

She was right. I would soon be struggling to hide us. I could already feel my magic blipping. I needed to reserve it for whatever fight lay ahead of us.

"Before the Seelie arrive." Finnian lifted a hand. "If we don't, Eldrin will attack them, and we're all going to die... except for *her*." He gestured to Lira. "Not that I'm upset over it. Lira's a rare Seelie that I like, but I'd prefer to live along with her."

"Father won't come for me." Lira exhaled loudly. "Not after I helped you two escape and chose the Unseelie over them."

Eiric snorted. "Your parents love you, believe me. But even if the king and queen cut you loose, Mom and Dad won't tolerate leaving us here, knowing the Unseelie could attack us."

I found myself approving more of Lira's Earth parents than her royal ones, though it wasn't hard since they'd had my parents killed.

"If we attack the guards for weapons, they'll alert the others." Caelan frowned. "And Eldrin will find us quickly."

Sheathing his sword, Lorne rubbed his hands together. "I know where weapons are stored outside the castle. They're guard grade and meant to serve a larger purpose. Even when he came into power under the ruse that Tavish had died, we kept the weapons. Eldrin suspected that Tavish would return and wanted his loyalists to have access to guard weapons. That's how the woman who hit Lira in the wings managed to have guard-grade weapons. A handful of guards pretended to remain on Eldrin's side and hid a few weapons in one of our homes, hoping you'd come back with Lira. Our hope was that she would be an ally and aid us in returning to our homeland without war."

"Loyalists?" My body tensed.

"He has coveted power since before your father died, Your Majesty. I know because I used to believe in his cause, thinking war was the only way to respond against the Seelie." Lorne rolled his shoulders back. "He had a group of followers even then and a plan to take the crown, but now isn't the time to discuss this."

As if Fate wanted to reinforce his point, Eldrin shouted so loudly that we could hear him even as far away as we were as he flew out of the window, "They're somewhere out here! I feel the faint pulse of his magic."

"I can lead you to the guard's house where we stored some of the weapons. He is loyal to you. No one outside our trusted group knows where they are. No one will betray us to Eldrin because watching Lira during the gauntlet changed their perception of her, the same as she convinced me she was worth having on our side."

Even at fifteen, I hadn't felt like everything was working against me like I did now. I should've seen that Eldrin had coveted my position before I even held it. At least there was a group of Unseelie who supported Lira, which meant they wouldn't have an issue with us ruling over them together. "Fine. I'll cloak us until we get there, but we need to hurry."

Lorne took the lead, and the rest of us followed. When I glanced behind us, I could see Eldrin searching the open area.

Our group flew low through the town, keeping to the shadows so there wasn't a dark spot moving through the light of the flickering street lanterns. My arms were growing tired from carrying Lira, but there was no way I would put her down.

As we flew past the darkened houses, I noticed that some fae were sleeping on the floor near their windows, ready to fight at the slightest alarm. It would've been comforting if I hadn't known many were prepared to kill Lira and me.

I couldn't hear Eldrin anymore, and a chill of warning ran down my spine. I pushed it away. My emotions were getting the best of me. We'd moved fast enough to put distance between us, and he'd have a harder time tracking us. He wouldn't expect us to head into the village.

Maybe we should get as far away as possible, but I couldn't run off and let the Seelie slaughter the innocent while searching for Lira and me. They'd have to find her because of their vow to the dragon prince.

Lira tensed, and I couldn't fathom her being with *him*. I refused to allow it. At the thought, blind rage wanted to take over, but I closed my eyes and focused on her touch and her wild roses, moonlight mist, and vanilla scent—my favorite in the entire realm. My body relaxed, but then a slight bulge grew in my pants, causing a whole different kind of problem.

"We're almost there," Lorne whispered, bringing my attention back to the present.

We reached a home in the center of the village, and Lorne dropped to the top-floor window. Even though I knew most of my people by name, I didn't know where everyone lived and wasn't sure whose home it was.

I followed close behind Lorne, wanting to shut off my magic so that Eldrin couldn't track us here. Moments after landing, I bent and set Lira down on the smooth floor, giving my arms some relief.

As Eiric, Caelan, and Finnian landed behind me, I pulled back the darkness so that the person who lived here could see us.

"Struan?" Lorne called. "It's me. We need those—"

My chest seized, and I pulled Lira behind me. This was a trap, and we'd all made a big mistake in trusting Lorne. Struan was one of Eldrin's most loyal guards, and he'd wanted Lira to die in the gauntlet.

Struan appeared, his face flushed black and his eyes flashing. He said, "You shouldn't have come here."

My wings fluttered, and a mild ache coursed through their base. Tavish pushed me behind him, startling me.

Refusing to cower behind my mate, I stepped to the side just as a man with a bruise-colored face came out of the hallway in front of us.

Stomach dropping, I remembered exactly who the man was and understood the tension and terror churning through our bond into me.

This was Struan, the guard who had gleefully placed the chains on my wings and wished me to fail in the gauntlet.

Why had Lorne taken us *here*?

Struan's eyes flashed. "You shouldn't have come here."

"Everyone, move back," Tavish growled as his wings stretched outward to hide Eiric, Finnian, Caelan, and me from Struan's view.

The swirl of Tavish's magic had an inky sensation, which meant one thing—he'd called on his nightmare magic to use against them. "I should've known not to trust you."

I batted past Tavish's onyx wing to see Lorne's face. I had a hard time believing he'd turn on us. If he'd continued to play me for a fool after I'd chosen to trust him again, I wasn't sure I would ever trust another Unseelie beyond Tavish, Finnian, and Caelan.

Lorne dropped his sword and wrapped his arms around his body. "My King, no." He took in a ragged breath. "I swear to you, it's not what you think."

Struan threaded his fingers into his pale-green hair and clutched his head, then sagged to his knees.

Small flutters of wings caught my attention as a little girl flew into the room. She couldn't have been older than ten, and her crystal-blue eyes widened as she jerked back. Her face blanched, and she opened her mouth.

Adrenaline shot through me, and I flew over Lorne and Struan and reached the girl in time to cover her mouth. "Please, don't," I whispered, pulling her back to my chest. She bit down on my fingers, digging her teeth into my flesh, and I wanted to scream.

I hissed, and Nightbane appeared beside us. He snarled, drool dripping from his teeth as he took in the threat toward me.

The little girl's jaw went slack, and I yanked my hand free from her mouth to see my honey-colored blood dripping down the front of the girl's pale-pink nightgown.

She whimpered, and her small body shook.

A lump formed in my throat as my stomach churned. "Nightbane, calm down. She's just scared."

"I'm not scared of anyone." She lifted her chin despite the way her body quivered. "Release my father from your illusions, or I'll kill you all."

Finnian squatted next to Lorne's sagging body and swiped the guard's sword from the floor. He pointed the edge of the blade at the young girl and beamed. "Aren't you a little shadowflare? Your bite is ferocious for one so small."

"Isla, go back to your room," Struan said slowly from where he cowered on the floor. "They aren't here to harm you."

"But I can't lose you, Father." Her bottom lip stuck out.

My heart shattered. Tavish could not continue down this road. *Tavish, we should leave.*

They know we're here, he replied, his irises turning the stormy gray that showed he was angry or out of control. In this moment, he felt both.

Eldrin already knows we're nearby, so it's not like being here will give Eldrin and the others an advantage. Memories of leaving my parents when I was around this little girl's age slammed into me. The pain of feeling abandoned was forever seared into my soul, even though it hadn't been the truth. No one deserved to go through that, especially not a young girl trying to protect her father from the strongest Unseelie alive.

When Tavish closed his eyes, I didn't need our connection to know the turmoil he was enduring, wanting to give in to my request but also feeling that, by doing so, he'd be exposing me to harm.

"If we release the illusions from your father, will you promise not to scream or cause us problems?" I lifted a brow and squatted next to her. "We were told you might have weapons you'd be willing to give us so we can protect ourselves."

Nightbane hunkered down at my side, ready to attack. He didn't snarl, but he clearly saw the girl as a threat.

She placed her hands on her hips and scowled. "You came to our house and attacked my father. What do you have to say for yourself?"

I mashed my lips together, trying not to laugh. Struan might be a douchebag, but he'd raised a brave and smart girl. "You're right. That's why King Tavish will release both your father and Lorne from their nightmares."

Eiric headed back to the window to keep watch.

"I suggest we depart before releasing our enemies." Caelan hovered over Struan, who was breathing raggedly on the floor.

"Wait. *You're* King Tavish?" Isla's jaw went slack, and she glanced from me to him. "And you're the sunscorched from the gauntlet."

"The one and only." Finnian winked at her. "Ever since Lira returned to Ardanos, none of us have been bored."

Isla's brows furrowed. "Then why are you hurting Father? He has always been in King Tavish's favor and always proclaimed that the king was a decent man to those who followed the rules." Her body stiffened. "But I don't agree with him now."

Shock filtered to me from Tavish, and Finnian rocked back on his heels. "Decent man? Not sure if that's how I'd describe him."

The magic rumbling through our connection faded as Tavish swallowed loudly. "Is that the truth?"

Struan inhaled quickly and straightened. "It is, Your Majesty."

"Then why did you tell us we shouldn't be here?" Tavish tilted his head, assessing every reaction.

"Because of my daughter." Struan gestured toward the little girl. "Lorne should've come alone and not brought all of you here. Eldrin is tracking you."

Satisfied that Struan wasn't an imminent threat, I moved back and threaded my fingers in Nightbane's fur to ease his worry.

"I... didn't..." Lorne gritted. "Have... a... choice. They need weapons."

The longer we remained here, the bigger the threat was to their family. *We need to get out of here. Eldrin will punish the little girl as well as the others.*

I had so many questions. Struan had seemed extremely loyal to Eldrin during my time in the gauntlet.

"Where are the weapons? We'll arm ourselves and leave." Tavish pulled his wings into his back as the last bit of his magic fizzled into nothing, releasing both men from their nightmares.

Isla spun on her heels and waved for us to follow. "They're in my room, back here."

"Her room?" Caelan's eyebrows rose.

"Please tell me the weapons aren't those toys Lira brought with her from Earth." Finnian shook his head. "They wouldn't even reach the heart."

Even in a dire situation, my pocketknife was a joke to him. In the human world, you could cause some damage with it if you caught someone off guard, but apparently, even toddlers here in Ardanos were trained with bigger knives.

"Yes, her *room*." Struan stood and tugged on his gray tunic. "No one would expect me to hide weapons there because her room is across the house from mine. If they questioned my loyalties, they'd expect anything I'd hidden to be near *me*."

That made sense, but Eldrin was smart. Things would've been a whole lot easier if he weren't.

"Come on." Isla gripped my hand, dragging me down the hallway. A small bathroom sat on one side, and her room was across from it.

Luckily, she'd taken the hand she hadn't bitten because

my injured one still smarted from her bite. I glanced down, noticing that some of my blood had dripped onto the floor. I pressed my hand against my shirt to keep more blood from spilling.

Nightbane ran in front of me, scoping out the area with Tavish at my back. When we entered Isla's room, a sharp ache shot through my chest.

Her room was bare, with only a small mattress set against the wall and a closet with a few outfits and one other nightgown. She had one pair of boots, and I realized how truly dire the people's situation was here. One small window allowed her to see outside.

Struan marched in and passed Tavish and me, heading into the closet. He squatted at the bottom and removed a dagger from his side, then slid it into a small divot in the grimy floor. A portion of the floor lifted.

Taking hold of one end, he pulled up the cover, and I wanted to groan. There were three swords, a sling like the one I'd used in the gauntlet, and a bow and arrows. We had seven people in our group, excluding Struan and Isla, and six weapons, including Lorne's sword. One of us wouldn't have a weapon, and the one who carried the sling would have to find something to use in it. This wasn't the mother lode I'd been hoping for.

"This is everything you have?" Tavish's head jerked back. "Is there anything else?"

"It was hard enough to get these." Struan grabbed the stash and tossed it at our feet. "We snuck them out over the past few days so Eldrin wouldn't detect anything. We believed you were dead."

I sighed, trying to make sense of everything. The more I learned, the more confused I got. "Then why were you hoarding weapons? Didn't you expect Eldrin to be your king?"

"We'd hoped—" he started.

Tavish's head snapped toward the window. "It's Eldrin. He's here."

"Guys," Eiric interjected. "We've got a problem. The guards are heading this way."

Blast. He must have tracked my illusion magic. Tavish snatched up the swords, leaving one on the floor. "They'll know you're working with us, so you need to protect your daughter. She's innocent in all of this, but if you betray me—"

"I won't." Struan lowered his head. "I am loyal to the rightful king. That has always been my stance."

My chest expanded with so much love for Tavish. He'd always cared about the innocents, but his giving Struan a second chance reminded me more of the boy I'd known before our worlds drastically changed.

When I peeked out, I saw four guards heading straight toward the window, and there were probably more since the window was so small it limited my view.

Take this. Tavish handed me one sword, his eyes burning brightly. *And, sprite, I need to know you'll do whatever it takes to keep yourself safe. Don't mourn these men who turned against us. They made that choice... not us.*

I nodded, not wanting to waste time with words. We hurried into the hallway, meeting Eiric, Calean, Lorne, and Finnian there.

"Give me the bow and arrows," Eiric demanded, holding out her hand. "I can use that."

I wanted to argue, but Caelan took the sling. The fact that Lorne had nothing didn't sit well with me, but that concern vanished when the rush of wings sounded right outside the house.

"Group together!" Eiric shouted and raised her hands, clutching the bow in one and the quiver in the other.

"What is she—" Struan started, but I didn't let him finish.

I took his arm and tugged him into the middle of our group. With his hold on Isla, she followed just as the roof began to shake. I wished like anything that I could help with my water magic, but with everything we'd gone through, I was drained.

Pieces of the ceiling fell on us as the guards flew in through the window and stormed toward us. I held up the sword, ignoring the ache in my fingers and the blood from the bite marks coating the hilt. The muscles in my back trembled, and my wings throbbed from the injury I hadn't finished healing.

Even with the ceiling falling hard on them, the guards kept moving forward, led by a female whose hardened eyes stared straight at me like I was the ultimate prize.

I probably was since Eldrin wanted my blood.

The ceiling above our heads broke apart, and Eiric threw the pieces at the guards as our group flew through the new hole in the roof.

My wings throbbed, and Tavish's arm wrapped around my waist, easing some of my weight. His carrying me would slow us down, especially since we were surrounded. There had to be fifty guards around us.

Eldrin smirked from behind two guards, flying slightly above their heads. "Dear cousin, you can't win. Surrender, and I won't kill Caelan and Finnian upon recapture. Fight me, and I'll make sure they perish in front of your eyes."

Get away as soon as you can, Lira. I'll distract them.

Rage boiled inside of him like I'd never seen before, and the thrumming of his magic took over. He said out loud, "I will *never* submit to you. No matter what, you won't capture us... not again."

Before I could do anything, Tavish released me, and his power channeled out of him. I could see the moment Tavish directed his nightmare illusions toward each person, and darkness slithered across my skin, hiding us. The problem was that it wasn't as strong as it had been, meaning he hadn't recovered.

A guard screamed and raced toward Tavish with his sword held high. He swung down, trying to end whatever terror he saw.

Ice shot from Finnian's hands in conjunction with him swinging his sword, and Eiric called her earth magic to aid her.

Everyone fought, and even Isla used her ice magic against the guards beside her father.

"Get the Seelie princess," Eldrin commanded. "And make sure she doesn't shed too much blood. We need it for the veil before the Seelie comes. She has to be in the same spot or near it. Better yet, anyone who has snow magic, blow it toward that section so we can see their outline."

Five guards soared toward me. I ignored the torment ravaging my body and lifted my sword. I refused to flee.

They searched for me, unsure where I might be with the darkness that cloaked me until the female guard used her magic. Snow pelted us as she said, "Look, the snow hits there and not the ground. Someone must be there."

My stomach knotted, and I realized I should've moved farther away.

The five guards circled me, and I tried to remember

every type of self-defense I'd learned from my time in Ardanos and on Earth. I'd been trained to protect myself.

The female nodded, and all five soared toward me at once. Only the woman had her sword out, while the other four must be planning to restrain me. I had to play this smart.

Lira, I said hide! Tavish shouted. *I can't hide us with darkness much longer. I'm using too much magic. He can't sense you if the rest of us stay here. Take the girl with you and go.*

I refuse to leave you like this, and she won't leave her father. If she was anything like me, she'd stay in one spot, and forcing her to leave would make it easier to find us.

The female guard swung her sword, and I lifted mine, the clash of metal confirming her suspicion. I kicked my feet out, hitting two of the men in the chest and using them to flip over. The other two guards crashed into each other as I turned myself upright again.

Unshed tears burned my eyes, but I gritted my teeth. The only way to end this was to kill Eldrin. Then the threat to the throne would be gone.

More snow spun around us as I turned, watching Eldrin track the magic surrounding us. This had to be it. I would take down the son of a bitch who threatened Tavish. The person who had done all of this to him.

With my sword at my side, I pushed through the agony and raced toward him. I wanted to catch him off guard the same way he had done to me in the tub.

I'd drawn the sword back, ready to drive it into his heart, when his head snapped in my direction. He flew backward, and my sword hit air.

"I know that isn't Tavish, but I can feel his magic coming off you." He smirked.

I gritted my teeth, though my wings were growing sluggish. The injury was catching up to me. I had to act fast, and I swung the sword again. Each time I moved forward, Eldrin moved just in time for the weapon to miss him.

Something behind him flashed brightly, like fire, and I paused.

Had the Seelie finally arrived? If so, I couldn't be happier to see my people. They had come in the nick of time.

"It's time to surrender, Eldrin," I said. Death would be too easy for him. He deserved capture and torture. "The Seelie are here."

Eldrin glanced around, and another line of fire pulsed closer. Fire that was thick and signaling an alarm. The Seelie wouldn't warn the Unseelie that they'd arrived, leaving only one explanation, especially with the sizable shape that could now be faintly seen slithering in the sky.

Dragon.

The frigid tendrils of fear that pulsed through our bond strangled me. I could feel the tugs of the darkness covering the eight of us, along with Nightbane below, as I made sure no guard could easily locate us. However, we had to determine how many guards had snow magic so we could eliminate them and hide more effectively. I was stretching my magic too far and could not engulf the entire force of guards with my nightmare illusions.

Something had to be wrong with Lira. The guard in front of me swung blindly, hoping to harm one of us, so I darted underneath him then shot upward and beheaded him. His blood sprayed, but I didn't pay attention to that or the yells of the nearby guards as they watched their friend die at the hands of an invisible force.

Luckily, ten guards were hovering near the back of the circle, not getting involved in the battle.

I found Lira close to Eldrin, but they weren't fighting... something I suspected even Lira would be capable of with *him* after everything he'd done to her.

The wildling.

I'd remedy that particular issue now.

A dragon is heading toward us, Lira connected, answering my unspoken question.

I jerked my head in the direction they were staring, and I gritted my teeth. Was it illusion magic? Why would a dragon be flying toward us? However, I wasn't chained, and my magic was flaring inside me. I should see through any illusion easily.

My heart nearly stopped beating. There could only be one explanation. The worst possible scenario that could happen in my entire world.

The ashbreath must have learned that Lira was here and had come to take her from me.

I released my hold on the snow, needing to conserve my energy. The darkness was more necessary. I needed Lira to leave and blasting hide. *Find Nightbane and go somewhere with him. I can keep cloaking you because of our connection.*

Lira shook her head as Eldrin spun around and swung his fist at her.

I opened my mouth to yell, and Lira stopped using her wings and dropped. But Eldrin's hand swung into her hair and clutched it.

I had to reach her.

A sharp throb bolted through the bond, and I rushed forward, slicing through any guard who got between us. I'd been trying not to kill all of them because we needed prisoners, but that changed when I lost sight of Lira.

Lira's wings fluttered, and fresh blood dripped from the wing injury she'd partially healed in the prison cell. The wounds had reopened.

Yanking her hair, Eldrin snapped her head upward and sheathed his sword.

He was trying not to make her bleed... not until he

could capture most of the blood. Instead, he pulled her up, and pain radiated through our bond.

A guard raced forward, about to get in my way, and I kicked him in the back. He slammed into the female guard fighting Eiric. Both guards dropped as I flew faster toward my mate.

Lira flapped her wings harder, the blood dripping more as she punched Eldrin in the testicles. Eldrin's eyes bulged as if he hadn't expected her to be so unconventional. It was one of the things I loved best about her—she thought outside the norm and didn't mind fighting dirty.

He released her and flew backward as he gripped his groin. But Lira's wings didn't hold her weight, and she dropped toward the village rooftops.

"Lira!" Eiric screamed as I pushed myself to catch her.

Blades clashed and guards spun toward Lira, able to locate her since she'd cried out.

My only goal was to catch my mate. I'd trust the others to help Eiric fight our attackers.

Not five feet from the slanted rooftops, I caught up and wrapped the arm not holding the sword around her, pulling her front to my chest. The jolt of our bond sprang between us, and I gritted my teeth, fighting the downward momentum.

Her expression strained as she panted. *I... I can't fly anymore.*

It's fine. We all don't need to fight Eldrin, especially with the ashbreath heading this way. I turned my head and saw that the beast had almost made it to our land. I could see his crimson scales and the smoke drifting from his snout.

Wings flapped toward us, and I glanced upward to see that the others had left the guards to fight themselves.

Eldrin was hunched over, but he was catching his breath, which meant he'd be back to tracking us in no time.

"We have a crater-size problem." Finnian flew to my side, staring at the dragon prince in beast form.

"God, he's huge," Eiric gasped, her breath catching as her green eyes locked on him. "And fucking strong."

"And here for my mate." I didn't appreciate the awe in her voice for the man who'd threatened to strip Lira from me and claim her as his own. The edges of my vision darkened as pressure built in my chest, but I wasn't sure if it was from that or fatigue. For all I knew, it could be from blasting both, which would be more problematic.

"She's shrouded in darkness, so she should be fine." Caelan kept glancing from the dragon to the guards.

"They're no longer here," Eldrin snapped. "Stop being foolish." He stared right at us, tracking the magical essence of the darkness.

Blighted abyss. I despised that he'd been born with royal magic.

"Lira can't fly, so you need to go on foot," I said softly to keep others from hearing us.

The dragon prince had made it to the edge of our island. We were flying out of time.

"Eiric, Isla, and Struan should go with her and get far away from the village and castle." The last thing I wanted to do was separate myself from Lira, but until Eldrin was dead, it was the safest choice. I believed Struan was on our side, and he wouldn't endanger his daughter. "Anywhere away from here and the cave. Somewhere no one would consider going."

"No." Lira wrapped her arms around my neck. "We can't separate."

"We have to. Eldrin will track us via my magic, and the

dragon will smell you if he gets too close. I need you to stay safe and free to be with *only* me." My chest tugged, the mate in me wanting to oblige her request. I didn't want to leave her side either, but that was futile. I needed her to be far away from the dragon prince and Eldrin. *If you remain, I'll be distracted, worrying about you, and I could get hurt.* I was able to say the words because they were true, but I wouldn't deny I was also using them to get her to agree with me. She didn't want me hurt either.

I could feel her frustration, telling me my words had swayed her.

Fine, but if you get hurt or captured, I need to know you'll tell me. Her cobalt-blue eyes shone even through the darkness, searching for the truth within me.

As if I could deny her request. *I promise.* I flew us toward the stone ground, and Nightbane appeared below us.

Who knew I'd come to tolerate the blasting cù-sìth? Something uncomfortable twisted in my chest as I thought about all the things I'd done to him as a pup.

"Here, I can carry her." Struan held out his arms. "Flying will get us away from here faster."

The thought of another man's hands on her made me want to kill everyone in sight, but Eldrin's commands became louder. They were heading to fight us once more. "Fine. Keep her safe."

I kissed her lips and passed her to Struan, then turned to face Eldrin just as the dragon flew over half the village, nearly upon us.

"I'll take care of her," Eiric vowed as she, Struan, Lira, and Isla flew quickly toward the ruined part of the island.

If I wanted them to have time to gain distance, the best thing I could do was reveal the four of us who were left.

We'd taken out over twenty guards and were still grossly outnumbered, but I hoped that the ten guards who'd been holding back would still choose not to engage in battle. Finnian, Caelan, and I were the best swordsfae in the kingdom, and all I needed to do was kill Eldrin.

"I'm pulling back the darkness from the four of us," I informed the others.

"Tavish," Caelan warned. "That's a horrible idea."

Before I could respond, Eldrin's loyal guard, Faelan, shouted, "There's Tavish. He's revealed himself."

The dragon prince roared overhead as five guards swarmed me. Faelan swung his sword, and I blocked it as Caelan, Finnian, and Lorne attacked three of the other guards focused on me.

A female guard jabbed while I was distracted, and the tip of her blade pierced my side before I could jerk back. As the blade slid free, Faelan rebounded and swung at my right hand, which held the sword. I turned sharply, his sword *swishing* by my arm. The female guard darted toward me, her sword held straight out, and I shoved Faelan into her blade, causing it to ricochet off his armor.

"Detain Tavish now." Eldrin gestured the other guards toward me just as Finnian slid his blade through Faelan's exposed neck and Caelan cut the wings off the female. The female dropped to the ground, and ten more guards moved toward us.

The dragon prince blew flames, engulfing three guards, and flew closer to Eldrin.

Eldrin's jaw clenched. He called out, "I don't know where the Seelie sunscorched is! Figure it out yourself. I'm dealing with escaped prisoners."

The remaining seven guards had paused but now continued toward us. The dragon prince engulfed five of them in flames, leaving two unmaimed. Finnian and I didn't hesitate. I shoved the sword through the guard's head as Finnian cut the other guard's throat.

Now, only five of the guards who'd attacked us were left. The other ten had continued to hang back.

"Fine. I'll help you locate her." Eldrin's nostrils flared, but he turned to his fifteen remaining guards. "Kill everyone but Tavish. We can find other people to work the lands."

Sword raised, Eldrin flew down to where we were hovering and waited for one of us to attack him.

No.

The dragon could pick up Lira's scent if he followed Eldrin down to where she'd been.

I barreled toward Eldrin and rammed him into the top floor of the cottage that faced the cave where the mushrooms grew for the people here. Eldrin grunted and elbowed me in the nose. After a sickening crack, blood poured into my mouth.

Tavish! Lira's voice popped into my head. *Did you get caught?*

Like he'd done to Lira, I fisted the back of his long white hair. *Keep moving. The dragon prince is here, searching for you.* With the hilt of my sword, I punched Eldrin in the face, unable to swing the blade at him this close.

"She was somewhere near here!" Eldrin shouted and bent completely over.

My legs spun over our heads, and I hit the wall I'd crashed him into upside down. Pain radiated down my back as Eldrin turned toward me with his blade.

"If it wouldn't weaken us so much, I would kill you right now," he snarled, placing the edge of the blade to my throat.

Still upside down, I allowed my feet to drop onto his shoulders and squeeze his neck as the tip of his blade slit my skin from neck to chin. Blood trickled from the wound into my face, joining the blood from my nose, and I jerked my feet to the side, trying to break Eldrin's neck.

He dropped his sword and allowed his body to spin with the move, then escaped my hold as I darted off and flipped upright.

Caelan appeared and stabbed Eldrin in the shoulder. Eldrin groaned as I touched my neck, the injury weakening my magic further. With the amount of magic I was using and the exertion, exhaustion was taking hold. The wound drained my energy and ability to channel my magic.

The ground shook, and rocks from the highest mountain peak tumbled down toward us, taking out two guards.

My stomach dropped just as the dragon roared even louder and took off flying.

I turned my head to see Lira on Nightbane's back, racing toward us. Eiric flew right behind her.

The dragon is coming for you. Fear gripped me, but adrenaline pumped through me, burning off some of the weakness. *I can't cloak you anymore.*

Caelan yanked his sword from Eldrin's body. "Do we kill him now or make a show of it?" he asked, but I couldn't focus on that. Not right now.

"Just—" I started, but a sickening grunt caused me to turn my head toward Eldrin.

He'd stabbed Caelan in one wing, and Caelan dropped to the stony ground.

"You will not win, Tavish." Eldrin slammed into me again, and I fell backward, my wings failing to gain traction as Finnian and Lorne clashed blades with the warriors above me.

I hit the ground, straining my back and wing muscles, but I punched Eldrin in the face. Something crunched, but

I didn't take the time to evaluate as I kneed him between the legs, following Lira's lead.

The ground shook and quaked from Eiric wielding her earth magic, but she'd used so much that I suspected her ability wouldn't last. Still, it let me know that she was protecting Lira. I shoved Eldrin off me and saw the dragon fly over Lira and Eiric. Lira had gotten off the cù-sìth, and her gaze darted everywhere, no doubt searching for me as the dragon and Eiric stared into each other's eyes.

Strange.

Five of the guards barreled toward Lira. I jumped to my feet and flapped my wings, ready to intervene, but something yanked on my foot.

"Eiric, Lira is being attacked!" I shouted, needing her to protect my most cherished treasure in the entire realm.

I flapped my wings, but something stabbed into my calf. I growled and kicked Eldrin, but I had to watch as Eiric tore her gaze from the dragon prince and leaped toward Lira.

This time, when Eldrin yanked, he dug his fingers into the wound, and my body crumbled. I spun around and placed the tip of my sword right above his chest.

"This is for attacking Lira and deceiving me," I gritted, readying to drive the blade through his heart.

Tavish, help, Lira connected.

Large, scaly wings flapped over us as the dragon took to the sky. I looked up and saw my mate dangling from the dragon's talons, her eyes wide and her blonde hair blowing wildly around her face.

The dragon prince was taking her.

Blighted abyss. I couldn't allow that to happen. I needed to kill him here and now before she got too far away.

Underneath me, Eldrin's legs moved sharply to the left,

toppling me over. Eldrin then took the same position I had, with his sword tip at my heart.

I couldn't seem to care at the moment, watching Lira grow smaller as the dragon flew away. My heart splintered with a pain I'd never thought I could feel.

If I didn't break free, I could lose my mate forever—and that couldn't happen. I gritted my teeth, readying to take care of Eldrin once and for all. He'd messed with the true king of Nightmare, Frost, and Darkness one too many times. It ended now.

ABOUT THE AUTHOR

Jen L. Grey is a *USA Today* Bestselling Author who writes Paranormal Romance, Urban Fantasy, and Fantasy genres.

Jen lives in Tennessee with her husband, two daughters, and two miniature Australian Shepherds. Before she began writing, she was an avid reader and enjoyed being involved in the indie community. Her love for books eventually led her to writing. For more information, please visit her website and sign up for her newsletter.

Check out her future projects and book signing events at her website.
www.jenlgrey.com

ALSO BY JEN L. GREY

Fated To Darkness

The King of Frost and Shadows

The Court of Thorns and Wings

The Kingdom of Flames and Ash

Rejected Fate Trilogy

Betrayed Mate

The Forbidden Mate Trilogy

Wolf Mate

Wolf Bitten

Wolf Touched

Standalone Romantasy

Of Shadows and Fae

Twisted Fate Trilogy

Destined Mate

Eclipsed Heart

Chosen Destiny

The Marked Dragon Prince Trilogy

Ruthless Mate

Marked Dragon

Hidden Fate

Shadow City: Silver Wolf Trilogy

Broken Mate

Rising Darkness

Silver Moon

Shadow City: Royal Vampire Trilogy

Cursed Mate

Shadow Bitten

Demon Blood

Shadow City: Demon Wolf Trilogy

Ruined Mate

Shattered Curse

Fated Souls

Shadow City: Dark Angel Trilogy

Fallen Mate

Demon Marked

Dark Prince

Fatal Secrets

Shadow City: Silver Mate

Shattered Wolf

Fated Hearts

Ruthless Moon

The Wolf Born Trilogy

Hidden Mate

Blood Secrets

Awakened Magic

The Hidden King Trilogy

Dragon Mate

Dragon Heir

Dragon Queen

The Marked Wolf Trilogy

Moon Kissed

Chosen Wolf

Broken Curse

Wolf Moon Academy Trilogy

Shadow Mate

Blood Legacy

Rising Fate

The Royal Heir Trilogy

Wolves' Queen

Wolf Unleashed

Wolf's Claim

Bloodshed Academy Trilogy

Year One

Year Two

Year Three

The Half-Breed Prison Duology (Same World As Bloodshed Academy)

Hunted

Cursed

The Artifact Reaper Series

Reaper: The Beginning

Reaper of Earth

Reaper of Wings

Reaper of Flames

Reaper of Water

Stones of Amaria (Shared World)

Kingdom of Storms

Kingdom of Shadows

Kingdom of Ruins

Kingdom of Fire

The Pearson Prophecy

Dawning Ascent

Enlightened Ascent

Reigning Ascent

Stand Alones

Death's Angel

Rising Alpha

Made in United States
Troutdale, OR
11/04/2024

24456822R00206